Finn

•••••• THE IRISHMEN BOOK ONE ••••••

NEW YORK TIMES AND USA TODAY BESTSELLING AUTHOR

MELANIE MORELAND

FINN
The Irishmen Book 1
by Melanie Moreland

Copyright © 2025 Moreland Books Inc.
Copyright # 1231926
ISBN Ebook 978-1-998471-11-9
Paperback 978-1-998471-10-2
All rights reserved

MORELAND
BOOKS INC.

Edited by Lisa Hollett of Silently Correcting Your Grammar
Proofreading by Sisters Get Lit.erary Proofreading
Cover design by Feed Your Dreams Designs
Cover Images by AdShooter
Cover content is for illustrative purposes only.

products of the author's imagination and are either fictitious or are used fictitiously. Any
similarity to real persons, living or dead, is purely coincidental and not intended by the author. Any trademarks, service marks, product names or named features are assumed to be the property of their respective owners, and are only used for reference. There is no implied endorsement if any of these terms are used. The author acknowledges the trademarked status and trademark owners of various products referenced in this work of fiction, which have been used without permission. The publication/use of these trademarks is not authorized, associated with, or sponsored by the trademark owners.

Readers with concerns about content or subjects depicted can check out the content advisory on my website: https://melaniemoreland.com/extras/fan-suggestions/content-advisory/

DEDICATION

To my dear friend Roisin
One of the bravest, warmest, loveliest people
I am honored to call friend.
Thank you for your help.

CHAPTER ONE

FINN

I glanced at my watch, then cast my gaze at the wall of monitors on the opposite wall. I could see and, if I wanted, hear everything going on in every corner of my hotel and casino, aside from the private rooms. I had no desire to know what went on behind the closed doors of my guests. Unless you were in a suite I put you in to keep tabs on you.

That was a totally different story.

The casino was steady, the restaurants prepping for another day of busy service, and everything was running smoothly. I clicked again so the entire wall became the lobby, scanning to make sure it looked perfect.

Guests were coming and going, the concierge desk busy. The front desk had a few people in front of it, and I did a quick zoom to make sure the staff was following protocol.

At least, that was what I told myself.

I took a moment to observe the lobby, waiting until a familiar head of bright-red curls appeared. I stared at the monitor, drinking in the smile and friendly expression on her face as she dealt with a guest. The warmth she exuded, the same warmth I wished were directed toward me, even though I knew she was off-limits. She had made that very clear, and I had to respect her wishes. I watched her for a few more moments, admiring her grace and beauty, reaching my hand out to stroke her cheek on the screen, recalling how soft her skin was. How silky it used to feel under my fingers. The way it felt when I pressed my lips there, whispering to her.

"Mo chroí."

As if hearing my thoughts, she looked up toward the monitor, her gaze feeling as if it were looking directly into my soul. The one only she knew. For a brief time, she had been the redemption, the gift I'd been given.

Until she'd left me.

Her gaze dropped and I shook my head, returning to the present. I focused my attention to the front door, waiting for my unscheduled visitor.

I didn't have to wait long. Roman Costas was nothing if not punctual.

He walked in, his shoulders back, head high, stopping to take in the much-changed front lobby.

When he'd owned the casino and hotel, it was modern, sleek, muted grays and creams. Streamlined furniture, thick carpeting underfoot.

When he sold it to me, I closed it for a year, remodeled parts of it, and reopened as O'Reilly's. I replaced the previous name of Maple II, as had been part of our agreement. He hadn't seen it yet.

I zoomed in to get a closer look at his reaction.

For a brief moment, I saw his shock and a slight sadness as he scanned the vast area, then his mask fell into place.

He walked forward, taking it all in. Gone were the glass and metal and carpet. Dark woods, soft colors, and heavy, thick-planked flooring were in their place. A massive rock wall was at the back, water cascading gently over the crevices to a pool below. Flanking the waterfall area were live trees and plants, the green stretching upward to the new, light-filled dome. The area was peaceful and serene. It invited our guests to sit and relax, close their eyes and forget about the city beyond the walls and glass. The dome was fitted with stained glass, the colors cascading all around, beautiful yet allowing the light to come in and highlight the plants and water. It was my favorite spot on the main floor.

It was *hers* as well.

Closer to the front was another alcove that contained a huge fireplace with chairs and sofas arranged around it. There were live edge desks at reception, deep armchairs, and muted greens and cream everywhere. No steel or metal surfaces anywhere. The ambiance of the entire hotel was now that of an Irish manor. Warm, welcoming, homey. Upstairs, I had added an Irish pub, the décor so realistic you'd think it had been there for years, not a matter of months. It was always busy and one of the biggest moneymakers in the entire building, next to the casino.

Whereas Roman had catered to the wealthy and grand, my hotel and casino were more down-to-earth. The money was still there, but muted. Covered with the feel of nature and home.

I watched his response as he took it all in, his gaze never stopping, no doubt cataloguing all the changes.

Then he looked right at the concealed camera and nodded, knowing I was watching him. I had to chuckle. That was one thing I had kept. His security systems were second to none, and he knew it.

He started toward the private elevator, then seemed to recall that he no longer had access to it.

For the first time since I'd met him, I saw Roman Costas hesitate.

I picked up the phone. "Escort Mr. Costas upstairs right away. Send coffee."

A moment later, my second was beside him, shaking his hand and indicating the elevator Roman had once considered his.

I stood and buttoned my jacket.

It was time to discover what this visit was about.

He strode in, his face impassive. He extended his hand. "O'Reilly."

I shook his hand firmly. "Costas."

"Hardly recognized the place."

I offered him a smile. "Rather the point."

"I like it."

I indicated the chair, and he sat, unbuttoning his coat and crossing his legs. A moment later, coffee arrived and I offered him a cup. He accepted and we sipped in silence.

"Good," he acknowledged. "Different."

"Irish," I said with a grin.

He laughed, shaking his head. "Of course."

He leaned back, appearing relaxed. "What have you done to the casino?"

"Very little, actually—a refresh, really, carpets and such. We redid the main parts. The lobby, the restaurants, the guest rooms."

He looked around. "The office as well."

I ran my hand over the desk I was sitting at. "This was my grandfather's. I had it brought over from Ireland."

"Stunning piece," he acknowledged. "Very different ambiance to the place now."

I nodded thoughtfully. "I don't want to compete with you, Roman. You run a very upscale casino. I'm appealing to the middle classes. Those who come for an evening to break the monotony of their run-of-the-mill lives. Staying in Toronto for a vacation and want to live it up a little. I still make millions, but in different ways." I shrugged. "The high rollers come to you. I'm good with that."

He finished his coffee, setting the empty cup on the desk. "I'm good with it too. I agree there are many types of gamblers and lots to go around." He cleared his throat. "Which is the main reason I'm here."

I rested my elbows on the desk. "Is there a problem?"

"Potentially."

"Fill me in."

He stood and paced, no doubt taking in other changes to his old office. "I assume you don't allow your men to gamble at your casino."

"No. I prefer them not to gamble at all, but if they do, not here. I want no whispers of favoritism or fixing games."

He nodded. "I have much the same rule, and I know my staff on occasion indulge elsewhere."

He sat down, meeting my curious gaze. "One of your men has been to the Maple twice in the past week. I'm concerned."

"Why?"

"I overheard him talking about a debt he is trying to clear up."

I withheld my groan. We both were aware that gambling more to pay off an existing debt rarely worked. It was an act of desperation that often led to negative consequences.

"Debt?" I asked. "Debt to whom?"

He sat back. "That's the troublesome part. The racetrack. Pedro Lopez."

I grimaced. "I've never met him, but I hate that lowlife. From what I've heard, he's trouble."

"As do I." He drummed his fingers on the arm of the chair. "He plays just within the rules. He's not under anyone's jurisdiction, but I have a feeling there's more going on there than horse racing. I've heard the rumors."

"As have I." I frowned. "I don't like the fact that one of mine owes him money. Or even that he frequents that place." I met Roman's gaze. "Name."

"Brian Murphy."

"Dammit," I replied, somehow not surprised at hearing that name.

He lifted an eyebrow in a silent question.

"His father, Jim, was one of my men. Brian's been a pain in my ass since he joined us." I rubbed my eyes. "Always just this side of too much trouble. Looking for the easy way to do things. Lazy."

"What I heard, he owed Lopez upwards of twenty. He was trying to win it to pay him. He did okay the other night and I imagine it was enough to buy himself a few days, but last night, he played poorly. I have a feeling, with the interest Lopez is charging, he's getting frantic. We both know that leads to bad decisions."

"How much does he owe you now?"

"Five."

"Fuck," I muttered.

"Not a huge amount, but enough that he can't cover it. I stepped in and cut him off." He shrugged. "He wasn't happy and got fucking mouthy. I decided I needed to tell you."

"You were right. I have to figure this out."

"Cut him loose."

"I can't."

"Why?"

"His father saved my life. Took a bullet meant for me. He never recovered and died later. I told him I'd look after his kids."

"More than one troublemaker?"

"No. His sister is one of my most loyal, exemplary staff. Very well-thought-of."

"You need to rein him in."

"I will."

"You want me to talk to Lopez?"

I shook my head. "Don't get involved, Roman. As much as I appreciate the offer, he's an unknown entity. You have a wife and a young one. A family. I don't want you on his radar."

He nodded, although he was clearly not happy about my answer. "I don't want anyone I know on his radar," he muttered. "I have a bad feeling about him."

"Roman," I added, waiting until he met my eyes. "I'll talk to Lopez. Clear up the debt, and Brian can work it off with me." I blew out a long breath. "I appreciate you coming to me instead of taking care of business the usual way. I'll deal with this. But Brian isn't allowed to gamble in your casino again."

"I made that very clear last night."

"I'll make sure his debt to you is cleared today. Niall will transfer the money. And he'll be warned about no more gambling. I've honored his father's debt."

"I agree."

"And as I said, I appreciate you coming to me."

He inclined his head in acknowledgment.

"Now, tell me. How is that little one of yours?"

His countenance changed, becoming lighter. The family man showing through.

"Getting bigger every day. He tests his mother and me constantly."

I laughed. "And your nonna?"

His smile was warm. "Happier than she has been in years. With Aldo, Luca, and me all having kids, I swear she looks younger than ever. She is constantly busy, happy, smiling."

I had only met his nonna and his wife once. Both were charming and brought out a side of Roman most people didn't know. He was incredibly protective of them, plus anyone he considered family, like his sister-in-law or Aldo's wife, Vi.

"Aldo was here last week with Vi. She did some shopping while he and I spoke."

Roman nodded, looking amused. "She's a firecracker."

I chuckled. "That she was. You should bring your wife for an evening. Dine at the new restaurant. Irish food is delicious." I winked. "I'll comp you some chips, and you can try your hand at one of my tables."

He laughed. "The dinner, I'll accept. I never gamble." He stood to leave. "And I'll extend the same invitation to you. Come to the Maple. Or even better, come to the winery. My nonna's cooking is not to be missed."

I shook his hand, surprised and honored. Roman Costas rarely let anyone on to his estate. "That's an invitation I'll accept. Maybe we can set a date when we meet with Luca in a few weeks?"

"Sounds good."

"Can I offer you lunch before you go?"

"I can't, I'm afraid. I have a busy afternoon. But I didn't want to discuss this on the phone and felt I needed to come here to tell you."

"Thank you for that. I'll take care of it."

He departed, and I switched on the monitors to watch him leave. He stopped to admire the water feature, studying it. Una approached him, smiling and greeting him. She indicated the wall, and he returned her smile then asked her a few questions. She was her usual animated self, describing the rocks I'd transported from Ireland and the way it worked. Her hands flitted as she spoke, her expressive face lighting up as she talked. The light around her caught her hair, and it gleamed red and gold. I was as fascinated by her hair as I was with her.

I found myself leaning closer to the monitor, my eyes

narrowing as I took in Roman's smile and how close he stood to her.

It took everything in me not to rush to the lobby and appear at her elbow, glare at Roman so he knew to back off. Then I reminded myself he was simply being friendly. Curious about the changes to the building he once owned. And Una was, as usual, being her warm, perfect self. Everyone was drawn to her. It happened without you even realizing it.

And the rock garden waterfall was one of her favorite features of the lobby. That and the fireplace. Even when she wasn't working, I often spied her curled up in one of the large armchairs, studying sheet music or reading.

I liked that she felt comfortable enough to do so.

I liked a lot of things about Una Murphy.

Except for her connection to her brother Brian. She loved and protected him fiercely. Always defended him. She had from the day I first met her. It was going to be a complication in what had to happen, and I wasn't looking forward to the fallout.

They finished their conversation, and Roman smiled at her. He was a good-looking son of a bitch, and if I didn't know how deeply in love he was with his wife, I'd be pissed off he was talking to Una. But I knew his heart and fidelity were deeply affixed to "his Effie," as I heard him call her, so I tamped down my jealousy.

Still, I was pleased when he nodded and left. I switched to an outside view and watched as he climbed into his car and drove off.

I shut off the monitors and called Niall.

"We have a problem."

"I figured as much when the great Roman Costas paid you a visit."

"We need to figure this out."

"I'll be there in five."

I hung up, staring out the window and to the busy city beyond it. My mind went over the current problem facing me, flipping through ideas of how to solve it with the fewest ramifications.

No matter what solution I came up with, someone was going to lose.

And I had no idea who.

CHAPTER TWO

FINN

Niall strode in, his face serious. He sat in the chair Roman had vacated, stopping to pour himself a cup of coffee. I swore he lived off caffeine.

I gave him a moment to enjoy his dark brew, thinking of our shared past.

Niall was my cousin. We were the same age, born a month apart thirty-eight years ago. Our mothers were sisters, and when mine died, his mother stepped up, trying desperately to fill in and offer me a little love and compassion that was lacking in my homelife.

My father was a low-level crime lord. His way of showing affection was using his fists and criticism. I was his favorite punching bag until I turned fifteen and, thanks to a sudden growth spurt, outweighed him by three stone and towered over his frame by a good six inches. The last time he hit me, I hit back—sending him to the floor in a mass of pain.

He never touched me again. I moved in to Niall's place, and Roisin made sure I was fed and cared for. When I turned seventeen, I left Ireland and came to Canada. I stayed with a distant relation who was part of the syndicate, and he got me into the ranks. I rose up the ladder quickly, my size and leadership taking me far. Two years later, when Roisin was ill, I returned to Ireland, made sure she had the best care and, when she recovered, brought Niall back with me. She had asked me to do so, wanting him out of Ireland and away from the dangerous criminal life there. She knew I was involved in the syndicate here but felt at least I could protect him. I agreed with her and knew he would be an asset with his street smarts and business intellect.

Together, we forged a path of power and wealth, and I became one of the heads of the syndicate.

When my father died, I sent word back to Ireland to cremate him and do what they wanted with the ashes. I had no desire to return and pretend to mourn. From what I heard, he was buried in a grave somewhere in the small town where I grew up.

I didn't care.

Niall's throat clearing made me look up. I met his brown eyes that regarded me steadily. He was darkness, his hair and eyes matching, his skin constantly tanned. Thick and muscled, hard and unyielding. My hair was ginger, and I was taller by an inch—a fact I never allowed him to forget—and my eyes were blue. I was broad and muscled, our builds much the same. I tended toward ruddy, disliking the sun that he loved to sit in. It only made me redder. He kept his hair short, while I preferred mine longer, usually pulled back away from my face. We both liked scruff, mine often growing into a beard until I got tired of it and shaved. Side by side, I was told we looked like we were related, although neither of us could see it. The only physical traits I thought we shared were our height and build.

"Sorry," I muttered. "Thinking."

"What's going on? And who is the cause?"

"Brian Murphy."

"Feck. What now?" he asked, his brogue coming out strong as it always did when he was upset.

I told him what Roman had divulged. He slammed his hand on the desk. "Dammit. He is always the troublemaker."

I scrubbed my face. "I know."

"So, twenty-five thousand? What the hell is he thinking? The interest alone I'm sure that sleaze is charging him will ensure the debt is never paid off." Again, he slammed his hand on the desk. "Stupid fecker."

"I have no idea."

"We can't allow this to stand."

"No."

"What are you going to do? Cut him loose and let Lopez have him?"

"I can't do that," I said quietly. "You know it."

He sat back, regarding me. "Because of Jim?" He paused. "Or Una?"

I met his gaze. "Both."

"You can't let this go."

"I'm going to pay the debt, and Brian will work it off with me. He's going to be taught a lesson, and if he doesn't learn it, I'll cut him loose."

"Once he pays the debt."

"Before, if need be." I took a sip of coffee. "Twenty-five K isn't a big deal to me. To him, yes. It's the principle."

"And the fact that he is playing with Lopez. He knows better. All the men do."

I nodded. "We have to visit him. He needs a warning as well. Brian isn't allowed at his track."

Niall pulled on his sleeves. "What is his punishment? Brian, I mean, for putting you in this position?"

"Depends on his attitude. Get me the cash plus whatever you think the interest is to Pedro Lopez. Transfer five to Roman. He refuses to take anything more. We'll pay the debt, and then later you can bring Brian to the warehouse." I never conducted business like this on-site. I kept the two as separate as possible.

Niall frowned. "Finn—"

I held up my hand, interrupting him. "I know."

"You need to stop basing your decisions on your feelings for her. No choice here is going to win you any favors."

"I'm aware."

"If you—"

I stood, cutting him off. "Enough, Niall."

He sighed, swiping a hand over his hair. "Fine. But I'm coming with you. So are two guards. Fully armed."

"Wouldn't have it any other way."

The racetrack was busy on a Friday afternoon. The crowds were loud, raucous. Cheering and drinking. Lots of money being spent. I looked around, curious. Horse races had never appealed to me. The dust and smell. The yelling. Even the bells and noises of my own casino didn't interest me. I preferred the muted sounds of a card game. The strategy behind the plays.

I climbed from the car, Niall flanking me, my guards on high alert. It didn't take long before a man appeared in front of me, another younger man behind him. "Mr. O'Reilly."

"I'm looking for Lopez."

"I am Luis. I'll take you to him. Juan, make sure Mr. O'Reilly's car is looked after. Offer his driver coffee." He paused as Juan spoke with Rory and directed him, walking behind the car as it moved away. "No firearms are allowed. And your guards are not needed. I assume you haven't come to cause trouble?" He let the question hang in the air.

I indicated for the guards to stay put. Niall was beside me, and I knew he had a weapon or two hidden on his person. I could take care of myself. Thanks to my father, I knew how to fight—and make it hurt. I had been well trained in that from an early age.

I followed Luis to an elevator. I looked around as we waited. It was over the top—the fake distressed wood, the large furniture, and the extensive use of color. The gaudy carpet reminded me of a circus. Despite the somewhat tacky atmosphere, a lot of money had been soaked in here. Bad money, bad taste, crossed my mind.

The elevator door opened, and Luis indicated for me to enter, allowing Niall to follow. Then he stepped in, using a pass to take us up.

The doors opened to an office that overlooked the racetrack. The same over-the-top décor was here as well. Pictures, bright colors, and the scent of incense made my eyes water. The man I assumed was Lopez stood from behind an ornate desk, making no move to come forward. We measured each other from across the room, and I felt Niall bristling with tension beside me.

Lopez was an average-sized man, thin, his head bald, his dark eyes beady. He was dressed in an expensive suit that needed a good tailoring, the shoulders too wide and the sleeves the wrong length. His tie was a wild pattern, no doubt meant to be fashionable, but it only looked out of place. His thin lips were drawn in a cruel smile, his scraggly mustache unattractive.

"Mr. O'Reilly. What an unexpected pleasure," he said, his accent thick.

"Yet, you were prepared," I stated, strolling forward. I towered over him, and I knew I outweighed him by at least sixty or more pounds. "And you know me by sight."

He smirked. "One must always be ready."

I cut to the chase. "An employee of mine owes you money."

"And who might that be?" he asked, playing dumb.

"Brian Murphy."

"Ah. Mr. Murphy. He has paid some of his debt, but not all." He made a tutting noise as if in disappointment. "He has asked you to take care of his balance?"

I didn't want to get into it with him. I didn't want to be in this office any longer than I had to be. I was going to need a shower when I got back to the hotel to wipe away the stench of the encounter.

"I will clear his debt today. He is not allowed back at your racetrack, Lopez. You understand? You deny him."

His eyes narrowed at the way I addressed him. "Mister" would never cross my lips, nor would his first name. He didn't deserve the respect.

He tutted again. "He has been a good customer. He simply had some bad luck."

I had no doubt he had. Lopez had made sure of it. I assumed that he let Brian win some races, building up his ego. Probably had a friendly face in the crowd, offering sure tips that worked at first as they fixed a few races. Brian, being Brian and liking the easy route, would fall for it. Build up his winnings, greedy and sloppy. Then Lopez pulled it away, knowing Brian would try to recapture his earlier "luck."

"I settle his debt, and it is over." I heaved out a long breath of air, hating to do this. "I'd consider it a personal courtesy."

His eyebrows shot up, and he stroked his mustache. It reminded me of a villain in a cartoon. "Finn O'Reilly asking me for a favor."

"*Not* a favor. A personal courtesy. Perhaps you have a client you would like to offer a night or two in Toronto as my guests. To return the courtesy."

"Perhaps."

"He is not allowed to gamble here again. I will make it clear to him as well."

He shrugged. "As you wish." He threw out a number, and I kept my expression neutral, glancing at Niall with a nod. The interest rate was exorbitant. Higher than I'd anticipated, but I knew Niall had it covered. Brian was going to pay heavily for this. He never would have gotten out of this debt. And God only knew what terms of payment Lopez would demand.

A moment later, Niall spoke. "Done."

Lopez smiled, his eyes cold and dead. "Perhaps we could do some business, Finn. Some cross-promotion, as it were."

I shook my head. "It's Mr. O'Reilly. And I want nothing to do with you or your brand of business, Lopez. I have no idea what illegal activities you run behind the scenes, but if I find out, you'll be sorry. Stay away from my people and get out of my world. It's the only warning I'll give you."

His already-cold gaze turned to ice. "Not good enough for the likes of you?"

I barked a laugh. "I'm no better than any man. But I have a feeling what goes on here isn't just racing. And I want no part of it. Or you." I turned to go. "You've been warned."

We exited, the elevator already waiting. We didn't speak as we headed toward the car. Once inside, Rory drove away quickly, and when we were clear of the track, I heaved a sigh.

"Something is going on there. Far too much money for a small track."

"Yep."

"I want to know what it is. I agree with Roman. It's gotta be bad." I snorted. "As if I would get into business with Lopez."

"You want me to get some men in?"

"Let's see what happens."

"He's not happy with you."

"I hardly expected him to be."

"He might try something."

"Then let's be prepared."

He pursed his lips. "I hope it's worth it, Finn."

I glanced out of the window, not wanting to discuss it. He let it go, knowing my feelings on the matter.

"Brian will be at the warehouse now."

"Then let's take care of that piece of business."

Brian had no idea until I stepped out of the car. His expression went from bored to worried in a matter of seconds. When he saw Niall and the guards, his face paled.

Like his sister, he had red hair, although his was darker. His skin was ruddy like mine, although his was due more to the freckles that covered his face. His entire body, actually. I had never seen a man with as many freckles as him. It gave him a boyish look that belied the lazy, temperamental man he really was. If it hadn't been for his family, I never would have put up with him this long.

His usual flippant attitude evaporated as I approached. We stood face-to-face, me silent and angry, him becoming more nervous with each passing quiet moment. I liked using silence as a weapon. People tended to start blathering and saying more than they intended. It worked with him when Niall handed him the transfer papers and he knew why we were here.

"It was one time, Mr. O'Reilly."

I lifted an eyebrow at his blatant lie.

"Okay, a few times. I was up! Rolling in cash. Then it fell apart."

"You know my rules about gambling."

"It wasn't at your place."

"Anywhere," I thundered. "And you go to Lopez? To a place we have no people, no jurisdiction? You're fucking lucky I'm not picking you up in a body bag and having to tell your sister how fucking stupid you were!" I roared. "You gamble up a debt with a man charging fifty-six percent interest? How the fuck did you think you were going to pay this off?"

"I thought my luck would come back."

"There is no luck, you idiot. He was playing you. And you fell for it. Then instead of admitting you had a problem, you show up at the Maple and lose money there too." I shook my head. "I should kill you just so your idiocy would stop hurting my head."

"You can't. My father—"

I cut him off. "My debt to your father is paid. In full. It has been for years. The only thing keeping you alive right now is your sister."

At the mention of Una, his face changed. The fear drained away, and he became cocky. "Well then, I guess we're good? At least the bitch can come in handy to look after your frustrations." He winked as if it were a joke. As if I planned on revenge-fucking his sister for his debt. My vision turned red, and I heard Niall's low groan of disbelief.

"Well, now you've fucking done it," he muttered.

I lost it, my fist crashing into Brian's jaw so hard, his head snapped back. His eyes rolled back in his head, and he fell, unconscious, to the floor.

Niall whistled under his breath. "Nice one."

"Pick him up. Get him in a chair and tie his hands. Wake him up." I shook off my jacket. "We're not done."

Brian groaned as his hands were released. I stood in front of him, my knuckles bruised and bleeding. My chest heaved from exertion, my anger still bright but my message received. His face was bleeding, his nose smashed, but it was his ribs that had taken the brunt of my fury. Not broken, but he was going to have trouble taking a deep breath.

I hunched in front of him, gripping his hair and lifting his head, forcing him to meet my eyes. "You understand me now, Brian? No gambling. You will pay your debt to me. Your cushy job just got ten times harder and will keep being such until your debt is paid. And the next time you disrespect your sister, I will end you. There is nothing between us, and for you to infer that also disrespects me. She is worth your weight in gold. Your father would be disgusted." I paused, going in for the kill shot. "And so disappointed in you. He had hopes for you. High ones. None of which you have lived up to."

His eyes widened, and I knew my words had hit their mark. Jim had been a good man. Tried to instill his beliefs into his kids, of hard work and loyalty. Una had learned her lessons well. Brian had been too eager to take the easy path. As the eldest, he should have been protecting Una, but it was the other way around. She would defend him to the death. I feared if the roles were reversed, he wouldn't offer the same sacrifice.

And I knew I was going to be the subject of her wrath once she found out what I had done to him today.

But he deserved it and more. If it had been anyone else, chances were they wouldn't be breathing.

"You go home and clean up. Be at the hotel on Monday, ready to start your new duties."

He had the audacity to speak. "Doing what?" he asked, a dribble of blood running down his chin.

"Running. Driving. Delivering. Working the warehouses. Whatever the fuck I tell you to do."

"That's grunt work!"

I bent down again. "Would you prefer the alternative?" I hissed, still angry.

His already-pale skin whitened. "No."

"Then be grateful for my leniency."

I could tell he wanted to mouth off. Tell me where to go. But for once, he kept his mouth shut, glaring instead at the floor. I could almost hear his curses inside his head.

"Clean him up and take him to the safe house. Watch him this weekend," I instructed, picking up my jacket and slinging it over my shoulder.

Brian had to push it. He always did. "Watch him," he mimicked under his breath.

He didn't see it coming. I delivered another blow to his stomach, one so hard, even I grunted.

He gasped, vomited, and passed out.

I looked at him in revulsion. "I need to head to my suite."

In the car, Niall was quiet for a moment. "You showed great restraint," he muttered. "I thought you were going to kill him."

I glanced his way. "I'm sure that's not how he'll tell his story."

"What are you going to say?"

I shook my aching hand. "The truth. Una is smart, and she knows the drill. I had no choice. I was going to let him walk with a threat and the new duties, but he had to mouth off. Twice." I shrugged. "He brought it on himself."

"Will Una see it that way?"

I shook my head, then stared out the window, knowing the answer.

She would not.

Niall didn't speak the rest of the way back to the hotel. I used my private elevator and headed to my suite, standing under the hot spray of the shower, letting the water run off my back to help relax me. I flexed my hand, trying to ignore the ache. I was pretty certain that Brian was suffering far more.

And he deserved it.

Simply thinking of his words made me angry all over again. I finished my shower and got dressed, glancing at the clock. It was just after five, and the one thing I knew would relax me fully wasn't available to me for three hours. I returned to my office, starting on the mound of paperwork. It would keep me busy until then.

At eight, I took the elevator to the main floor, striding through the lobby to the music room. I slipped in the back, the lights already low, and made my way to the alcove that was for my use only. I sat down, a tumbler of whiskey waiting for me, the bottle ready for another when I was. I sat back, sipping the golden liquid, the Irish liquor coating my throat. Hearing the piano music starting, I opened my eyes, resting my elbows on the table.

Una walked onstage, a vision. Gone were the simple hairstyle and uniform. In their place, a figure-hugging dress that touched at her waist and hip, the low neckline showcasing her incredible breasts. The emerald green of the dress highlighted the red of her hair that was swept up in a sophisticated knot, wisps of curls and long tendrils floating around her face and neck. Her creamy skin glowed under the lights, and I waited, barely breathing, until she opened her red-stained lips and began to sing.

Instantly, I was transported to another time and place as she sang a traditional Celtic song. Her voice was pure, soaring in the high notes, haunting in its richness. I listened, enraptured. It didn't matter how often I heard her sing. How many times I heard the same sets. Each one was magnificent. Old songs, new ones. Celtic folklore. Reworked popular songs. She made each one her own. Every single one reached me on a level I couldn't explain to anyone. She didn't know I was there. I came in just before she started, and I would leave as she took her bow. I sent flowers every week without a card.

Respecting her wishes, even as it killed me.

I loved her with a passion I didn't know I was capable of. Desired her. Wanted her time and attention.

I was totally and utterly obsessed with her.

And she wanted nothing to do with me.

So I stole these moments. Created a place where she could showcase her talent, letting her think it was part of the plans for the hotel all along, when, in fact, I'd made it for her alone. Others graced the small stage during the week and when she was away as well. Just as popular and loved as she was.

But not by me.

And they never would be.

CHAPTER THREE
UNA

He was there. As he always was, sitting in the dark in the back alcove, watching me. I sensed his presence even if I couldn't see him. The same way I knew he was observing me at the front desk. I could feel his eyes on me. There were times when I was sitting by the waterfall, and I knew he had zoomed in on me with one of the security feeds. Or spotted me while walking through the lobby. He rarely stopped, and if he did, he was courteous, polite, and distant. The consummate boss.

Exactly what I requested of him, even if it made me sad.

Finn O'Reilly was everything I wanted in a man, except for one thing.

His ties to the underworld and the violent environment he chose to live in. I had been forced to live that way my entire life, hating every aspect of it. I swore once I was old enough, I would leave it behind me and find a regular life. One not filled with blood and fear.

And every day, I strove more and more toward that goal.

I finished my set, bowing to the applause. The green of my gown shimmered in the bright lights as I stepped from the small stage, heading toward the private room in the back. I planned to have something to eat, sip some tea and honey to soothe my throat, and rest until the next set at eleven.

It was the same every Friday and Saturday night. The moments I lived for. I loved to sing and had since I was a child. It was the one thing no one ever criticized me for.

I wasn't the world's best singer. I had no aspirations of a career in the music industry, but I loved the chance to lift my voice and make people smile. Here at O'Reilly's, I was given that chance every week. They had other performers the rest of the time, but Friday and Saturday were mine.

A gift from Finn. One of the few I would accept since I knew how much he enjoyed my performances. I felt it was an equal partnership. He took what I could give, and I did the same by accepting the spots.

In my dressing room, I ran my fingers over the blossoms that waited. They arrived every Friday without fail. Without a card. But I knew who sent them and why. I felt the sadness seeping into my chest, and I shook my head to clear it of the morose thoughts.

I had made my choice.

A knock at the door startled me. Few people were able to get back this way. I had tried to mingle with patrons at first, but a few were too handsy. Too close. I learned quickly I needed to isolate myself to rest and to stay safe. I didn't like being touched by strangers.

I stood, going to the door. "Hello?" I called.

"It's me," a voice said quietly, the low tone and Irish brogue instantly calming me yet causing my heart to race at the same time.

I opened the door. Finn stood on the other side, tall and broad, his hair glinting in the lights. He wore it tied back today, the waves still evident in the sweep of the knot.

I stepped back, silently bidding him to enter. He brushed past me, and I felt the heat of his body, his scent hitting me, masculine and enticing. I breathed him in deeply, shutting the door and giving myself a moment to school my features.

"Mr. O'Reilly."

He clasped his hands behind his back. "Finn," he replied with a frown, waiting.

"You're my boss."

"I'm also your friend. I am Finn to you when we're alone."

I hated the way his voice sounded as he said, "when we're alone." It was an unspoken promise that stirred memories I refused to think of. Instead, I cleared my throat.

"Is there an issue?"

"You looked tired. I wanted to check on you. Make sure you're not overdoing it."

I sat down at my makeup table, and he perched on the large chair in the corner. It wasn't a big room, and it now seemed minuscule with him in it. His hands rested on his thighs and he looked casual, but his fingers were knotted in a fist, and I saw the tic of his jaw as he waited for my reply.

I waved off his concern. "I'm fine. It was a busy week at the desk. I was worried about Brian, so I didn't sleep well. He didn't come home for a few days, but he texted me earlier and said he was fine." I shrugged. "I guess he was off doing whatever it is he does for you."

I hated that he worked for Finn. That my brother was a part of that dark world I was trying to get away from. I couldn't escape it yet, but soon, I would. I would leave it all behind me.

Finn shifted, looking uncomfortable. "First off, as much as I would like to point out your brother is a grown man and should be living on his own, not sponging off his younger sister, I will refrain."

"Thank you for your restraint," I murmured, trying to resist rolling my eyes. I knew Finn's thoughts on Brian.

"Second, your brother was not working for me the nights he chose not to come home." He took a deep breath. "I need to tell you something. Something you're not going to like."

"Is Brian okay? Is he—"

Finn cut me off. "He's fine. A little bruised. His ego wounded more than anything."

"I don't understand."

"Your brother got himself into trouble. He gambled where he shouldn't and racked up a bill he couldn't pay."

I felt the blood drain from my face. Finn leaned forward. "I paid the debt, Una. He owes me now, and he will work it off fairly. But I had to teach him a lesson."

"You're the one who bruised him?"

"Yes. I wanted to tell you before you saw him and he told you whatever bullshit story he made up about why."

"You hurt him."

"Not as badly as he would have been hurt by the man he owed money to. Money he didn't have." He sat back, serious and unrepentant. "I couldn't let it go."

"You mean you wouldn't."

"You know the message it would send out if I did, Una. I didn't break anything. He'll be sore for a few days, and he'll remember what happens when you disregard the rules and run up bills you have no way of paying."

"How much?"

"Pardon me?"

"How much is his debt?"

"I paid off thirty-five thousand."

The sum shocked me. I knew Brian liked to bet on horses, play some cards, but thirty-five thousand dollars? I looked down at my hands that were now shaking, knowing what I had to do.

"I will pay you."

"What?" Finn hissed.

I lifted my gaze to his. "I have twenty thousand saved. I will pay you. The rest you can dock my wages."

He shook his head, leaning forward. "Over my dead body. This is not your debt to pay. Stop saving him, Una. He is not your responsibility."

"He is. He is my brother."

"Your older brother. It's his job to care for you—to look after you—not the other way around."

"I will pay his debt. I don't want us owing you anything."

He stood, fury dripping from his tone. "*You* don't owe me anything."

I stood as well, suddenly weary. "You know, I tell myself that all the time. But it's a lie. I owe you everything, don't I? You gave me the job in every hotel you own so I could learn how to run my own place. You let me sing because it makes me happy. I know you helped with the apartment I found. The driver that you insisted all the late-night employees get, yet I seem to be the only one who has it. I owe you for all that. And now Brian owes you money." I met his angry gaze. "I will pay that debt, Finn."

"You know why I do all those things, Una. You owe me nothing."

"I can't give you what you want."

"I know, *mo chroí*," he murmured sadly. "But it doesn't change my feelings."

"Please leave," I whispered, my throat suddenly thick. It always affected me when he used that term. "I'll get the money to you."

"I will *not* accept it. This is Brian's obligation. I only came to tell you so you knew the truth. I promised you the truth always."

"I know."

He stepped forward and wrapped me in his arms. For a moment, I allowed myself the indulgence of feeling his warmth. It was odd how safe I felt in the embrace of a ruthless crime lord. It was as if nothing could hurt me—which was so far from the truth it was laughable. Being anywhere near Finn O'Reilly's orbit put me in danger. Even worse, it put him in danger as well.

Which was why I had to step back. Distance myself, even as I felt the physical pain of withdrawing from him.

"Please, Finn."

"No. This is between Brian and me. Do not interfere, Una. Let him grow up and deal with the consequences of his actions."

He stepped past me, stopping. For a moment, he said nothing, then he uttered my name. "Please, Una. I'm doing what is best."

I looked up. "For whom?"

"Him. You. All of us."

Then he pressed his mouth to my forehead, his lips lingering in a long, sweet caress.

And he was gone.

FINN

I sat in the darkness of my suite, whiskey in hand, staring out onto the bright lights of the city below me. Unlike Roman, who'd had a room here but lived elsewhere, this hotel was my home. I had a full suite on the top floor, larger than most condos in the city. It was totally self-contained, although I was the first to admit I rarely used the well-equipped kitchen, never once had sat at the dining table to eat, and the guest room had never been occupied. I had no life outside of my businesses, and it was wisest to live where I had access to everything I needed. I ran the hotel and casino. The warehouses and other office buildings I owned were used for various aspects of my world. Many illegal. I had trusted men who ran my operations. I had many people who paid for my protection. There were deals and bribes. Palms that needed to be greased daily.

I also had real businessmen who looked after my legal entities.

Many thought that being a member of a syndicate was dangerous and exciting. While at times it was dangerous, it was more paperwork and overseeing than anything. I had people who did the reinforcing when needed. My reputation helped keep that to a minimum. I ruled with a strong, firm hand, making sure to keep those around me in line. The ones who chose not to follow were eliminated. It kept me safe, and it kept all the others depending on me safe as well.

But it wasn't my businesses on my mind right now. It was the woman I'd held earlier. The one who was permanently etched into my heart and wanted nothing I could offer her—too afraid of the consequences of loving me.

I sighed as I drained my drink, then poured two more fingers of the whiskey into my glass. I shut my eyes, letting my thoughts drift back to the day I first met Una Murphy.

I made a habit of knowing my men's families. Making sure they were looked after. Jim Murphy was from the old regime, but he was loyal and trustworthy. I went to his house as a guest. He had invited me for dinner, and I made sure to accept those sorts of invitations when extended. It gave me a chance to see my men be themselves. See how they interacted with their own family. It told me a great deal about the sort of person they were.

I knew his wife was deceased. That he had a nineteen-year-old son and a daughter who had just turned eighteen. His intentions for his son were clear—to join his father in the ranks and be one of my men. The daughter, I had no idea about. I knew little about her. Often, that was the case in syndicate families. The males were doted on, while the women faded into the background. Expected to marry and produce children. Sometimes marriages were arranged, but I refused to be part of that. I believed a person should be allowed to love and live with whom they chose. Whom their heart chose. Some families were more progressive and the women were treated as equals. I applauded that. I expected, given Jim's old-fashioned ways of doing things, his daughter would be part of the former.

What I didn't expect was the old soul that dwelled in the young girl. From the moment she met me at the door, she acted like the matriarch of the family. Made sure I had a drink, sat primly, chastising her older brother like a mother when he'd run his mouth too long. She was articulate and well-read. She made and presented a roast dinner a much older person would have had trouble pulling off. One that reminded me of meals from long ago back in Ireland.

She was still a child, yet I caught glimpses of the woman she would become, and I had a feeling she would be a force to be reckoned with. I found myself talking to her, asking her about her studies, her goals.

"I want to run a hotel," she informed me. "The very best. Small. Exclusive."

"The hospitality industry is hard work."

"I'm aware. I plan to take courses, then work in as many hotels as I have to in order to learn from the best."

I was impressed with her mind-set.

"Where?" I asked.

"Tobermory or Niagara."

"Given this a lot of thought, I see," I said. "Expensive proposition."

She lifted her stubborn chin. "I will save. Work hard. Get a job. Two, if I need to. Get a singing gig on the side."

I was intrigued. "You sing?"

For the first time, her father interrupted our conversation. "Like an angel."

Even her brother nodded. It was obvious that Brian Murphy had one goal in life and that was to follow in his father's footsteps. He wanted nothing to do with the corporate world. He wanted the life of a soldier. I knew that was one reason for this invitation. Jim wanted me to meet Brian. To have that connection, so when he finished school and came to me for a job, I would take him on.

Oddly, I felt nothing for her brother. No interest either way. He didn't impress me. His father insisted he go to community college before joining the ranks, in case he changed his mind. But Brian barely made passing grades. He had little ambition and even less personality. His younger sister impressed me completely. I was twenty-eight at the time, and I felt as if I were speaking with a woman my own age, not a teenager.

We had finished dinner when a neighbor came by, asking for help from Brian and Jim. "It'll only take a few moments," she assured them. I offered to help, but Jim waved me off.

"Una will make you coffee. We will be back soon."

I sat at the kitchen table as Una efficiently tidied up. Unable to sit and not help, I picked up a tea towel to dry the dishes.

"Oh, you shouldn't," she protested. "Dad wouldn't like it."

I laughed. "I've done my fair share of dishes."

I found myself enjoying the domestic moments with her. And I liked hearing her talk. Small inflections of an accent on occasion, no doubt picked up from her parents, gave her voice a lilting sound when she spoke that was somehow soothing.

"Do you like school, Una?"

She shrugged. "The classes, yes. The other students, not so much."

"Why?"

She paused, lifting a hand to wipe away a stray curl from her forehead. I had to fight not to do it for her. "I feel old next to most of them. Our interests aren't the same."

"I understand."

She turned her face, her lovely eyes curious. "You do?"

I nodded. "I felt much the same growing up. As if I lived a different life."

"Yes!"

"What do you do for fun?"

"I read. Sketch. I like to run."

"Where do you run?"

"The track at the school. I'll be off to have a run soon."

"But it's getting late."

"The track is well lit, and there are always others there," she said, brushing off my concern.

"It's not safe," I insisted, stepping closer.

She smiled. "My dad has taught me to defend myself. I carry pepper spray. I can fight hard. And I'm alert. If the track is empty, I come home and run on the treadmill. But I like to run outside."

"Please be careful."

She tilted up her head, a small vee between her eyes. "I will be."

The same curl fell across her forehead again, and I reached up, tucking it behind her ear. It was soft to the touch. I suddenly became conscious of how close we were standing to each other. How small she was compared to me. How enticingly sweet she smelled.

Awareness hit me. She was eighteen. Alluring, lovely, intelligent, and interesting.

And eighteen fucking years old.

I stepped back, dropping into my chair just as Brian and Jim walked in. I averted my eyes as Una held out a tray of coffee and a plate of cookies. "Take it to the living room. It's more comfortable," she told her father. "I'll finish here."

Sitting with her father and brother having whiskey and coffee, I could make out her humming in the kitchen and I wanted to hear it again. I wanted to talk to her again. Listen to her voice. Hear her plans. Her soft laughter.

All of which were impossible. I had no business feeling this way for a child. I was grateful when she called out, informing her dad she was going for a run. I waited a few moments, then made my excuses and departed.

I drove to the school and watched her run. Made a call, stationing a man to watch the track nightly, ensuring her safety. Then I did the only thing I could do—I left and never returned. She was eighteen. Off-limits in every way possible.

Yet, I never forgot her.

The next time I saw Una was years later at her father's funeral. She was almost twenty-six and as compelling as I remembered.

The loyalty I'd seen in him was correct. He'd stepped in front of me, taking a bullet that should have killed me. Instead, it put him in a wheelchair and ended his life in a long, drawn-out decline. I paid for all his medical needs, which grew over time, and I offered as much support as he would allow. Somehow every time I went to see him, Una was out. I often wondered if it was because she blamed me for her father's condition. I couldn't fault her, but for some reason, it distressed me.

Brian had been working for me for a while, a decent enough soldier, although I often suspected without his father overseeing him, he would be trouble. I was worried what he would do now that his father's influence was gone. Yet, I owed it to Jim to keep him on. He had asked me to look after his children, and I always honored my word.

I didn't recognize Una at first. She was eight years older and no longer a child. She had grown and matured. She was all woman, and her beauty stunned me.

The day I had first met her, her hair had been tied into a thick braid over her shoulder. Now, it was loose in a mass of brilliant red curls that hung down her back. The simple black dress she wore highlighted her hair color and the paleness of her complexion. She looked tired, sad, and older than her years. I knew she'd taken a leave of absence to care for her father. I'd tried to intervene, but Jim was stubborn and refused, insisting that his daughter had it under control. I had to admit, at times, I wondered if it was Jim or Una who refused my help. Remembering her dreams, I hated the fact that she'd put them on hold to care for her father. I could only hope she found her way back to them. I wanted to help her with that.

As I stopped in front of her, offering my condolences, her eyes widened, and I took in her features. Her cheeks were full, her chin stubborn. Her beautiful green eyes were fringed with dark lashes, set under delicate eyebrows the same red as her hair. She had a smattering of freckles over the bridge of her nose, with one prominent, dark one to the side of her right eye. It gave her a sultry look, like a beauty mark. Her lips were plump and rosy but looked ragged as if she'd been chewing them in nerves.

Still, she was lovely. Even in mourning, there was no denying her beauty.

Or the fact that she was no longer a child.

I took her hand, feeling a strange sensation when our skin touched. Her gaze flew to mine, and I knew she felt it too. I closed my large palm over hers, and I held it tightly, unwilling to break our contact.

"Una," I murmured. "I'm sorry for your loss."

"Mr. O'Reilly," she replied stiffly. "Thank you for coming."

"Finn," I responded. "You call me Finn."

She indicated the back of the room. "There are refreshments."

I glanced around, noticing everyone was looked after. Her brother was in the corner, surrounded by his friends and some of my other men. Older soldiers were there with their wives or children to pay their respects. They all seemed to have someone.

Who was there for her?

"May I get you something?" I asked. "Maybe you could sit for a while."

She frowned. "Sit?" she echoed. "I have to make sure all is being handled."

"Your brother should be helping," I said, feeling annoyed.

She smiled sadly. "Brian misses Dad terribly. He needs his friends right now."

"What do you need?" I asked before I could think.

She blinked. "I'm fine."

I highly doubted that. I reached for her elbow, and she let me escort her to an empty table. "Sit."

I headed to the buffet table, marveling at the food laid out. I filled a plate and carried it back to her, then got two coffees and brought them over. I sat next to her, pushing the plate closer. "Eat, please."

She looked shocked. "You don't have to wait on me, Mr.— " At my glare, she cleared her throat. "Finn. I'm fine."

"Good. Then eat a sandwich."

She picked up an egg salad, nibbling on it. I took one, devouring it in two bites. "Tasty," I observed. "Different."

"I add horseradish," she said absently.

"You made the food?"

"Most of it. A few neighbors helped."

I sighed. "Why didn't you have it catered?"

She frowned. "It wasn't necessary. Besides, Dad always liked my cooking. It felt as if it was the final thing I could do for him."

The last sentence was spoken so quietly and with so much emotion, it hit me in the chest.

"Una," I said gently, taking her hand again.

She let out a small sigh, a tremor coursing through her.

"Tell me what you need."

"I'm fine," she insisted. "I'll get through today and make sure everything is in order, then I'm going back to work."

"Good. Still planning on that hotel?"

"Yes. I have more learning to do, but I'm getting there."

I glanced down, surprised to see our fingers still entangled. I didn't want to let go of her. I wanted more time. I was shocked to realize I wanted a lot of things with Una Murphy. But I knew I had to move carefully.

"I have an offer for you."

She frowned. "Oh?"

"May I take you to dinner tomorrow to discuss it?"

"Um…" she whispered, trying to withdraw her hand.

"Please," I added.

"Okay."

I drained my whiskey, standing and shaking my head to clear it of the memories.

That had been the start of our journey. One that began slowly, ended quickly, yet was never going to stop—at least for me.

CHAPTER FOUR
UNA

When my second set was done, I changed and hurried to the waiting car, anxious to get home. I lived in a small complex in Etobicoke. Mine was an older building with only sixteen units in the four-floor structure. There were three other buildings, and we shared a parking lot. We actually had trees and grass around the area, and the buildings were close to a park. It was quiet and safe, and I liked it. I didn't own a car, but Brian used my spot. It was an easy walk to the subway, which I used daily, except for the late nights when a driver was provided to take me home. I had to admit, I was always grateful not to have to take public transit and walk home at that time of the night.

Finn had told me about the building when I'd mentioned I planned on moving, and when I went to see it, I was pleased at how nice it was. I put in an application, thrilled when I was accepted. It took me a while to realize one of his companies owned the entire complex and Finn had made sure I got this place. It was just another debt I owed him.

But right now, I was concerned about something else. Something far more severe.

Inside my apartment, I headed to Brian's room, ignoring the dirty dishes in the sink and the leftover food containers on the counter. I knocked on his door, not bothering to wait for him to tell me to come in.

I pushed it open, snapping on the light. Brian groaned from the bed, obviously not happy about being woken up.

"Fuck, Una. I'm sleeping. Whatever it is can wait."

I crossed the room, pushing on his shoulder. "No, it can't."

He rolled over, grimacing in pain. I stepped back at the sight of his bruised face.

He pulled himself up, running a hand through his hair. His chest was marked as well, wrapped in bandages, the dark bruises peeking out from the wrap.

"Holy shit," I breathed out.

Brian reached for a cigarette, and I slapped his hand away. "I told you no smoking in the apartment."

He rolled his eyes, picking up a piece of gum and chewing. "It's been a bad day."

I shook my head. "What were you thinking, Brian? Gambling?"

He huffed out a dry laugh. "Oh, so he told you, did he?"

"He did."

He slid from the bed, holding out his arms. "Look what the bastard did."

"He could have let the other guy punish you. You wouldn't be standing." I swallowed hard. "Or breathing."

Brian waved his hand. "I had it under control. Fucking Finn had to remind me who was boss."

I crossed my arms. "He *is* your boss. And mine."

"After our father died saving his life, you would think that would give me some leeway."

I shook my head. "He paid off your debt, Brian. Thirty-five thousand dollars. You put him in a terrible situation."

"And he beat me."

I had to admit, he looked terrible. "Who wrapped your ribs?"

He sat down with another grimace. "Niall had me looked at. The doc wrapped me up and gave me some painkillers." He rubbed his eyes. "And I had to listen to Niall's fucking lecture on how I got off lightly and I should be grateful." He huffed an angry breath. "I still have to fucking pay the debt off. Fuck. Thirty-five K to Finn is lunch. He could have let it go." He looked at me. "He would if you asked him, Una."

I shook my head. "No, he wouldn't. And I'm not asking."

He narrowed his eyes. "Jesus, you too. I thought at least you'd take my side on this."

I had thought so too. I was furious with Finn for beating Brian. "I tried. I offered to pay him the money I had saved, but he refused."

Brian looked uncomfortable. "About that…"

I frowned. "About what?"

He shut his eyes. "My debt was higher."

My blood turned cold. "Higher?"

"Yes. I paid him some with what I won at the Maple. But he added more penalties and interest since I couldn't pay it all. I made another payment of twenty."

"Where did you get the twenty?" I asked, my voice shaking.

He didn't look me in the eyes. "I hacked into your computer and got into your account. I sort of borrowed it."

I stepped back, covering my mouth with my hand and stifling the gasp. "No!"

"I was gonna pay you back, Una. I was on a streak!"

I shook my head wildly, the tears in my eyes burning. "That was for my future."

"I'll pay you back."

"How?"

"I'll figure it out."

I wiped under my eyes, unable to believe what he'd said. Finn's words over the years came back to me. He hated how I coddled Brian. Always took his side. Defended him. Cared for him. "He'll drain you dry," he once informed me.

And he was right. My own brother had stolen from me. My entire life savings. And I had a feeling he didn't really care.

"I want you out," I said, straightening my shoulders.

"Oh, come on, Una. I'll get your money. You can't throw me out. Where will I go?"

"I don't care. Not here. And you will pay me back." I threw out the only threat I had. "Or I'll tell Finn you stole from me."

"You wouldn't."

"I would. Finn's right. I've been your mother too long, Brian. It's time for you to stand on your own two feet. You have a car. And thanks to Finn, a job. Go and act like an adult. Get your own place. Move in with one of the crew you like to hang with. I don't care."

"Right now? You're kicking me out right now when I can barely walk?"

"You will leave in the morning."

"You're being a bitch, you know that, right?" he snarled. "Dad would be so ashamed of you."

"No, Dad would be ashamed of you. He was a man of honor. He would understand why I have to do this."

"Would he understand you're taking Finn's side over mine? Your brother? He always said family first."

I refused to let him know how his words hurt and how torn I was feeling. "You reap what you sow, Brian."

He glared and stepped closer, wrapping his hands around my arms. He squeezed, his fingers digging into my skin. His eyes were dark and furious, his mouth curled into a sneer. My brother was gone, and in his place was the cold soldier he enjoyed being.

"Brian Joseph Murphy!" I snapped. "You're hurting me. Stop it now!"

He let go, and I stumbled back. Never once in my life had he hurt me physically. My dad didn't believe in hitting women, and he'd drummed that into Brian's head.

When had that changed?

I turned and headed to the door, my voice shaking. "You're gone in the morning."

He left before eight, the slamming of the door echoing behind him. He tore his room apart, leaving a mess behind him, acting like a petulant child. He had lots of names for me, cursing and constantly muttering between his groans. I was tense until he left, unsure if he would try to hurt me again. I rushed to the door and locked it behind him, engaging the dead bolt, then let out a shaky breath as I leaned my head on the wood.

I'd barely slept all night, upset and worried. More than once, I reached for my phone to call Finn, but I stopped myself. Brian was on his phone, hitting up his mates for a place to stay, no doubt calling me more names as he spoke.

He'd barely looked at me as he left, tossing his key to the table.

"Thanks for nothing," he'd muttered.

I slumped in my chair, my cup of tea growing cold on the table beside me. I rested my head in my hand, feeling weary and emotional. Drained. More than once, I glanced at my runners, thinking I needed to go and pound the pavement for a while. It always helped clear my head. But I was too tired to bother.

Memories of Brian when we were young played in my head. Before Mum died, even with what Dad did as a job, we were just a normal family. Brian doted on me. Everyone did. I was the baby. He was my big brother, and I adored him. When Mum died, it changed somehow, and he acted younger than I was. Less caring. More dependent. And I allowed it, needing to channel my grief into some other place. I did it by caring for him and Dad.

I spent the day wandering my apartment, straightening the guest room, doing laundry. I wasn't hungry, but I had some tea and crackers midafternoon, knowing I had to go to the hotel and sing that night. Normally, Fridays and Saturdays were my happy days. I got to perform. Let my voice loose and enjoy. But today, I was finding no joy, only obligation.

But as they said, the show must go on. I showered and dressed casually, walking to the subway and sitting in the back row, the car mercifully empty for this time of day. As the stops rolled past, I recalled meeting with Finn for dinner after my father's funeral, his offer.

"I bought a hotel. Two, actually," he informed me.

"Oh. I had no idea you were interested in that sort of business."

He smiled at me as he poured us some wine. We had met at a small restaurant, Finn not pleased that I wouldn't allow him to pick me up. But I was trying to draw a line somewhere. It was hard to remember that, though, while he sat across from me, his dress shirt stretched tightly over his chest and arms and the sleeves rolled up, exposing his strong forearms. He looked good. Better than good. The schoolgirl crush I'd had on him all those years was still there, only now, it was tinged with the awareness of adulthood. I understood the glances he stole when he thought I wasn't looking. The frank approval in his eyes as he watched me. The flare of desire I caught on occasion when I would laugh or tap my bottom lip. He watched me intently, making me feel as if I was the only person in the room. He didn't seem to notice other women staring at him.

I had to admit, I liked it.

"I don't think you know much about me, Una." He paused as he set down the bottle. "Yet."

The one word was laden with promise. I had to clench my hands on my lap to stop the tremble that went through me.

"And these hotels?" I asked. "Where are they?"

"Both here. In Toronto. They are smaller boutique hotels that have been mismanaged. I've hired new staff and done a lot of renovations." He took a drink of wine, studying me. "I'd like you to come work for me. Help me run them."

I almost sputtered. "I'm still learning myself."

He chuckled. "I've followed you, Una. Top of your class. The first hotel you went to, you rose up fast. Your old employer sang your praises. Hated that he lost you."

I sighed. "I wish I hadn't left."

"Why?"

"I wanted to work for Embers. The hotel had such a good reputation. But my manager is horrible. So terrified someone will surpass or replace her that she micromanages everything. The first word out of her mouth ninety percent of the time is no. She resents the fact that Alison, the hotel owner, handpicked me and offered me a position just under her. I'm getting nowhere—except frustrated."

"Then accept my offer."

"How do I know it would be different?"

He crossed his ankle over his knee, meeting my eyes. "I guarantee it would be, Una. I expect you to work hard and take advantage of the opportunity. You will learn under a great mentor. Then when you're ready, I'll send you to the next hotel in a higher position. I want to give you the opportunities you deserve."

"Why?" I asked, my voice suddenly breathless.

He sipped his wine, his gaze never leaving my face. "Because I saw the spark in you years ago. It's still there, but it's dimming. I want to bring it back to life." He set down his glass. "And I want to be part of your life."

"Finn," I whispered.

"I want to ask you out again. Only this time, not to offer you a job."

"I don't want to be involved with someone who is…" I trailed off, unsure how to explain.

"Date me, *not my choice of living," he said.*

"Are the two not connected?"

"Give me a chance." He slid his hand along the table, taking mine. "You feel that, Una? That connection? It was there when you were eighteen. So strong that I had to stay away. But it's still there, and we're both adults now."

My heart beat rapidly and my breathing picked up. I felt it too. He had woken something in me all those years ago. An awareness. A craving that had never been satisfied. The moment he took my hand, something in my chest eased. The second I walked away from him, the ache started. I was too young then to understand, but I understood it now. And I wanted him.

I had sensed him the entire time at my father's funeral. Watching me. Staying close. Always looking. Every time I glanced around the room, I met his intense gaze. Knew when he was close. Felt sad when he left and took that intensity with him. It was as if my soul needed him. As if I needed him.

"I don't know if I can." I swore I would never date anyone in the syndicate. Never get close to one of the men.

"Do you hate me because of your father?"

"No," I gasped. "My father made his decision long ago. I disliked it, but it was part of him. I just don't know if I want it to be part of me. If I could live in a world where the person I cared about was in danger all the time. It destroyed my mother."

"Give us a chance. My life is mostly nonviolent. I am careful. My men are careful. We want peace."

"Tell that to the bullet that hit my father."

He frowned. "That was a disgruntled, drugged-up asshole looking for revenge. It's not a daily occurrence." He paused. "Things have changed, Una."

I sighed, making the mistake of meeting his eyes. They were locked on me. Intense, passionate, and focused. I wanted to feel that intensity every day. Give in to the hunger he brought out in me. Rethink the rule I had set for myself so long ago. Somehow, I knew he would be worth it.

"Okay," I whispered.

"To the job or me?" he asked.

"To the job," I replied. I knew it was time to leave Embers. Audrey Ford would never be the mentor I hoped.

"And this?" he asked, indicating our hands.

I looked down, realizing I was clutching on to him with both hands as if he was a lifeline.

"You know you hold all the power here, mo chroí.*"*

I swallowed. "We can try."

His smile said it all. "Perfect."

I stepped from the stage amid the loud applause. I had laid my heart out on the stage tonight. Let my pain bleed out through the lyrics. I sensed Finn during the second show, but he was gone before I finished. I made my way to the dressing room, wanting nothing more than to change and head home. Soak in the tub with a dram of whiskey. Not the posh kind Finn and Niall drank, but reliable Jameson. It never let me down.

I walked into the room, knowing he was there before I flicked on the light.

"Finn," I said wearily. "Not tonight, please."

He sat in the corner, his presence once again filling the space. "You look exhausted. What's wrong?"

With a sigh, I sat at my table, making quick work of removing my makeup. I wore it lightly at work, but under the bright lights of the stage in the music room, I needed more. I disliked it. I was silent until I scrubbed off the last of it, changing behind the privacy screen in the corner. My yoga pants and soft shirt touched my overheated skin gently. I felt as if my nerves were on the outside of my body, and I was worried about breaking down in front of Finn. I refused to do that.

"You got your wish," I finally replied, sitting back at the table, smoothing on some moisturizer. "Brian moved out this morning."

"Good riddance."

I turned on him, angry. "If you dislike him so much, why do you keep him on?"

"He's a decent soldier. He could be great if he applied himself. But he was used to riding around on your dad's coattails. And you coddling him. Being on his own will be good for him."

"Whatever you say, Finn." I reached for my sweater when Finn cursed and shot out of the chair, dropping to his knees in front of me. He took my arm, turning and inspecting it.

"What the hell," he muttered. "Who—" He stopped speaking, his eyes narrowing, his mouth a slash of anger on his face. "I'm going to fucking kill him."

I stood, shaking off his grip. "You are going to leave him alone. Do you hear me? We had an argument. I kicked him out. He grabbed me, and I bruise easily."

Finn stood, towering over me. "He laid hands on you. That is punishable by death. I don't care if he's your brother."

"You hurt him, and I will walk, Finn. Out of this hotel, out of this city. You will never see me again, do you understand?"

Pain flashed over his face.

"Leave it. It's between him and me. It's done."

"I can't stand the thought of you hurt," he admitted.

"Taking your side over his hurt me. Kicking him out hurt me. I'm tired and drained, Finn. I can't do this with you. Not tonight. Not right now."

I reached for my purse, but he stopped me, dragging me into his arms. His warmth, his scent, wrapped around me. I could hear his heartbeat under my ear, the steady thump soothing. I felt the gentleness in his touch. The pressure of his lips moving on my head as he offered me the only comfort I could accept. For a moment, I relaxed. Melted into him. Nothing mattered outside this moment. This room.

I lifted my head, our gazes clashing. I recalled everything from our past, every moment of our brief interludes. Time seemed to melt away in that instant. I was caught in the intensity of his eyes, the pain and desire that swirled in them.

Then his mouth was on mine, and I was transported back in time. To the first kiss we shared. The intimacy of the moment. The possession of his mouth. The passion he brought out in me. I whimpered as I wrapped my arms around his neck, and he lifted me, still kissing, his tongue twisting and dancing with mine. He licked deep into my mouth, groaning. I gripped the back of his neck, the need for him becoming overwhelming.

Then my phone rang and shattered the moment. I startled, pushing back, and he set me on my feet. "That'll be my driver."

"Let me send him away."

Clarity hit me. I could nod, and in minutes, Finn would have me upstairs in his suite. We'd be naked and all over each other in no time.

And I would be caught.

I stepped back, reaching for my purse. "No. I can't."

He pushed his hands into his pockets. "I know."

"I'm sorry," I offered.

Then once again, I ran from Finn O'Reilly.

CHAPTER FIVE
UNA

Rain beat incessantly against the window. I sat in my chair, pulling my legs to my chest and covering them with a blanket. I clutched a cup of tea between my palms. I had been up early and ran three miles, hoping to dispel the sadness in my chest. It relieved some tension, but the ache didn't leave. I made it home just before the downpour started.

The skies were a dark gray, filled with water that poured from them, much like the pain that was filling my chest.

If only it could open up and release the emotion. Drain it away and leave a sun-filled space behind. I laughed quietly at my strange musings.

That wasn't going to happen.

I rested my chin on my bent knees, watching the deluge outside. I thought of the first date I'd had with Finn.

He picked me up, bringing me flowers and taking me to a quaint, family-owned restaurant. I looked around surprised, and he smiled at me. "My choice isn't what you expected?"

"No," I replied honestly. I had thought he would take me somewhere fancy and over the top. Exclusive and rich. I much preferred this intimate setting.

"I like quiet places," he explained. "I've been coming here for years. Great steak and even better whiskey. Simple and delicious." He winked. "Better doesn't always mean pricey, Una."

I blushed at his teasing.

After asking, he ordered us each a whiskey, then we chose our entrees. He was pleased when I ordered a steak like him, although smaller.

"Thank God you aren't one of those women who orders a meal and water and then picks at it. Eating is not a crime."

I shrugged, sipping my whiskey. It was decadent, far smoother than the stuff I drank at home. "I'm not much like other women. I've been surrounded my entire life by men and a no-nonsense attitude. I like food. I like whiskey. Why hide that?"

He lifted his glass, touching the rim to mine. "Amen to that. You are a breath of fresh air, Una."

Something about the way he said my name made my chest tighten. It was spoken in a low, intimate tone. As if his tongue were caressing it before he said it.

I had to shake my head to dispel my odd thoughts.

"I put in my notice," I informed him. "And met with Connie."

He nodded. "She told me. She was impressed as well."

"I liked her. I start on Monday."

"I'm aware."

"Finn—"

He chuckled, setting down his glass. "I already know what you're about to say."

I tilted my head, waiting.

"There will be no special treatment—in fact, I plan to have little to do with the day-to-day running of the hotels other than being the owner. That is what I expect the staff I hire to do. Which is why I only hire the best."

I waved my fingers between us. "Isn't this going to muddy those waters?"

"No. My private life is that. Private. Who I date has no significant impact on the hotel. I will rarely be in the

building. I don't make the decisions—Connie does. I won't be directly supervising you. What happens between us stays between us." He held up his hand. "And before you can ask, yes, Connie knows we're involved. She is married to the manager and there is no issue there, so all is good, Una."

"Involved?" I asked, raising an eyebrow. "It's our first date."

He waited until our appetizers were set in front of us. He cut into his sizzling shrimp, taking a bite and chewing slowly, a pleased expression on his face. "Delicious."

I tried my baked feta, spreading it on the warm toast, humming at the taste. "Agreed."

He leaned closer, meeting my eyes, his serious. "The first of many," he insisted.

"You're so certain," I mused.

"There was something the very moment I met you," he replied. "You were too young and there was no way I would have acted on it, but I felt it again when I saw you at the funeral." He paused. "I have never been able to move past that feeling, Una. Move past you. And this time, I didn't want to take a chance and lose you."

We were silent as I mulled over his words. I ate more of my appetizer, enjoying the saltiness of the feta and creamy garlic on the toast points. I saw Finn eye my plate, and with a smile, I handed him one of the delicious morsels. He ate it with gusto, placing a shrimp on my plate in return. It was garlicky and spicy, the shrimp bursting with flavor.

"I felt it too," I admitted quietly. "Young or not, I felt something for you."

"Then we're on the same page."

Dinner was smooth and enjoyable. Talking to Finn was easy. He listened to me. Really listened. He asked questions, answered mine honestly, thoughtfully.

"So do you still like to run?"

I nodded. "I do. It clears my head. I sometimes run in the park across from the hotel after work, but there's another park by the house."

He frowned. "Is it safe?"

"Yes. Lots of runners, bikes, and people taking their dogs for a walk. The paths are well lit, and I only run in the daytime," I replied, my heart warming a little at his concern.

"Good. I wondered after they tore down the school."

"You knew it was torn down?"

He sighed, wiping his mouth. "I worried, Una. About you running there in the evening."

"You didn't have to worry, Finn. They actually hired a security guard. He was there every..." I trailed off, something on his face giving him away.

"That was you?" I asked.

He nodded. "I had to stay away, but I had to make sure you were okay."

"Finn," I murmured.

"You already meant something. I needed to protect you."

I blinked at the feelings he evoked. I felt warm, protected, and seen. My dad had been caring, but once he'd shown me how to defend myself, he seemed not to worry. Brian never noticed or cared what I did or where I went. Neither of them thought of my safety the way Finn had. It made me feel loved in a way I didn't know I needed.

"Thank you," I murmured, laying my hand over his. He smiled and squeezed our fingers together, then lifted my hand to his mouth, kissing it.

"I'll always look out for you, Una."

The warmth deepened.

Our entrees came, and Finn changed the subject. We talked about other things—books, the headlines, music. Any question I asked, he answered. Any opinion I gave, he listened.

"I'm still worried," I admitted over dessert.

He ran a hand over his face. "I know, but Una, things are not the same as they were in your father's early days. I know you saw a lot of ugly events. But I run a tight ship. I promote peace, as do others of my generation. We work together for the most part. None of us want our loved ones dead or living under a cloud of fear all the time."

"There is still violence."

He sat back, resting his ankle on his knee. "And there always will be. Whether we're together or not. I try to control the violence. I know sometimes it rears its ugly head, but it's less than it used to be. Things have changed, Una. What we do, how we do it, has changed. I have more legal businesses than not. I oversee and keep peace in my territory. My crimes involve other worlds. Art. Currency. Machines. And those profits feed the ones I use to keep peace."

"I swore I would never date anyone in your world. I wanted to get as far away from it as possible."

A frown marred his face, and furrows deepened on his brow. "So, you're changing your mind?"

I sighed, tracing my finger over the pattern on the tablecloth. "That was before you," I admitted. "I feel such a..." I trailed off, unsure how to express it.

"Connection?" he asked quietly, reaching out to take my hand and stop its restless movement.

"Yes."

"I feel it too, Una. I have from the moment I met you. Your brother and father faded into the background, and I couldn't have cared less that they were even in the room. I was captivated by the old soul in the eighteen-year-old body. The wise woman speaking in a girl's voice. I have compared you to every woman I have met since that day, wondering how they seemed so ordinary next to you."

"I'm sure you didn't let that stop you from enjoying their company," I teased, yet hated the thought of him with someone else.

He shrugged. *"I've never been a monk, but I think you'd be surprised at how few I enjoyed, as you put it. How empty I felt with them. How simply being in your presence tonight has filled me in ways I can't even explain."*

"Finn..." I whispered.

He gripped my hand. *"Promise me you'll try. If you're worried, talk to me. Give me a chance, Una. Get to know me. In return, I promise you complete honesty. I'll never lie or sugarcoat things. You will always know where you stand with me. Honesty is very important."*

His gaze was powerful. Focused entirely on me. I could feel his passion and need. Felt it reflected in my soul.

"Or am I too old for you, Una? Ten years is a lot."

"No. I don't care about that. I have never felt my age."

"Or acted like it," he agreed. "So, what are you saying?"

"I'm saying yes."

"I need you alone. Now."

"I don't get to finish dessert?"

He was already on his feet. "I'll get you one to go."

A knock at my door brought me from my musings. I stood, shifting the blanket off my lap. I set down my cup of cold tea and headed to the door, peering out the peephole. I sighed, resting my head against the wood. "What now, Brian?" I asked.

"Let me in."

"So you can yell and call me names? Mess up the place some more?"

"Apologize."

That surprised me. I opened the door, stepping back to let him in. He looked tired, the bruising on his face dark and angry-looking. He met my eyes, his brown-colored gaze much like my father's.

For a moment, neither of us said anything. Then I waved my hand. "Come sit."

He followed me to the living room, sitting on the sofa. He was clean, his hair brushed, and despite his injuries, he looked calm.

"I was a jerk. An asshole. I'm sorry."

He sounded sincere. I nodded, letting him talk.

"I was in over my head. I broke all the rules, and you're right. Finn could have done much worse. I'm sorry for what I did. For stealing your money."

I indicated the backpack he had with him. "You can't come back."

"I know. But I wanted you to know I meant it. I'll pay you back. I'll figure it out." He drew in a deep breath. "I was wondering if I could leave my backpack, though. Juan's place is small, and I need this safe." He glanced at me, then back at the bag.

"What's in it?" I asked, suspicious.

He paused, then sighed. "Some of Dad's old shirts and things. Some pictures. They're all I have left, Una. I just want them safe. I'll stick them in the closet so they won't be in your way."

Instantly, I felt awful.

"I didn't know you had some of Dad's things."

"Stuff he had in his locker and car. They were things he touched every day, so they're important." He opened a zipper, showing me a photo of the three of us when he and I were young. It was faded and bent. "Like this."

I traced the images, sentiment welling inside me. If this photo and whatever else meant something to him, he wasn't lost. The man I knew he could be was in there somewhere. I handed it back to him. "Yes, you can."

"Thanks. Just until I find a place of my own."

I nodded, and he left the room, returning a moment later after putting the bag away.

"So, do I know this Juan?"

"No. I met him a few weeks ago on one of my jobs."

"Ah."

"He also does some side delivery gigs, and it gives him some extra cash. He's gonna get me in, and I'll give you that money."

"Side deliveries?" I asked skeptically.

"Like DoorDash, but for businesses. He takes documents that need signing from one business to another—that sort of thing."

"Oh." It sounded innocent enough. "Nothing that will compromise your job with Finn?"

A look flashed over his face. One of annoyance—but it went quickly.

"No. Just a side gig so I can pay you back."

There was silence for a moment. "All right," I said quietly. "I would appreciate that."

"I was scared and acted irrationally. I shouldn't have hacked into your account. I thought I could handle it and I would make back what I lost." He looked sad. "I didn't want you to know and be upset with me." He laughed ruefully. "I guess that didn't work out so well. Now you hate me."

"I don't hate you," I protested. "You're my brother, and I love you." I swallowed. "I'm just not sure I can trust you."

"That's fair. But you will again." He smiled. "Maybe we could start with a cup of tea? I'll make it."

"The last time you made the tea, you broke the bag and added too much milk. It was lumpy and cold."

"At least I tried. How about you make the tea, and I'll get the biscuits?"

I smiled. He was trying. "Sounds good."

The next day, the front desk was busy with weekend guests checking out and new ones checking in. I divided my time between there and pitching in at the concierge desk. I loved helping people get theater tickets or a reservation to a nice restaurant. I used all the contacts I had made over the years to get what I needed, often trading upgrades and other perks to return the favors. One of my ticket contacts loved the high tea we had on Sundays, and I often comped her in to say thanks and stay in her good books when I needed hard-to-come-by seats to a popular show.

I felt him before I saw him, his intense presence filling all my senses. I glanced up from behind the desk, meeting Finn's direct gaze. My breath caught in my throat as it always did at the sight of him. Tall, broad, his suit fitting him like a glove, showcasing his wide chest and shoulders, the deep forest-green highlighting his dark auburn hair that was pulled off his face with a strip of leather as it usually was. The snow-white of his shirt set off his coloring, and he looked every inch the owner of all he surveyed.

I remembered how soft his hair felt between my fingers. How it tickled my skin as he kissed his way along my body. The way those broad shoulders and wide chest felt as I lay on top of him, his arms encasing me, holding me tight. Safe.

Until, in the blink of an eye, it changed.

I shook my head to clear it of the thoughts invading my brain. I forced a smile as he approached.

"Good morning."

"Una," he rumbled. "How are you today?"

"I'm well. Yourself?"

He nodded in return, our polite, distant smiles lying to everyone around us. Boss and employee. Nothing else.

But simmering under the surface was so much more. And it took everything I had to push it down and hold it back.

I feared the day that no longer worked.

I would have to disappear from this hotel and his life completely.

"Everything going well?" he asked.

Beside me, George spoke. "She is working her magic again. Even I couldn't get the tickets she just procured for the penthouse guests. I arranged dinner for them, and they will have a night to remember tomorrow."

Finn looked pleased. "You both do me credit. I'm sure Mr. and Mrs. Wellington will thoroughly enjoy their stay."

The guests were new. Wealthy and used to getting what they wanted, yet not rude about it. They had been pleasant to deal with and appreciative of everything we had arranged, which was a nice change. Often, guests were less than pleasant—especially if you couldn't find exactly what they demanded.

"I arranged a special high tea this afternoon in their room. Dinner and access to the casino tonight," I informed him. "George got reservations at Crème, and I managed tenth-row center for the musical they wanted tomorrow. He is meeting friends in the lounge for a catered lunch, and she is getting the full spa service on Wednesday. They have a car at their disposal for shopping tomorrow afternoon."

"Excellent. Great work by you both. Thank you."

George beamed and I nodded, looking away from Finn's penetrating gaze. I wondered if I would ever get used to his presence and react to him in a normal way.

Odds were not in my favor.

"Una," Finn murmured.

"Yes?" I asked, bringing myself back to the present.

"I need a word with you later, in my office, please. Say, at two?"

"Of course."

He smiled and moved on. I watched him walk away, admiring how he moved. I knew he was observing, noting things in the lobby he would want addressed or admiring other items that pleased him. He was a good employer. Strict and exacting, but fair. Offering praise for good work. Reprimanding in private—never embarrassing staff in front of others. Always professional and in control.

Unless we were in a room alone together. Then he became far more personal. With a quiet sigh, I returned to my work, wondering what he wanted to see me about.

I supposed I'd find out soon enough.

FINN

There was a quiet knock at my door, and I smiled at Una's punctuality.

"In," I called.

She entered, bringing with her the sun. Figuratively, of course, although I swore the room got brighter when she entered it—any room. She had an aura of light around her.

"You wanted to see me?" she asked, trying to sound nonchalant.

I indicated the chair in front of my desk. "Sit, please."

She did so, crossing her legs. I tried not to ogle her, no doubt failing. The uniform for the hotel was simple. Light-colored blouses or shirts, deep-green skirts or pants. A waistcoat if you wanted. A necktie was optional, but today, not only was Una wearing a skirt, she had a flirty little bow tied around the neckline of her cream-colored blouse. And she had chosen one of the lacier blouses we offered, making her look feminine and sexy. Her hair was gathered up off her face, hanging down her back in a cascade of bright-red curls. She was irresistible.

She cleared her throat, and I had to grin. She'd caught me.

Patiently, she waited and I sobered. "I wanted to ask how you were."

"You did so this morning."

"With George present. You know what I mean."

"I'm fine." She hesitated. "Brian came to see me yesterday to apologize for his behavior."

"I see. I saw him this morning, and he thanked me for giving him another chance." I withheld the information that I'd grabbed him by the collar and threatened to end him if he ever so much as touched her again. He knew I was serious and assured me he would never do so again—although I didn't like the look in his eye or his attitude. He was on edge and almost twitchy. He wasn't to be trusted anymore, and I wondered how much longer he'd be part of the crew. Something was going to give—one of us would snap.

"Oh." She leaned forward, looking pleased. "Maybe this has shaken him up, Finn. He'll do better. Stand on his own two feet."

"I don't share your enthusiasm, but for your sake and his, I hope so."

"He could," she insisted.

Unable to resist the draw anymore, I stood, rounding the desk and sitting beside her. "Una, your father used to call you intuitive. He said you could read a person instantly, and he was right. I see how you sum up a guest. You always know the ones who need extra attention. More pandering. You gravitate toward the right people for friends. Your instincts serve you well for everyone—except your brother. Your love for him blinds you to his faults." To take the sting from my words, I reached out and tucked a strand of hair behind her ear. "And he is so lucky to have you in his corner. I only hope he is all you think he can be and that he doesn't let you down."

She closed her hand over mine, holding it in place. "I have to," she whispered. "He is all I have left in this world."

"No, you have me," I whispered back. "You will always have me, *mo chroí*. Let me in again. Try. I promise you will be safe. I will keep you safe."

Tears filled her eyes. "I can't, Finn. They shot you in front of me. And your men. Trying to get to me. I made you vulnerable, and I couldn't live with myself if you died because of me."

I wiped away the tears under her eyes. "I'm already half dead living without you."

"Move on and find someone else."

"I can't. I love you, Una. I will always love you. That is never going to change."

"Then I need to go."

"No," I demanded, tamping down my panic at the thought of her gone. "You stay here. Close. I won't bother you."

She stood, bending and pressing a kiss to my head. She held my eyes, then walked to the door. "That's the problem, Finn. You never bother me. But I can't—I can't do that again. I'm sorry."

And she walked out.

Early evening faded into night as I sat in my office. Niall was out of the building, and no one bothered me as I stared out the window, drinking whiskey and thinking. Remembering when we started. How bright and complete my world felt.

I had wined and dined Una for a week. A week of conversations over the table. Texts and calls. I went for a couple of runs with her. We didn't talk much, but I did enjoy the way it felt to be by her side, our pace matching once I shortened my stride a little. I teased her about it, making her laugh, which, in turn, made me smile. I did love her laugh. I also liked how her ass looked in her tight leggings, but I kept that information to myself.

Then she offered to cook me dinner, and I asked her to make it at my condo. I rarely spent time there, but the thought of having her there, in my space—filling it with her scent, the sound of her laughter, the aroma of her cooking...creating a memory I could relive—was too much to resist.

Over dinner, she told me she was ready to sell her father's house and move in to a place of her own.

"I know a great building," I informed her. "Clean. Affordable. Good neighborhood. I can give you the manager's name."

She beamed at me across the table. "Thank you."

"What about Brian?"

"He's looking for his own place." She sighed. "He's having trouble moving ahead without Dad. I'm looking for a two-bedroom place so he can stay until he finds his own."

I bit my tongue so I wouldn't tell her he would never move out if she let him in. He would sponge off her for as long as he could.

After dinner, we sat on the sofa, enjoying the fireplace and the quiet music. On impulse, I stood and took her in my arms, dancing around the room. She was tiny in my embrace, making me feel like a giant. A protector. I pulled her closer, smiling at her hum of approval. Looking down, I met her eyes, the green glowing in the dull light. Bending, I captured her mouth, kissing her. She sighed as she wound her arms around my neck and kissed me back. I picked her up, still moving as she wrapped her legs around my waist, and I deepened the kiss. She gripped my hair, pulled the knot out, and ran her fingers through the shaggy mess.

"God, I love your hair," she murmured. "It's so sexy, Finn."

Right then, I swore I would never change it. I cupped the back of her head, my hand filled with her curls. "Back at you, Una. You are so beautiful."

She whimpered, crashing her mouth to mine. With no thought, I walked to my bedroom, unable to tear my mouth from hers. I laid her on my mattress, hovering over her.

"Tell me you want this. You want me," I demanded.

"Yes."

I ran a finger down her cheek. "Once I have you, you're mine, Una. All mine."

She caught my hand, kissing it. "I already am."

That was all I needed to hear.

I kissed her, hovering over her on the mattress. I lost myself to the taste of her. The scent of her skin as we shed our clothing. How she felt so right molded to my body. Her softness cradled my muscled form, curving around me perfectly.

I buried my face into her neck, groaning as she touched me, the feeling of her hands on my skin like nothing I had ever experienced. How this tiny woman could affect me so deeply was a mystery.

"Finn," she whispered. "You're so beautiful. Everything about you."

"Even the scars?" I replied, trying to keep it light.

"Even the scars. I hate seeing them, but they tell me you survived."

I gathered her hair from around her face. "That's what I did until you came into my life, mo chroí. I survived. Now, I want to live. Feel. Experience everything. With you."

She crashed her mouth to mine, stroking, finding me hard and aching for her.

"I've never..." she confessed, her voice low.

My breath caught. She would be mine. Completely and utterly mine.

The caveman in me roared in satisfaction.

"I'll use a condom," I assured her.

"I'm on birth control," she replied. "I want to feel you, Finn."

I nuzzled the soft spot behind her ear. "That'll be a first for me as well." I had never gone bare with a woman. It was only right somehow that I experienced that with Una.

We kissed and touched endlessly, getting to know each other. She explored my body eagerly, caressing and discovering. Her touch branded me as hers. Her lips claimed me. Her hesitant fingers on my shaft were almost my undoing.

Her mouth that followed was.

Never had I experienced anything so erotic. The flick of her tongue, the gentle suction of her lips, the way she grew bolder, cupping my balls and letting me guide her.

Until I couldn't take it anymore and I returned the favor, listening to her gasp of shock turn into a low whimper of pleasure. She was sweet and musky on my tongue, a feast for all my senses.

Then when she was ready, I hovered over her, sliding into the heat and tightness waiting for me. Slowly. Carefully. Allowing her to adjust.

"Are you all right?" I asked quietly when I was fully seated inside her.

"Finn," she murmured. "Finn, it's so good. Please. Show me."

I moved, easing out and back in, listening to her moan. "Yes."

I slid my hand under her back, pulling her up to my chest, and sliding in deeper. Her eyes widened, and I began to move. She grasped at my neck, gripped my arms. Buried her face in my neck, chanting my name. Begging for more. I groaned as she tightened around me. Fought off my orgasm until I couldn't hold back and I joined her in the pleasure, cresting high as I held her, rocking into her and feeling complete and at peace for the first time I could recall.

And I knew I would never be able to let her go.

A knock at the door interrupted my thoughts. I called out to enter, and Niall walked in. He looked surprised.

"You are in here," he muttered. "You didn't answer your cell, and I knocked twice."

"Sorry," I replied. "Deep in thought." I waved to the decanter. "Help yourself."

He poured a finger of whiskey, sitting down and taking a sip. His brow was furrowed and he looked tired.

"Problem?" I asked.

"I was at the warehouse checking on things."

"Shipment okay?"

He nodded. "But something is off."

Niall and his instincts had never let me down, and I trusted him completely.

"With?" I prompted.

"Brian Murphy."

I wasn't surprised to hear his name. It kept cropping up and not in a good way.

"How?"

"He's acting strangely. Almost cocky. On edge."

"I thought he was twitchy earlier."

Niall tilted his chin in agreement.

"Anything missing?"

"No. I don't think he's stupid enough to steal from you. But I get the feeling something is up."

I told him about the conversation I'd had with Una a

few days prior. "She thinks he is getting ready to turn over a new leaf."

He snorted. "I think he's planning something. Or thinks he is."

"Watch him."

"I intend to."

I studied him briefly. "What else?"

He rubbed his forehead. "Mum," he replied.

I sat up, worried. "What is it?"

He shook his head. "I don't know. She sounds odd on the phone. Insists she is fine, but I FaceTimed with her and she looked drawn."

"Did you call the troublemakers?" I asked, referring to Maggie and Connie, her best friends.

He nodded. "They said she was fine and I was making too much out of a bad day." He scrubbed his face. "I think they're lying and in cahoots so as not to worry me. Which worries me more."

"Call Dr. Watts in the morning and check in. Although, with what we pay him, if he were worried, he would have called."

Niall drained his glass, looking thoughtful. "You're right, he would have."

"But you're still worried."

"I am," he admitted. "She sounded... I don't know. Different."

"Fine. I'll arrange the jet, and you fly there tomorrow."

"Finn, we have a shit-ton going on right now."

I shook my head. "Nothing as important as your mum."

He sighed. "I told her I'd come, and she told me off. Said I was being silly and seeing things not there. She said she was fine and that I caught her on a bad day."

I frowned. That sounded exactly like Aunt Roisin. We had wanted her to come live here with us, but she refused to leave Ireland. Niall bought her a new house in the same small town, but right on the water—modern and airy, with a garden she loved to putter in. When she refused it at first, stating she would know none of the neighbors, I bought the house beside her and moved her two closest friends in, who'd already shared a house since their husbands had passed. She had settled in well, but her health had been declining the last couple of years. We made sure she had the best care possible and had people keeping an eye on her as much as we could.

"You're due for a visit anyway," I pointed out. "It's been a while."

He looked out the window. "I hate going back," he admitted. "I feel as if all my mistakes from my youth are there, waiting for me."

"You've moved past all that shit," I replied.

"Yet I feel sixteen when I get there."

I took a sip of my whiskey, knowing exactly what he meant. I rarely went over, but when I did, I felt as if the past were all around me. The only good thing about going was seeing Aunt Roisin, and even that lost its luster after a few days. Niall kept his trips short, and mine were even shorter. But he tried to go twice a year, and I made it a point to go every eighteen months or so. We preferred it when we could convince her to come here. She would stay a month or so then head home, saying she'd had enough of the big city and the noise. The last visit, she'd brought her friends, and it took Niall and me months to recover. Three old Irish women intent on seeing everything they could, regardless of travel, crowds, or time constraints, proved to be a challenge. Never mind their love of whiskey and getting into trouble. I swore it was payback for when Niall and I got into scrapes when we were younger.

"Don't regret your decision," I said quietly. "She's been doing well, but you never know."

"I wish she would just come here and stay."

"We both do, but her life is there. Her friends. The shops she knows. The pub. She wouldn't be happy here long-term, Niall. You know that." I took another sip. "Any more than you would be happy living there. You've changed and outgrown it. She wants nothing to do with the big city other than the occasional visit, but she wants you happy."

He lifted an eyebrow, and I chuckled. "*Us* happy. She likes her life there. Let her live it. See what the doctor says and make a decision."

"I will." He crossed his ankle over his knee, studying me. "And what were you sitting in the dark thinking of? Or should I say, who?"

"Feck off."

He laughed, shaking his head. "You are never going to let go of her, are you?"

"I can't. It's impossible."

"You have everything, Finn. Find someone who wants to share that with you."

"I can't move on, Niall. I tried. Una is it for me. If all I can do is be her friend, stay in the background and make sure she's safe, then it's enough."

He stood, pulling down his sleeves. "You're lying to yourself, cousin. It isn't enough—and one day, you are going to want more, no matter what you tell yourself."

He headed to the door. "And you are going to have to make a choice. Live in the past filled with regrets or find some happiness."

Then he was gone, leaving me to my thoughts.

The next morning, Niall strode in, his expression calm.

"What did Dr. Watts say?" I asked.

"Dr. Watts said everything was fine with her levels at her last visit. She has another appointment next week, and he promised to keep me in the loop." He grimaced. "He reminded me she wasn't a young woman anymore and she is slowing down."

I met his gaze. "He's right, but she's your mother."

"I know. I called her today too and she seemed brighter, so maybe I did catch her on a bad day. I sent her flowers." He scrubbed the back of his neck. "I'll keep in touch and monitor things."

"Good plan. And if you need to go, the plane is at your disposal."

"Thanks, Finn."

"Family," was all I said.

He held out his hand. "Family."

I was restless that evening, unable to settle and my head aching. I went for a drive, finding myself parking in front of Una's building. I could see her light on behind the blinds, and I went upstairs, smiling in thanks at the person who held the door open for me. They had seen me around enough to know I was okay to let in.

Una looked surprised when she opened the door. "Finn?"

"Hi."

"Are you okay?"

"Sure." Then I paused. "May I come in?"

She stepped back. "Of course."

I walked in, inhaling.

"What are you cooking?"

"Oh," she said with a smile. "Stew."

"It smells incredible."

"I was about to eat. Would you like some?"

"*Mo chroí*, I would love a bowl," I replied. "And you know I love your cooking."

She headed to the kitchen. "It's simple."

"Simple is perfect."

I sat at the table, watching her, feeling myself relax. She always had that effect on me. She hummed as she moved around the small space, stirring the pot on the stove, slicing some bread and bringing it to the table. She paused, looking at me. "You look tired."

"Long day. Niall and I are a bit worried about his mum."

"Why?"

"We think Aunt Roisin isn't doing as well as she insists she is."

She placed a bowl in front of me, laying her hand on my shoulder. "I'm sorry. I know how much she means to you."

I tilted my head, resting it on her hand. "Thank you. Niall was concerned and got in touch with her doctor and her friends. They thought he was overreacting, so he's staying here and will keep a close eye on the situation. If anything changes and he needs to go, I'll get him there as fast as I can."

She squeezed my shoulder, drifting her hand up through my hair. It was all I could do not to groan at her touch. Moving away, she filled a bowl for herself and sat down beside me. "Eat, Finn. It'll help your headache."

"How did you know I had a headache?"

"You get a little pinched line right here." She tapped her forehead. "And you can see it in your eyes if you look hard enough."

"You're the only one who ever does."

She was quiet. "Eat. Please."

I picked up my spoon, wondering if she knew I'd do anything she asked of me.

Always.

The food helped, the company even more so. Una talked about some new song ideas she had and how much she was enjoying the front desk and working in the concierge area.

"Cleo wants to bring you up to management," I informed her. "She thinks you have all the qualifications you need to be a real asset in running the hotel behind the scenes."

"Already?"

I chuckled as I finished my second bowl of stew. "You've proven yourself, Una. Every challenge. You did at the other hotels as well. Connie hated to see you go. Albert, even more, from the last hotel. Everyone you work with speaks highly of you."

She nibbled on her bottom lip, looking worried. "I like the front desk."

I laughed. "Philip likes you. You're his favorite and he'll hate it when you go, but he knew you would. George, as well. You can call Cleo and go talk to her. It's the next step." I picked up my glass, draining the water from it, trying to stop the bitterness in my voice. "Soon, you'll leave us all."

She met my gaze. "You know it's always been my dream to have my own hotel."

I shoved down my sadness at the thought of her leaving. "I know. And I know you've been saving for it."

A shadow crossed her face, and her smile was forced. "Having enough for my dream will take me longer than I thought. I'm not in any hurry."

Something was off in her voice. Her shoulders were stiff and drawn back. "What changed? I know you have a budget, and you've always been good at following it."

She shrugged. "Sometimes life happens."

"What does that mean?"

"Nothing."

She stood, reaching for my empty bowl. I wrapped my hand around her wrist. "Una, I know you. What has happened? Do you need a raise? Is there a problem?"

She looked away, sitting. She traced a pattern on the table, not meeting my eyes.

"Una."

She looked up.

"Tell me."

"My savings... I loaned it to Brian."

I narrowed my eyes, instantly suspicious. "You *loaned* it to him?"

"Yes. He admitted his debt was larger than you knew."

"Una," I bit out. "I knew the figure from Lopez himself. The only way the debt was larger was if Brian paid some of it off before I found out. And since you were shocked when I told you about the situation, that means one of two things. You lied to me about not knowing, or he took your money without your knowledge. Which was it?"

She lifted her eyes to mine, and I knew.

"He fucking stole your money."

"He's going to pay it back. He promised."

"Yes, he is. Every penny plus interest. I'll make sure of it."

"Finn, stay out of it. It's between us."

"No—"

She stood, angry. "I didn't want to tell you because I knew how you'd react. This is between Brian and me. Stay out of it."

"And when he doesn't pay you back?"

"Then I helped my brother."

"When are you going to open your eyes, Una? Stop letting him take advantage of you!" I roared.

"He's my brother. My family. He's all I have left of my dad," she said, her voice broken. "I have to help him."

I rose to my feet, staring down at her. "You are too good for him. He's going to drain you. Financially, emotionally. I fear for you if you don't break away from him."

"My brother doesn't scare me."

I shook my head. "Then you're deluding yourself, Una. You refuse to allow me into your life based on the what-ifs, yet you allow him full access, when his what-ifs and past behaviors are far more dangerous to your well-being. Why can't you see that?"

"It isn't only the what-ifs," she replied, her eyes glimmering. "I was there, Finn. I witnessed your world firsthand."

I shut my eyes at the pain in her voice.

"So, it's easier to live without me than take a chance with me?" I asked quietly.

"I can't be the cause of your demise."

I chuckled without humor. "Since you insist my world is so violent, then someone is going to take me out at some point."

"Don't even say that!" she yelled, jumping to her feet.

"They could come after you to get to Brian," I pointed out.

"He is of no consequence to anyone," she insisted, crossing her arms. I knew the mulish look in her eyes far too well. She wouldn't listen to me. When it came to her brother, she never would. I bent and brushed a kiss to her forehead.

"Thank you for dinner, *mo chroí*. Until the last few moments, it was the best evening I've had in a long time." I paused. "I miss you. I miss us."

"We didn't have enough time for there to be an *us*."

I shook my head. "Always so stubborn. There *was* an us. There *is* an us. I hope one day there will be a forever us. Once you realize it, I'll be waiting."

"If you hate my brother so much, why do you want to be a part of my life?" she asked.

"I don't hate him. I loathe how he uses you. I detest how you allow it, but I understand it. It's how you show your love. I don't think he deserves it."

"But you do?"

Her words stopped me. I lifted my hand, trailing my fingers down her cheek. "No, I don't. But I am a selfish man, Una, and I want it. I want your love, your laughter, your body. I want your world to begin and end with me. I want your every breath and thought. I want to possess you. Love you. I want to give you everything you need to fulfill your dreams and watch you soar." I smiled sadly. "As long as I'm part of them."

"Finn," she whispered, her eyes wide, her chest rising and falling rapidly.

I bent close so our mouths were almost touching. Near enough I could feel her breath on mine. "I want you. I love you. I'm waiting. Don't make me wait much longer."

"What will you do?" she breathed out, her voice shaky.

I crushed her to me, kissing her until she was trembling. Breathless. Unable to stop the desire that filled her eyes.

"I will take what is mine, and this time, I won't let go."

Then I left.

CHAPTER SEVEN

UNA

I gave up trying to sleep. I had tossed and turned most of the night, Finn's words, his actions, repeating themselves over and over in my head.

I'm a selfish man.

I want your love, your laughter, your body.

Us.

Forever.

This time, I won't let go.

I made a coffee, curling up in my chair, once again letting the past wash over me.

After that first night, Finn and I'd become inseparable, and before I knew it, two months had flown by. Calls, texts, dates, flowers. Dinners that ended up with us in bed. Dates that ended up with no dinner. Weekends spent never leaving his condo. He was insatiable. An incredible lover. Patient, thorough. I could ask him anything, and he would teach me. Show me how to touch him. What to do. How to find my own pleasure. I had never known passion the way it was with him.

Brian was ambivalent that we were together, yet seemed angry over the fact that it gained him no favor in Finn's eyes. He liked to make small digs, hinting that Finn was simply using me and would eventually grow tired and move on.

I ignored him.

We spent more of our time at Finn's condo than the new place I had moved in to, and Finn kept slyly suggesting I give it to Brian and move in with him.

Life couldn't have been better.

Until reality stepped in.

The night began like any other night. Finn took me to one of our favorite places—a small café with great food, good music, and a fabulous wine list. He wanted to celebrate our two-month anniversary, and there were flowers on the table and my favorite bottle of wine.

He listened to me go on about my day, excited about what was happening at the job. The one he'd helped me get. Over dessert, he laughed when I told him I'd tried to get into the wrong apartment the night before.

"I'm there so little, I tried to get into 319 instead of 419," I informed him. "You have me so crazy I can't even remember where I live!"

He leaned over and kissed me. "You should be living with me."

I shook my head. "Too soon, Finn O'Reilly."

He kissed me again, his eyes dancing. "I've waited years, mo chroí. *I think my patience needs to be rewarded."*

"Then take me home."

He stood, holding out his hand. We were headed toward the door when it happened. I heard the sound of gunshots and shattering glass. People began screaming. Finn cursed, drawing a gun I had no idea he was carrying, shoving me behind him and yelling at me to get down. His men outside were returning fire, and as fast as it began, it stopped, the echoes of the shots lingering in the eerie silence that fell. I staggered to my feet in shock, staring at Finn. Then in horror at the blood that was soaking through his shirt.

"Una," he gasped. "Are you hurt?" He stepped toward me, and I grabbed at his arm.

"Finn, you need to sit!"

"Why?"

"You've been shot!"

He glanced down, looking surprised. He looked up, frowning. "That explains the pain."

Then he collapsed.

The ride to the hospital was a blur. His men had bundled him and me into a car, not waiting for an ambulance. We were met at the entrance to the ER, and Finn was whisked away. I stood in shock outside the doors they took him through, unsure what to do. Moments later, Niall arrived, taking charge. He wrapped me in his overcoat and sat me down, leaving one of the men with me. He spoke to the doctors then kneeled in front of me.

"They're taking him to surgery, Una."

"He'll be okay?" I asked, my voice barely a whisper.

His face was grave. "They're doing the best they can."

"He'll be okay," I repeated, more firmly.

He nodded. "It's Finn."

"It's Finn," I echoed.

I paced for what felt like hours. I heard snippets of the conversation—enough to know what had happened.

"Who was it?" Niall demanded of the men. "Who did you see?"

"I didn't know him," Rory, his driver, spoke up. "But I recognized the tattoo on his arm. It was from Diego's gang he chased out of town."

"Dammit," Niall responded. "I knew they'd return."

Rory's eyes skittered to me. "I don't think it was him they wanted to take out. I think they were aiming elsewhere to send a message."

I swallowed at the lump in my throat.

Someone with a grudge against Finn decided to take away the one thing that seemed to mean a lot to him.

Me.

The gunfire was to kill me.

Instead, he took the bullet.

Just like my dad did for him.

Niall pressed a coffee into my hand, and I grabbed at his wrist before he could leave.

"Did you retaliate?"

He stared at me a moment. "It's started. They'll all be eliminated before dawn," he said quietly. "Don't be afraid, Una. You're safe."

He walked away, and I shook my head.

I wasn't afraid for me. I feared for Finn.

I was a liability.

I'd heard my dad talk about leaders and their families. How the right person could strengthen and uphold the other, making them more powerful. But they had to be careful never to reveal that connection since it could be used against them.

Finn had been transparent with his feelings to me. It had almost cost him his life.

I had to break it off when he recovered.

No matter how much it hurt me.

Because I loved him too much to let him die because of me.

An odd noise alerted me to someone at my door. I walked over, peeking through the keyhole to see Brian. He was looking down at something in his hand. I opened the door, surprising him.

"Oh—you're home. I knocked," he said, sounding nervous, his hands closing into fists in a repetitive gesture. "I thought you'd be at work."

"I have the later shift today. What were you doing—trying to pick the lock?" I asked, teasing.

He held up his phone. "I was texting you."

"Oh." I glanced at my watch, seeing it was just after eight. I had been lost to my thoughts for over two hours. "It's early for a visit."

"I was in the neighborhood and wanted to come say hi." I stepped back, and he came in. "Any chance of a tea?"

"I was just having coffee," I replied.

"I'd take that too."

"Sure." I headed for the kitchen, and he leaned on the doorframe, watching me, his gaze dark and never settling. "Can I use the bathroom?"

I sighed, shaking my head. "You don't have to ask."

"I feel as if I do."

I grabbed a cup, waiting as it filled with steaming coffee, then made myself another one. I carried them to the living room, frowning when Brian reappeared from his old room.

"The bathroom is down the hall."

He took his cup, sitting down, his knee bouncing. "I was checking to see if I'd left behind an extra phone cable in my backpack. I broke mine."

"Any luck?"

"No. I'll buy one."

He slid his hand into his pocket and handed me a wad of cash. I took it with a frown. "What is this?"

"Money toward what I owe you. It's only a few hundred, but I'll keep paying you."

"Where did you get this?"

"I told you, I'm working extra jobs." He took another sip of coffee. "In fact, Juan and I are thinking of opening our own business." He met my gaze. "I'm going to leave Finn's crew."

I felt my eyes widen. "Have you told him that?"

"No. Not yet. He won't give a shit anyway."

"You owe him a lot of money."

"And I'll pay him. But I'm tired of being treated like a chump," he snarled. "I've been his whipping boy long enough."

I was surprised at his tone and how quickly he became angry.

"Why do you dislike him so much?" I asked.

He ran a hand through his hair. "Why don't I? He keeps me down, like a nobody. No promotions, no rewards. I'm just a grunt. After what Dad did for him, he should be fucking showing me gratitude. And you..." He trailed off, his anger getting the better of him. "He should be looking after me too. Not just you. I deserve it."

I frowned. "You deserve it?"

"Yeah, I do," he spat.

"Well, I hope the conversation goes well," I soothed, feeling nervous. Brian was off today. Wound up tight. I could feel his agitation, and it was making me anxious. I didn't want to provoke him.

He slammed his coffee cup down on the table, leaning forward. His anger rolled off him. "Do you, Una? Or do you hope he beats me again? Puts me in my place?"

"Your place?" I repeated, anxiety becoming fear.

"Below you. Never good enough. Always under Una, the perfect one."

I forced a laugh. "I'm hardly perfect, Brian. You know that."

He stood, towering over me. "Not to him," he sneered. "He thinks you fucking walk on water. Even after you broke it off. He gets you a job in the new hotel. A place to sing. He's always around. Fucking watching. Like a fucking pervert."

"I don't know why you're so angry right now, Brian," I said, forcing myself to stay calm. "But I think you should leave."

For a moment, I thought he was going to explode. Then he sighed, every muscle loosening in his body. He shook his head.

"Sorry, Una." He straightened. "Thanks for the coffee. I'll get you more money as soon as I can."

He walked out, and as soon as the door shut, I was out of my chair, snapping the dead bolt and leaning on the door, my heart racing.

What the hell was that all about?

I wasn't sure, but I knew I needed to talk to Finn.

FINN

No phone call that happens at four a.m. brings any good news with it. Niall's voice was thick when I answered.

"What happened?"

"Mum. She had a stroke." He paused, and I heard him swallow. "It's bad, Finn."

"How bad?"

"Bad."

"I'll get the plane ready. I'm coming with you."

"Thanks."

I hung up and scrubbed my hand over my face. I called my pilot with instructions to file a flight plan and let me know how quickly we could depart, then I rested my head in my hands.

I wasn't worried about the hotel. My managers would run it while I was gone. The casino staff would look after that side of it. But my territory—with both Niall and me out of the country, that left us vulnerable.

I shook my head and sighed. I really had only one option. I scrolled my contacts and called the one person I could trust. He answered on the first ring, his voice as awake as if he'd been waiting for my call.

"O'Reilly?"

"Roman, I need your help."

"Tell me."

An hour later, Roman Costas was in my office, dressed, looking as if he'd just stepped off the runway. He listened as I explained everything, my instructions basic since he knew even better than I did what had to happen in the hotel, the casino, and even the territory.

"Everything is peaceful and smooth. I want it to stay that way."

"Any issues? Personnel? Crews?" he asked.

"Nothing."

"Murphy?' he asked. "The brother?"

"Well, a pain in my ass, as always. He isn't happy about his demotion. Or the money I am making him repay. But he's toeing the line." I took a sip of coffee. "Although Niall noticed he was on edge the last week. Jittery."

"I'll watch him."

"Good."

"And the sister?"

"Under my protection. She is to be kept safe above all else. Happy."

"I figured as much." He leaned forward, resting his elbows on his thighs. "I'm going to divide my time between here and Niagara. Aldo and I will make sure this place is covered, your territory is kept under control, and I will make sure your Una is safe."

"I appreciate it. I owe you."

He waved his hand. "Working together was always part of the plan. I wish you a safe journey. When do you leave?"

"Two hours. Just enough time for me to take you around and introduce you to the key people. One of my top men will take you anywhere you need to be and give you access to anything you require. You can reach me day or night."

He nodded. "Only in an emergency."

I stood. "Let's do this."

An hour later, I headed to my suite, grabbing my bag and packing quickly. Niall was with Roman and Aldo, finishing up the introductions. I made a few calls, then snapped my suitcase closed. I sat down and dialed Una for the third time, waiting impatiently for her to answer. I wanted to tell her I was going myself, not leave a message. I really wanted to see her, but she was working a later shift today, and there wasn't time to go to her place before the airport.

"Hello?" she answered, breathless.

"It's Finn. Are you okay?"

"I was in the shower. I kept hearing the phone ringing. Are you all right?"

"I'm flying to Ireland shortly."

"Oh, Finn," she replied, her voice soft. "I'm so sorry."

"Roisin had a stroke—a bad one. Niall needs me. She needs me. I don't have much choice."

"Of course not—they are your family. You have to go. Oh, I wish I were there with you."

"So do I."

There was a pause. I cleared my throat.

"Roman Costas is running everything while I'm gone. If you need something, you call him. Anything."

"I'll be fine."

"Una. Anything. You understand me?"

"Yes." She hesitated. "You can call me anytime too, Finn. If you need to talk or a shoulder. I'm here."

"I know, *mo chroí*. I know." I took a deep breath. "We're going to talk when I get back, do you hear me? Really talk."

"Finn..."

"My patience is done."

Her intake of air was fast.

"Done," I repeated.

"I heard you the first time, Finn."

"Just so you understand. Life is too fucking short, Una. I'm not spending it without you anymore. Think about it while I'm gone." I paused. "*Tá mé i ngrá leat.* I love you."

I hung up before she could reply.

CHAPTER EIGHT

FINN

The plane trip was smooth and mostly silent. Niall was lost in his thoughts, no doubt worried and upset. He and I weren't good at discussing feelings. He knew I was there, would offer any support I could, and that was enough for him.

The onboard staff stayed away, offering food and drink we accepted, although the food was mostly picked at.

The drinks, however, were replenished a few times.

I spent the flight checking emails, texts, checking in with Roman and getting told off for doing so.

> For fuck's sake, O'Reilly. It's been 6 hours. What kind of catastrophe are you expecting in 6 hours? Look after your family. I have it in hand.

Somehow his message made me feel better.

I leaned my head back, thinking of what I had said to Una. Why I had said it. I hadn't planned it. It simply came out.

But it was the truth. I was tired of pretending. Pretending she didn't mean what she meant to me. Pretending that I was fine with being on the fringes of her life. Worrying constantly that one day I would see her with another man. One who didn't deserve her—who would never treat her like the queen she was. She needed to be adored, cared for, protected. Lavished with gifts and love. Fucked on a regular basis and made love to other times. And both done by a man strong enough and clever enough to know the difference.

And the only man suitable for that job was me.

I recalled waking up in the hospital, Una hovering over me, pale, scared, and panicked. I was weak and in pain, barely able to talk. Niall was a constant shadow behind her, assuring me quietly the threat had been eliminated and that Una was safe. I was in and out of it for days, the loss of blood and the length of surgery taking its toll.

When the haze began to lift, Una was there. Helpful, careful, always encouraging.

And distant. She kept her emotions in check and stayed

close enough to care, but not feel. She held herself back. I hated every second of it.

I was released a week later and settled into my condo, grateful to be among familiar things. Una busied herself in the kitchen as I spoke with Niall and some other key members of my team.

"Who?" I finally was able to ask, no longer worried about prying eyes or ears.

"Diego Cortez. His brother was killed when we clashed with his gang."

"He was killing civilians for fun," I snarled. "In my territory. Spreading his poisonous drugs."

Oliver, one of my head soldiers, looked grim. "He liked bloodshed. The whole gang did."

"How many men?"

"We lost two. Grant and Simon."

I grimaced. Both were loyal. Grant was a bachelor but had a sister. Simon was older and widowed but had two grown kids.

"We've taken care of the families? The funerals?"

"Everything is handled."

"Stupid fecker. His brother was a casualty of a war he

started. I didn't go gunning for him." I rubbed my eyes, feeling weary. "But he came after Una."

"And paid the price." Niall looked fierce. "The gang no longer exists, except for a few low-level foot soldiers who shit their pants and ran like children. I made sure the word was out that if they returned, death would greet them."

I nodded, feeling exhausted already but refusing to show weakness in front of my men. "Do we expect retaliation?"

"No," Oliver replied. "Our locals are grateful they are gone. Business is picking up again, knowing the poison is off the streets."

I leaned my head back, shutting my eyes for a moment. I hated drugs, and we didn't deal in them. I especially hated low-grade drugs that killed. And the people who pushed them.

Like many of my generation, I dealt in high-end, nonviolent ways of making money. I left the rest to the street gangs—as long as they stayed out of my turf. Drugs were debilitating and I wasn't stupid enough to think none were around, but I turned a blind eye at times, knowing it was better to be aware of what was happening in order to maintain control.

I sighed. "Keep your eyes and ears open. Let it be known I'm alive, well, and still running the territory. No weakness."

Niall chuckled. "Trust me, the rumors are already out there."

"Good or bad?"

"That you shot five men after being shot yourself. How you walked into the hospital and refused to wait for surgery, making the doc pull the bullet from your shoulder right there."

I had to laugh. "No anesthetic?"

"None."

"Sounds about right," Una spoke up from the doorway. "Superman Finn." She clapped her hands. "Enough. He needs his rest."

All my men deferred to her, not a single one even glancing in my direction to make sure it was all right to leave. Niall stayed behind.

"Mum needs to hear your voice. She's pretty upset."

"Why'd you say anything?" I groaned.

He leaned close. "We didn't know if you'd make it, Finn. I had to ease her into it, dammit."

"I'll call her tonight."

"I told her you were on the mend and in good hands. She still needs to hear you."

"Tonight," I promised.

"Okay."

Una brought me some soup, helping me eat it since my arm was still taped to my body. The bullet had gone in below the shoulder on the left side. Another few inches either way, I would have been dead. As it was, it damaged some muscles and tissue and had been a bitch to get out. The stitches pulled every time I moved, and it felt as if my shoulder and chest were on fire.

"Your doctor will be here tomorrow to check on your progress. You'll start physio in a few days," she said quietly.

"Good. Then we can put this behind us."

She didn't reply. I reached for her hand with my good one, frowning at how cold hers was.

"Una," I said, waiting until she met my eyes. "I'm sorry. I'm sorry for what you went through."

"You almost died trying to protect me. Two men died." She shook her head. "That is exactly why I didn't want to be in your world, Finn."

"I know."

"I swore I would never get involved with a syndicate man. I believed you when you said it was different."

"It is—usually. That was an anomaly, not the norm. I

swear to God it was. He was a drugged-up hothead and made a stupid decision."

"And next time, he might not miss."

"I will never allow anything to happen to you."

She slid from the bed, shaking her head. "Not me. You, Finn. If you had died protecting me, I would never forgive myself. I refuse to be your vulnerability. To be used against you."

"Don't, Una. Don't say it."

She sighed. "We both know it, Finn. I can't stay. I won't leave you until you're on your feet, but I can't stay. I need to be what we were before my father died."

"Strangers?" I snapped. "That is impossible."

She smiled, even as tears glistened in her eyes. "Polite acquaintances."

"I can't do that."

"You have to. And you will."

"What makes you so sure?"

She paused, a tear rolling down her cheek. "Because I'm asking you to do that for me."

And she left the room, the silence deafening in its stillness.

Because she was right.

The pilot announced that we would be landing, pulling my thoughts back from the past.

From one loss to potentially another.

I wasn't sure how I would handle this one.

I had never gotten over the other.

All hospitals smelled the same. Medicinal. Underlying bleach fumes covering the stench of decaying walls and illness. I hated them with a passion.

And knowing what was waiting for us made it even worse.

Roisin was a silent form under the blankets and machinery. Pale and waxen, she looked older than I had ever seen her appear. Vulnerable and small.

Niall sat beside her, taking her hand in his and pressing it to his forehead. I stood behind him, my hand on his shoulder as he wept.

Her specialist came in, and we spoke of results, prognoses, possibilities.

None of it good.

I arranged a room close to the hospital, and Niall and I agreed on a schedule so she would never be alone. I had a feeling getting either of us away from her bedside would prove fruitless, but in theory, it worked.

We sat in that dim room, forcing ourselves to talk. Speak to her. Hoping she knew we were there.

Our cousin Sullivan, ten years our senior and a barrister in Edinburgh, came when we called, looking somber and sad.

"Sully," I greeted him with a handshake and a backslapping hug. "Good to see you, although I wish not under these circumstances."

He hugged me back, staring over my shoulder at my aunt. "Jesus, I only saw her two weeks ago when I came to Dublin for the office. She was right as rain. Fussing over me, telling me I needed a wife and I worked too hard. She refused to let me take her to lunch and insisted on cooking a Sunday roast for us."

"And no doubt sending you home with the leftovers."

"Aye. I ate like a king for a week." He wiped his eyes. "How's Niall?"

"I finally got him to rest." I snorted, shaking my head. "In the room across the way that was empty. The hotel room is sitting unused. Neither of us has been there."

"Any change?"

"Well, she isn't worse. She muttered a little yesterday and squeezed Niall's hand, so we're taking that as a good sign."

"Go get a coffee or take a walk. I'll sit with her, man. You look like death warmed over." He lifted one shoulder. "Pardon the expression."

"I'll take you up on that. I'll only be gone a short while. I have my phone with me, and Niall will be back in a minute. I heard his alarm go."

He nodded. "Off with you."

The fresh air felt good on my face, and I inhaled it deeply, ridding my lungs of the scents of the hospital. I walked the block, needed to feel the stretch in my legs and arms as I swung them. I got a coffee and bun from a local shop and sat on the bench outside, checking my phone. I saw a missed call from Roman, and I returned it, waiting until he picked up.

"Costas."

"It's Finn."

"How are things?"

"About the same. My cousin arrived, so I'm out on a walk to clear my head. Is there a problem?"

He paused. "Not sure if you'll think it's a problem or a solution."

"That sounds ominous."

"Brian Murphy."

I shut my eyes. "What now?"

"He picked a fight with one of the crew. It took Oliver and me to pull him off. He was high, Finn. Out of his mind on something."

"Fuck," I muttered. I had a zero tolerance for drugs. "When did he start on that shit?"

"You mentioned he seemed off. Oliver noticed his behavior too." He sighed. "He mouthed off, disrespectful and belligerent. Then basically told us to fuck off—he was done. He had a lot of anger in his departing words."

"You let him walk?"

"I had no idea on your policy for crew. I didn't run mine the way the elders did."

I knew what he meant. There was no retirement package in the old days unless you left in a box. Now, we handled things differently, but I had never had anyone leave this way. A few who wanted something different were allowed to go and relocate, but I still had their loyalty. I'd never had Brian's. I never would.

"I'll deal with him when I return. Make sure he has zero access."

"Everything—passcodes, locks, security, anything he might have known, has been changed. He was checked before he left the building, and he walked with nothing."

"Have you told Una?"

"No. I was waiting for your direction."

"I'll let her know. She might already have heard since he'd run to her first with a cover story."

"Ah. It's like that, is it?"

"She protects him. Always has."

"I know a bit about that. Effie had a sister..." He cleared his throat. "It didn't end well."

I scrubbed my face. "Hmm. Watch over her carefully."

"Will do. If it's any comfort, no one is upset he is gone. Apparently his attitude has been bad, and he's not missed."

I ran a hand through my hair as I stared at the busy street around me. "I won't miss dealing with him. I did my duty to Jim," I confessed. I stood. "I'm heading back to the hospital. I'll check in again in a couple of days."

"Right." He hung up.

I sighed as I headed back to the small gray building. I probably would have handled it the same way as Roman. I wouldn't kill Brian, although he would probably have been taught a lesson for the disrespect. I wondered what he would tell Una or how she would react when I called her.

I reached the hospital, putting it out of my mind. I had more important things to think on now.

Roisin opened her eyes that evening. She was confused, weak, and could barely speak, but it was a step in the right direction. The next morning, she was brighter, actually smiling, her color better. I hoped we were over the worst of it and that she would continue to improve. I sat beside her after sending Niall to the hotel for a shower and some much-needed sleep. I stroked her hand, smiling as she clucked her tongue at me, her voice tremulous and raw. Her speech pattern was slow and she hesitated over her words, but the doctor hoped with therapy and time she would recover.

"You need rest too."

"Hush, Aunt. I'm fine."

"I have...a different opinion...on that."

I rolled my eyes. "I wouldn't be so lippy. You're the one lying in the hospital." I picked up her hand and kissed the knuckles. "If you wanted a visit so bad, you only had to ask."

She huffed and was quiet for a moment. "How's that... redheaded beauty of yours?"

I frowned. "Not mine."

She huffed again. "Still on that...nonsense, are we?"

"It's complicated."

"Your generation makes it...complicated," she mumbled.

"Is that so?" I replied with a smile. Even though she could barely keep her eyes open and her speech was slow, Roisin was determined to tell me off.

"If you love her, tell her."

"She knows."

"Then...what's the problem?"

My aunt knew what I did. Who I was. She had lived through it herself and didn't shy away from the truth.

"My world."

She attempted to roll her eyes, but since they were half shut, it didn't really have the proper effect.

"Go to sleep, Aunt. Stop meddling."

She squeezed my fingers after a fashion and, with a sigh, fell asleep.

I quietly rose from the uncomfortable chair and walked to the window. It was an overcast gray day. I glanced at my watch, knowing Una would be home, getting ready to head to the hotel later for her performance.

I dialed her number, simply the sound of her soft hello easing something in me.

"Una," I murmured.

"Oh, Finn. How is she?"

"Awake. Weak. Stubborn as hell."

"You sound exhausted."

"I am," I admitted. It was something I would only tell her. "Shattered."

"You need to rest."

"I have to look after Niall. Roisin."

"Who is looking after you?"

"This call has helped." I leaned my head on the glass. "I miss you, *mo chroí.*"

"Oh, Finn," she whispered again.

I'd planned to tell her about Brian, but I couldn't. This call was about her. Me. Us. I didn't want him in the middle yet again. I would call her tomorrow while I was alone.

For a moment, the line was silent, then she spoke again.

"Are you still done?"

"Done and over."

"Okay, then."

"Sing for me tonight."

"I will."

"Is ceol mo chroí thú," I murmured. Music of my heart. She always would be.

I hung up.

UNA

I hated that Finn was gone. And I hated the fact that I hated it even more. The hotel seemed dimmer, and somehow knowing he wasn't checking on me occasionally made me feel oddly vulnerable.

He sounded so lost and alone on his call. A weakness I knew he would only allow me to see. I wished I could hold him. Let him rely on me for strength for a change.

I was tired of fighting my feelings. Fighting him. I hated his job, but I loved the man. He had been nothing but patient. Loving. Kind. Doing everything in his power to ensure my happiness, even as I kept him at arm's length. His words, his powerful statements, rolled through my mind as I dressed.

"I'm half dead without you."

"I'm done being patient."

Not once, even the day I'd walked away from him, had he ever shown me anything but love. Understanding. And the bottom line was that I had accepted all his gestures, knowing deep in my heart why he was making them. Ever hopeful I would return to him. Waiting, his emotions on hold for me to grow up and realize that what I wanted was right in front of me.

That, between us, if I listened to him and we worked together, we would figure out our future.

I wiped away my tears. He was too far away for me to tell him. To apologize. To beg his forgiveness and let his love surround me. I had made him wait for so long, and I didn't want him to wait anymore.

I knew in that moment I needed him as much as he needed me. I was his light, and he was the dark I was drawn to, because with him, I was safe.

The songs I chose that night were deep and sorrowful, the pain I was feeling bleeding through the notes my voice carried into the room. Roman Costas showed up at my dressing room door after the first show, looking concerned.

I was surprised to see him but allowed him entrance.

"Is there a problem?"

He frowned. "That's what I'm here to find out. You sounded very emotional. You made my wife weep as you sang. Vi even got emotional, and that's rare. Are you all right?"

"I'm fine."

He crossed his arms. "Miss Murphy, I was left with three very strict instructions from Finn. Take care of his casino. Make sure his territory remained peaceful in his absence, and above all, be certain Una Murphy was safe, protected, and happy. If I have to tell him you're upset and despondent while under my watch, things aren't going to go well for me."

I waved him off. "Finn called and he was upset. I wish I were there."

He studied me for a moment, then nodded as if making a decision.

"Would you join my wife and me for a drink before your next set? She would like to meet you, and I think you would like her. She is a ray of light in my life, maybe she can brighten yours today."

Somehow I knew he wouldn't take no for an answer, so I agreed. He excused himself, his phone pressed to his ear, and I took a moment to compose myself.

Then I joined Roman and his wife, Effie, for a drink. His right hand, Aldo, was present with his wife, Vi. She and Effie were obviously close although they were two exact opposites. Effie was petite, with long, dark hair and stunning blue eyes. She spoke quietly, but her smile could fill a room with light. She was kind and effusive, and her love for Roman was obvious. He, in turn, looked at her as if she was his entire world.

Vi was tall. She towered over me, and she had short hair that hugged her head and gleamed under the lights. She was funny and droll. Laughed loudly, teased Aldo and Roman. She praised my voice, informing Roman he should have me come to Niagara and give a special performance.

"She would pack the house!"

I smiled and waved off her praise. "I'm happy here."

The others started bickering and teasing, but Effie leaned close, her voice a pleasant hum. "You don't seem happy tonight, if I may be so bold. Roman told me your Finn is away, dealing with family issues. You are missing him?"

I bit my lip, unsure of what to say. But her blue eyes were kind and patient. Friendly.

I nodded. "He is, and I hate the fact that I'm here and he's there. That I can't do anything for him." I rubbed my hands together. "Not that I could do much."

"Your presence would be a great comfort to him, I'm sure."

I blinked. She smiled in encouragement. "There are ways to get there quickly." She indicated her husband with a tilt of her head. "And people who would ensure it happened."

"I'm not sure I have that right."

She patted my hand. "From what Roman tells me, you do. You would be welcomed and loved even more for it. You have only to ask."

I glanced at Roman just as he turned his head, meeting my eyes. He studied me for a moment.

"Say the word, and I'll handle it."

I drew in a bracing breath, knowing what I needed to do. "I need to get to Finn."

"A car is waiting. I'll announce your next set has been canceled."

"My passport is at home."

"You can go there, pack quickly, and still be at the airport in time."

I frowned. "You already arranged it?"

"As soon as I heard your first song and after speaking with Finn earlier, I knew it needed to happen." He smiled at his wife with affection. "Effie encouraged it."

"Thank you."

He inclined his head. "Go. He needs you."

I stared up at the gray building, weariness making my eyes blurry. Roman had taken care of everything. The car he had waiting took me home, and I threw a few things into a bag, left a note on my neighbor's door asking her to water my plants, grabbed my passport, and was back in the car in twenty minutes. I was whisked right to a private plane, and before I could really comprehend what was happening, I was airborne. I dozed and read, the hours passing swiftly.

Another car waited for me at the airport, taking me to the hospital once I spoke with the customs person who came on board. Roman sent me a text with Roisin's room number, and I headed up to the sixth floor. Outside her room, I looked around, but no one was there so I opened the door and peeked in. A pair of blue eyes so like Finn's peered at me from the bed, and the woman's face broke into a smile. One side of her face still drooped a little so it was crooked, but it was warm.

"Come in, Una."

I had met Roisin more than once. She had always seemed larger-than-life, but in the hospital bed, she was small and frail-looking. She still had oxygen being pumped into her via cannulas, and an IV was attached to her left arm. Finn had told me there were some issues with movement on her right side, and I could see it on her face and the way her mouth moved. They hoped it would improve.

I tiptoed forward, shocked to see the room empty. I set down my case and went over to the bed where she beckoned. Leaning down, I pressed a kiss to her soft cheek.

"He'll be so glad...you came," she murmured.

"Where is everyone?"

She swallowed. "Niall and Sully are out finding me a good cup of tea—" she inhaled and paused "—and a biscuit. We finally convinced Finn to nap. He's—" she pointed to the door "—across the hall."

"Oh." I was pleased to see her speech was better. Slow and hesitant at times, but fairly clear.

She grimaced. "I need them to stop hovering." Another sigh. "Every time I open my eyes, one of them is staring at me, waiting for me to take my last breath."

It took her a moment to get the words out, but her tone was quite scornful. I bit my lip to stop my laughter. "They love you."

"I'm well aware. They are all too big and too explosive —" she waved her hand "—to be cooped up in this room. They're supposed to take turns, and they all refuse to leave." I handed her the cup she indicated, and she took a sip of water. "The only way I got a moment's peace was the nurse telling them she needed to bathe me. They went searching for my tea." She winked. "I already had a sponge bath this morning."

"I see."

The door opened, and a tall man walked in. He was as broad as Niall and Finn and just as handsome, although older. His hair was salt-and-pepper, cut short on the sides and longer on top. He had a trimmed beard and mustache that set off full lips. He had the same air of danger around him as Finn and Niall carried, confidence making his shoulders straight and his walk a smooth swagger. He frowned, almost growling.

"And who are you?"

"Oh, ah..."

Roisin interrupted. "Mind your manners. This is Finn's girl."

He looked surprised. "I wasn't aware he had one."

Roisin shook her head. "Do you men ever talk? Really talk?"

He set down a steaming cup and a small bag. "If you mean braid each other's hair and wax on about feelings, only on Wednesdays." He smirked. "We missed it last week, thanks to you, woman."

He turned to me, taking my hand. "Sullivan Black at your service. Finn is a lucky man. You are ravishing."

I frowned. "You're full of it, aren't you?"

He chuckled. "Witty, too, I see."

Niall walked in, shocked to see me. He recovered, allowing me to hug him. "He'll be pleased to see you."

"Where is he?" I asked, feeling anxious.

He opened the door, escorting me across the hall. "Here." He put his hand on my arm, pausing. "Tell me you've come to your senses, Una. That you're not going to hurt him again."

"I don't want to."

He drew in a deep breath. "You're a smart girl, so I have never understood your decision. He would die rather than see you hurt."

"I don't want that to be on my conscience."

He huffed a low laugh. "First off, it's his decision. And second, do you think that you walking away has changed that?" He made a clucking noise. "You are either blind, or I gave you too much credit."

"I was too afraid to make that choice."

"If you needed him, he would burn down the city to get to you. Don't you realize you are safer with him than without?"

"I don't want to be a distraction."

He leaned close. "Open your eyes, Una. *He's* safer when you are with him. Less distracted. More focused because he knows you're okay."

I stared at him. "I never thought... I didn't know—"

He cut me off. "Now you do."

"I love him," I whispered.

"Then tell him. He needs you, Una. He always has."

"I need him too."

He opened the door. "Go get him."

CHAPTER NINE

FINN

I woke, loath to leave the pleasant dream I was having. Una was beside me, stroking my hair the way she knew I loved, and humming. It was such a real dream, it lingered, even after I blinked open my eyes.

Her lovely green irises looked down at me. She smiled, her voice quiet in the room.

"Hello, Finn."

I sat up, dragging her into my arms. I didn't care if we were alone or what else was happening in the room. I needed her close. I needed to know she was real. That I wasn't hallucinating.

Her low gasp seemed genuine. The feel of her pressed against me was equally compelling. But it was the sensation of her mouth on mine, the taste of her, that convinced me I wasn't dreaming.

No dream, no matter how good, could possibly be this incredible.

I kissed her with all the emotion I was feeling. The fear and worry. The isolation and loneliness that had been building, being away from her. The love I felt.

And she kissed me back, her fingers buried in my hair, holding me close and whimpering as I tugged her as tight to me as I could.

Panting, I drew back. "Una, *mo chroí*—how?"

"Roman helped me. He arranged everything."

"I owe him."

She looked at me, her lips swollen, her cheeks flushed, and her hair messed from my hands. "You needed me. I could hear it."

"I always need you."

She ran her finger over my cheek. "More than usual. You were looking after everyone, and you needed someone to look after you."

"There is no one I would rather look after me." I gathered her close, swaying us. "Thank you."

She sighed, resting her head on my chest.

"I won't be able to let you go again. You know that."

"I know."

"And you'll stay?"

She looked up. "I'm done punishing myself. Hurting you. I'm sorry. I—I was scared."

I cupped her face, the torment in her voice deep. "I know. We move on together now. We'll sort it out. All of it."

She nodded. "Together."

I kissed her again, a gentle press of our mouths.

"Have you seen Roisin?"

"For a moment. I met Sully."

I chuckled. "Lucky you."

"Handsome man."

I growled. "Not that handsome."

"He looks like you, but older."

"Well, he is a decent-looking bloke, I suppose."

She laughed, little puffs of air against my neck. "Jealous?"

I pulled back, looking down. "I want you to see only me."

She smiled, looking beautiful and tired at the same time. "I do, Finn. My eyes are always on you when you're in the room."

I liked that. More than I should.

There was a discreet knock, and Niall peered in. "Mum wants to see Una before you drag her to the hotel and ravish her." He grinned. "Her words—not mine."

I chuckled. "The queen has spoken."

Una slipped from my arms and stood, swaying a little. I knew she was tired. The trip over was exhausting, no matter how comfortable the plane was. With the time difference, she'd only be able to stay awake a few more hours.

She went ahead of me, and I sent a brief text to Roman.

> The package has arrived. Thank you.

He was quick to reply.

> No thanks needed. I charged the plane and everything to the hotel. Your woman—your expense.

I chuckled at his dry wit.

> No problem. I am still in your debt.

I laughed at his final words.

> And I will never let you forget it.

Somehow, I was okay with that.

Una sat with Roisin, spooning her some soup and talking to her quietly. Sully had found a shop close by and brought the soup as well as some decent coffee. The three of us sipped the dark brew, not saying much. Roisin was still pale and weak, but better. Talking easier. Eating in addition to all the sleeping.

"I have to get back," Sully said, sounding regretful. "The practice is busy. I have a huge caseload."

Niall nodded. "We appreciate you coming. I know Mum did as well."

"I'll keep close tabs when she is released."

"We're arranging around-the-clock care," I muttered, my eyes locked on Una. Her hair gleamed in the dim light, and the sound of her voice was like a balm to my soul.

Roisin was eating up her attention, having given me a pointed look when we had walked back into the room. I had bent down to kiss her, and her whispered, "*Not so complicated now, eh, boy?*" made me grin.

I knew Una and I had a lot to talk about. The past, the future. Our relationship. Her damn brother.

But for now, she was here, and I was content.

"Okay, Finn?"

I shook my head, looking at Niall. "Sorry, was lost in thought."

"Sully and I are staying here for the night. You take Una to the hotel. Come back in the morning, and I'll go there then. Sully is heading back to Edinburgh tomorrow afternoon."

"Are you sure? I can stay and you take Una to the hotel and make sure she gets to my room."

Niall and Sully chuckled. "Right."

I rolled my eyes. "We are both here for Roisin. She didn't fly all this way to be 'ravished,' as you stated earlier. I am quite capable of controlling myself."

Sully laughed. "Then yer blind, mate. She keeps eyeing you from under those lashes. Imagining, no doubt, what you'll do when you're alone."

Just then, Una began to sing. Perched on the edge of Roisin's bed, holding her hand, she was singing one of my aunt's favorite Celtic songs, her voice low and sweet in the room. Roisin's eyes were shut, and she smiled, looking peaceful and content. My heart swelled in gratitude for Una's tender care toward her. The three of us tried, but we failed at the gentle stuff.

"Jesus, never mind," Sully muttered. "I'll take her to the hotel."

"Feck off," I replied. "She's mine."

"She looks like that, sings, and loves you?" He clapped my shoulder. "Lucky bastard."

"I know." I shut my eyes, listening to the beauty of Una's voice. The way she wove the lyrics and music, making it almost swirl around the room.

"I think I'll take you up on that offer," I announced.

Niall smirked. "As if there was any doubt."

Sully groaned. "How about you and Niall go to the hotel? Leave me the singing angel. I could listen to her all night."

"Nope," I replied, staring at Una, suddenly needing her alone. "She's coming with me."

Sully sighed. "Like I said, lucky bastard."

He was right.

Una sat back, cupping her cheek in her hand, resting her elbow on the arm of the overstuffed chair in our hotel room. While she'd showered, I'd ordered some sandwiches and tea, grabbing my own shower once she sat down to eat. I pulled on some sleep pants. She wore the dressing gown the hotel provided, her red hair an explosion of color against the white terry towel.

"Have you had enough?"

She smiled. "The tea is lovely and the tart delicious."

"You only ate half a sandwich."

"I had some food earlier. Really, Finn—don't fuss. I'm fine."

I leaned close. "I get to fuss now. I get to do anything I want, right, Una?"

She laughed. "No. I am not giving you free rein. You'll have me locked in your suite, spoiling me, no doubt pregnant, married, and chained to the stove before I can even blink."

"Not true," I replied, my eyes dancing at her teasing. "I'd get you a cook."

She smiled, reaching out and tapping my nose. "Funny man."

I grabbed her hand, kneeling in front of her in the chair. "You're here. I'm thrilled. We're going to sort out the situation here, then head back to Canada and figure out how to entwine our lives again. I am perfectly fine with you moving in right away. I love the thought of marrying you...and, frankly, thinking of you pregnant with my child? I want to throw you down right here and start."

Her eyes widened to the point of hilarity.

"But," I added, "I know we need to take it a step at a time. As long as you are part of my life, Una, we'll figure out the steps. I want you happy."

"I want you happy too."

I turned my head, pressing a kiss to her palm. "*Mo chroí*, I have you back. I am happier than I've been in a long time."

"I'm sorry," she whispered. "I was so scared after what happened. So sure we were better off without each other. That I wouldn't have to carry the guilt of being the reason for your death." She swallowed. "I couldn't even admit to myself how much I missed you. It felt as if you had died at times. It felt as if I had as well." Her voice trembled. "And I was so selfish, Finn."

"How?" I asked tenderly.

"I let you give me my dream. Working in the hotels, the singing." She shook her head. "Even putting up with Brian."

"I was equally as selfish. I could keep you close. Make sure you were okay. See you on a daily basis. Listen to you every week and pretend it was me you were singing to."

Tears began to glimmer in her eyes. "I hate myself for hurting you."

I drew her closer. "Enough. You're here. You made the decision to come when you knew I needed you. Even when you left me before, you refused to go until I was able to care for myself. I knew then you loved me."

"I do. I love you so much," she whispered, tracing my scar with her finger. "Seeing this makes me scared again."

"Don't be scared. No one is after me. You are safe. Tell me you know that."

She ran her fingertip over the mottled skin, catching her bottom lip between her teeth. Leaning forward, she pressed a kiss to the scar, her lips soft and warm against the imperfect blemish. I groaned low in my throat as she slipped from the chair so our knees pressed together. Her lips stayed on my skin as she kissed her way along my shoulder and up my neck. I grabbed her arms, hissing her name as she nipped at my earlobe, drawing the skin between her teeth and nibbling.

"Una," I warned as she pressed on my thighs and nestled between them.

"I've missed you," she whispered in my ear. "Let me show you how much."

I let out a curse as I pulled her into my arms, covering her mouth with mine. She tasted of tea and sweet tart. Una. Her mouth was heaven, and I kissed her with everything I had in me. Our tongues twined, tasting and seeking. Exploring and reacquainting ourselves with each other. I grabbed at the sash of her robe, yanking it open and pushing it off her shoulders. Her skin was warm and silky under my fingers. Her hair was a heavy mass in my fists as I ravished her mouth. She ran her hands over my back, up through my hair, tugging and pulling as she pushed herself closer. I dragged her up my thighs, splitting her legs wide, my cock trapped between us. I cupped her rounded ass, loving how she felt against me. Her tight nipples rubbed against my chest, and I felt the heat of her as I slipped my fingers between her legs, feeling her slickness.

"Oh God," she gasped as I teased her clit, already hard and throbbing for me.

"Not God," I growled. "He has no place here tonight with what I'm going to do to you. Finn. Call my name when you come, Una. Scream it. Always my name."

I worked her, feeling her orgasm approaching. Desperate to feel it, to feel her, I lifted her up, freeing my cock between us, settling her back, then nudging it against her entrance.

"Tell me you want me."

"Yes. Please. Finn, *yes*."

Inch by inch, I sank into her. Her head fell back as I reclaimed what was mine. What had always been mine. Locked inside her, I was home. She surrounded me like a raging summer storm. Drenched and warm. A deluge I never wanted to escape. She begged me for more. To move. To make her come.

"Finn, Finn," she chanted.

"Yes, *mo chroí*. Listen to your body sing for me," I praised her as I thrust as deeply as I could. She rolled her hips, matching my rhythm, whimpering my name. I covered her mouth with mine, unable to stop kissing her. Needing her taste in my mouth to ground me to her. I shifted, changing the angle, and she moaned as I went deeper. She flung her head back, arching her back, once again taking more of me. All of me until our bodies were flush. I groaned in satisfaction at the intensity of the feeling. Her soft body against my harder one. How her breath felt on my skin. The way her hands caressed me. Lingering, light, her touch perfect. The hot, tight grip she had on my cock. I lowered my head, taking one hard nipple in my mouth, then the other. She gripped my arm that banded her to me, whimpering. I slid my fingers along her folds, gathering her desire, teasing the tight ring of muscle of her sweet ass. I loved her reaction when I did that, the small pucker reacting to my touch, almost quivering. She shivered as I played, dipping in my smallest finger, caressing and stroking, finally sinking the digit in, feeling the muscle clench and contract. Una went rigid, coming hard, tightening around me, more wetness making me move faster, the feel of her muscles clenching and spasming around my cock too much.

I buried my face in her neck, kissing the damp skin, growling her name. Praising her. Feeling another tremor race through her as she orgasmed again, her keening cry another sort of music to my ears.

We moved until we were exhausted. Sated. Once again complete. I gathered her close, holding her tight. For a moment, there was no sound but our breathing and the distant noise of the traffic out on the street. We were locked in our own world—one I never want to leave.

Wordlessly, I rose to my feet, keeping her wrapped around me. I carried her to the bed, slowly disentangling our joined bodies. I gazed down at her, a smile pulling on my lips, before heading into the next room. She was half asleep, already curling into the pillow, her bright-red hair spread around her. I returned with a cloth, cleaning her gently, whispering adoring words. Then after cleaning myself, I slipped into bed with her. I pulled her into my arms, feeling the peace she brought with her. All the noise in my head stopped with her beside me. My body relaxed of its own accord, having her close. I pressed a kiss to her head.

"*Tá mé i ngrá leat,*" I whispered. "*As amhrán mo chroí.*"

"I don't know what that second one means," she admitted, sounding sleepy.

I kissed her softly. "You, Una, are the song of my heart."

"Oh, that's beautiful." She sighed. "I love you too," she added, then fell asleep, safe and content in my arms.

Where I planned on her being every night for the rest of my life.

CHAPTER TEN

UNA

I woke in the night, disoriented and unsure. I blinked as I took in the dark room, relaxing when I felt the heat and strength of the man behind me.

Finn.

I was in Ireland with Finn.

With a sigh, I snuggled back, smiling as his arm tightened.

"All right, *mo chroí?*" he asked, his voice a low rumble in my ear. He kissed the skin on my neck, making me shiver.

"Yes, I'm—" My reply ended with a low gasp as he cupped me, and I realized he had his hand between my legs and what had woken me was his gentle stroking.

"You're soaked," he murmured. "You've been fidgeting the past ten minutes." He bit down on my lobe. "Begging me."

"Oh. *Oh*," I groaned as he touched my clit, strumming it gently. I arched my back as he slid one finger, then two inside me, pumping slowly, drawing out my pleasure. "Finn," I whimpered.

"You want more?" he asked, a rough edge to his voice.

"Yes."

"Lift your leg, drape it back over my hip."

I did as he said, shivering as I felt his cock pressing into me. Solid, hot, and filling me completely. He rocked into me, nothing hurried or rushed. I shut my eyes as pleasure rolled over me, his fingers still working my clit as he pumped into me.

"Give me your mouth," he demanded, and I turned my head as he rose over me, capturing my lips. His tongue mimicked what his cock and fingers were doing. Stroking, pressing, going deep, then retreating. Driving me crazy with desire.

The darkness of the room and the quiet made it all so intimate. There was only the sound of our skin sliding together, his hushed words, the feel of his strong body moving with mine. The sensation of his hair falling over my face, no doubt tangling with mine. I fisted his thick waves in my hand, feeling my orgasm beginning to build.

"That's it, Una. Come all over me again. Drench me. My hand and my cock." He sped up his movements, burying his head into the side of my neck and biting down as he rolled my clit between his fingers. The sting of his teeth in my skin and the pinch of his touch sent me over the edge, and I cried out as my orgasm blossomed like a flower opening for the sun. Full, ecstatic, rich with beauty and color. He gentled his touch, then pulled his hand to my pelvis, pressing down as he climaxed. The feel of his release and the way he touched me brought on another spasm, this one slow and easy, like a wave kissing the sand. I shuddered and gasped, calling out his name. He roared out mine as he pumped into me, filling me completely.

Then we stilled, our harsh breathing filling the room.

"Jesus, Una," he murmured, his voice ragged. "I mean, fuck. I—"

I giggled at his breathless statement, unsure if it delighted me more that he was speechless or if he felt the same way I was feeling.

Overcome.

He lay back, pulling me close again. "I'm too tired to get a cloth."

"I'm good with that."

"Good. You can sleep full of me."

"Messy," I commented, not really caring at this point.

"They'll change the sheets in the morning."

"Hmm."

"God, I missed you," he said, pressing a kiss to my shoulder. "I missed the way you fit me so well and waking up with you."

"You, ah, didn't let other women spend the night?" I asked, hating to hear the answer.

He stiffened, reaching over and snapping on the light. He gazed down at me, his fierce gaze pinning me to the sheets.

"There has been no one since you, Una."

"But it's been—"

He cut me off. "I love you. I have loved you this whole time. Do you really think I would disrespect you that way? There has been no one else. There never will be. Ever."

He furrowed his brow. "Is that what you've thought all this time? That I moved on and took lovers?"

"You had every right to," I whispered, trying to fight

the grateful tears. "You moved to the hotel, and I assumed—"

"I moved to the hotel because I couldn't bear being in my condo once you left me. You were everywhere. I sold it and moved to the hotel to be close to work. Close to you. I never once thought of bringing a woman there or even thought about being with another one."

"So many beautiful women were always looking at you. I saw the keycards they slipped you. The way they looked at you. Do you know how many of them tried to bribe me for information on you or give them a room key or even divulge your room number? It made me ill every time."

He shook his head. "Any keycard I was given was promptly thrown away. I was never even tempted, Una. Not once."

"I'm sorry. You're so, um, virile, and I just thought..." I trailed off at the blazing fire in his eyes.

"You thought wrong. You, Una. Only you. And obviously, I need to prove to you how much I've missed you. How often I thought of you as I stroked *myself,* wishing it were you."

"I'm sorry," I repeated.

He bent low and kissed me, no anger behind it, only tenderness. "I plan on proving it to you. Over and over again. Until you believe me."

He shifted, sliding between my legs, already hard. I inhaled sharply.

"Again?" I whispered.

"Always," he replied. "Until you feel how much you were missed." He kissed me. "How loved you are."

I wound my arms around his neck.

"I'm good with that."

Hand in hand, we walked into the hospital room. Roisin was sitting up against the pillows, looking better. Her color was returning and her eyes gleamed. Her hair was freshly washed, and she smiled when she saw us. If you looked, you could see the droop to her eye and mouth, and the way her arm curled into her lap. But she was improving.

"Finn—darling. Tell me that is decent tea." She made a clucking sound with her tongue. "You would think they could do an acceptable cup here, for heaven's sake. I'm still in Ireland after all."

Finn chuckled, pressing a kiss to her head. "Tea, yes. Una picked you out a scone too. She had one yesterday and said it was delicious."

I sat beside her, opening the tea and breaking off a piece of scone and handing it to her. "You sound better this morning."

She nodded, chewing the scone and swallowing. "The doctor was pleased when he came in. Surprised."

"I'm not," Sully said with a laugh. "It's Roisin Black. Nothing is going to keep her down for long. And God forbid you take away her speech. She's not having that shite."

I grinned, meeting Roisin's dancing eyes. They looked like Finn's. Niall's were dark like his father's apparently. Sully had inherited the same deep-brown color from his father, who was Niall's uncle. Finn had explained all the relationship lines to me. Once Finn went to live with Roisin, they hung around together since Sully lived a few doors away. Although older, Sully treated them as equals.

"He was never a jerk," Finn explained. "We were tight then. Still are now."

Roisin tried to wink, the flutter not quite right yet, but I saw the affection in her gaze as she looked at the three men in her hospital room. They all adored her, and the feeling was obviously mutual.

She sipped her tea and finished her scone. She sighed, leaning back on the pillows. "Sully, what I told you. Please repeat to my son and nephew. It's too many words right now."

He shook his head. "I'm not sure I'm in agreement with Roisin about this, but I will express her wishes. She has a small cottage in Scotland she inherited years ago."

Niall looked surprised. "Mum, you never said anything. From whom?"

She shrugged. "An old friend. You never met her."

Sully continued. "I go and check on it from time to time. I've stayed there, and so has your second cousin Bonnie from Canada. It's a small place. Otherwise, we rent it from time to time—only to people we know."

Finn and Niall exchanged a look but let him finish. "Your mum wants to give it to me. Since I'm there and all. She says neither of you would be interested, but I don't want to take away your inheritance. It could be worth a good amount to the right buyer."

Roisin spoke up. "And I said it isn't for sale. I promised Lenore I would keep it in my family."

Niall frowned. "If that's what you want, that's fine, Mum." He looked at Sully. "I'm not worried about an inheritance at all. I'm certainly not concerned about a cottage I didn't even know existed. I'd like to see it someday, though."

Finn nodded. "Me as well. If Roisin wants you to have it, it's fine. No objections. She's right—you're in Edinburgh. We're half a world away. If you can use it and enjoy it, you should have it."

Sully scrubbed his neck. "I appreciate that. I enjoy going at times. It's on the edge of a small village and right by the water. Rustic. I go to clear my mind on occasion."

"Then take it with my blessing," Niall stated. "You're family. It's a gift from Mum, and I will respect that."

Finn nodded in agreement.

"I want to give it to him now, not wait until something, ah, happens," Roisin stated. "Have it all legal and binding."

"He's the right bloke," Finn said with a smile. "He can sew that up easy, right, Sully? A walk in the park for you."

"Arse," Sully said, flipping the finger.

Finn chuckled, reaching for my hand. "Do whatever Roisin wants." Then he looked at her. "And no more talk about something happening. You're getting better, and you're going to be around for a long time, you understand?"

She smiled, blowing him a kiss. "I understand."

Later as she napped, Sully showed the guys a few pictures of the cottage. It was small, with an open living area and kitchen at the front, and one bedroom at the back. Weathered and worn, it was still charming, the little front porch overlooking the water.

"Only a ten-minute walk into the village," Sully explained. "I take the train, stop at the local store for some food, and walk to the cottage." He chuckled. "But there is no one around. It's quiet and peaceful."

"Do you know anything about this Lenore?"

Sully lowered his voice. "Your mum helped her escape a bad marriage. Assisted her in finding the little cottage and a job. Even after her husband died and she was safe, she stayed there. Never remarried, had no kids, but what I have heard, she was a favorite in the village and lived a happy life. She was older than your mum and, when she passed a few years ago, left it to Roisin. She's been there a few times but says it's too isolated for her."

"I'm glad you like it and can use it."

Sully nodded. "It is a bit of a sanctuary for me, I admit. I had planned on offering to buy it from her estate when the time came. And I'm happy to do so—"

Niall cut him off. "No. She wants you to have it, and that's that. I'm not upset at all." He chuckled. "Frankly, it's a bit too, ah, cottagey for me."

Finn laughed. "I wouldn't mind seeing it, but I agree with Niall. I'm more a Ritz kind of man myself."

I snorted. "Spoiled babies. No room service, no big-screen TVs. I think it's charming."

Finn grasped me around the waist, pulling me close, his voice a low promise in my ear. "I'll take you to see it. Stay for a few days. With nothing to interrupt us, I might enjoy that."

I turned my head and kissed him. "I'll hold you to that."

The doctor came in and sat with Niall and Finn, explaining the next steps.

"Rehab," he said. "Speech and body. We can do outpatient or refer her to a rehab hospital. I discussed it with her earlier and she insists on going home, but I explained she can't live alone right now."

"I hired two full-time caregivers. Both experienced. She'll have good care at home. Can we arrange for the rehab at home?"

"It's, ah, expensive," the doctor said, sounding nervous.

Niall laughed. "Whatever it is, I'll cover it. Only the best for my mum. But I want regular updates. And visits from her medical team." He paused. "I will happily arrange a very generous donation to the hospital to ensure it happens." He leaned forward. "I already spoke with the hospital administrators. My mum gets the best care. Whatever you need to provide that, you let me know, you understand?"

Roisin was napping, and I was sitting beside her, letting them talk to the doctor. I had never heard Niall speak that way. Commanding, in control, slightly threatening. Finn was always the one who did the talking. Now I saw why they made such a good team. How he sat next to Niall, simply nodding, looking intense and silent.

They were quite the sight.

"Of course, Mr. Black." He cleared his throat. "I would rather she be in the rehab hospital, but I understand her desire to be at home. Patients do tend to do better when in their own environment."

"And she will. I will make sure the caregivers follow the guidelines and she does the work needed while in the comfort of her own home."

"Right. Excellent. Then we will be keeping her a few more days and I will discharge her. I'll make sure everything is in place."

"Thank you."

He left, looking happy to do so, and Finn chuckled. "You were pretty intense."

"It's my mum."

Finn clapped him on the shoulder. "I know."

Niall sat back, furrowing his brow. "You should head back, Finn. I need to be here a few more days, but I know you have an empire to run."

"Nothing is more important than Roisin," Finn said, his voice firm.

"And I'll look after her. If you head back to Canada and plan on coming back for a visit soon. We need to be more aware of time." He rubbed his face, and his voice caught. "She's not always going to bounce back."

I slipped from the room, wanting to give them their privacy. Niall had been a pillar of strength, but I had a feeling right now he needed Finn to be the strong one for him.

A few moments later, solid arms came around me as I stood looking out the window.

"Is he okay?" I asked.

"Yes. Relieved and needed an outlet for a moment."

"His big brother."

Finn laughed quietly. "I suppose. I am a few weeks older."

I turned in his arms. "So, we're going back?"

He nodded. "I'll arrange the flight. Niall thinks he'll follow next week. I know he wants some time alone with Roisin, and he'll make sure she is settled back at home before he leaves."

"That'll be a hard goodbye." I cupped his face. "For both of you."

I felt the way his jaw tightened. "I have to believe she will come back from this. That with rehab, proper meds, and caregivers, she'll be around a long time. But yes, this will be a difficult goodbye."

I wrapped my arms around him, and he lifted me, burying his face in my neck. I held him as tight as I could, grateful I could be the strong one for him for a change.

Finn was quiet in the car as we left the hospital. He

held my hand, staring out the window. I frowned as we drove along, turning to him after a while.

"Aren't we going to the airport?"

"Tomorrow morning."

"Then where are we going?"

He smiled. "I wanted a few hours with you in Dublin and a night alone in a hotel."

"We've been alone."

He shrugged. "And on call. The rest of today and tonight belong to us. I'm being selfish."

I cupped his face. "I would hardly call that selfish."

He shook his head. "But it is. I want you all to myself. Once we get back, the reality there is going to set in, and life will be all too busy. The next few hours, I'm claiming."

I smiled. "Okay."

I left Finn alone to sort out his thoughts, knowing he needed the time. I rested my head on his shoulder, startling awake when he kissed my head, amusement lacing his voice. "We're here, *mo chroí*."

He stepped from the car, offering me his hand. I peered at the small hotel in wonder. It was pretty, with ivy-covered walls, the stonework peeking out smooth and old. Finn guided me inside, where a beaming man greeted him. They shook hands and Finn introduced me.

"Una, this is my general manager, Seamus O'Malley. Seamus has been with me since I bought this place."

"Welcome, Una. Enjoy your stay. Your suite is ready, Finn."

"And my other request?"

"Handled. Everything you asked."

"Good work." He accepted an envelope, and we headed to the elevator.

"This is your hotel?"

"One of them," he said with a smile. "I wanted you to see it."

He swiped the keycard and pressed the button for the top floor. The doors opened to an opulent hallway, and he guided me to one of two doors, swiping the key. Inside, I gasped as I took in the space. Large and open, it was luxurious yet warm. Comfortable-looking furniture, a fireplace, and thick rugs welcomed us. A small kitchen set in an alcove was state-of-the-art. The bedroom boasted a four-poster bed hung with beautiful material that swept the floor and a sitting area with another fireplace. The bathroom was sumptuous, with a sunken tub and a multiheaded shower. The colors were a rich blend of blues and greens, with creams and burgundy. The fabrics were heavy and a feast for the eyes and the woods detailed and intricate.

It was exquisite.

"Finn," I breathed out. "I can't even—"

He wrapped his arms around me. "Awesome, isn't it? It's my favorite room of any hotel I own. It is rented to very few people." He pressed a kiss to my head. "Sully borrows it if he wants to impress someone."

"A woman someone?"

"I don't ask." His grip tightened. "Is my woman impressed?"

I turned in his arms. "Very much so. Overwhelmed, if I'm being honest. I'm not used to this level of, ah…"

"…wealth?" he finished for me.

"Yes."

He leaned against a plush chair. "I know it's not something you're used to or even comfortable with, Una, but for today—" he inhaled and gazed at me seriously "—for today, can you let me spoil you? Accept what I want to give you. Just for today. I need that."

"You need that?"

"Yes. I feel ten feet tall when I give you something you like. I want to feel that the rest of the day."

"Nothing over the top."

"As in?"

"Jewelry I'll never wear. Diamonds. Cars. A hotel of my own. Overly extravagant."

His eyes glinted. "Anything else?"

I sighed. "What did you have in mind?"

"A little clothes shopping. Maybe a handbag or shoes." He leaned down and nipped my neck. "Something lacy and silky that only I get to see?"

I looked up at him, smiling. "I'd love to see you in something lacy and silky. What color are you going for? Green to set off your hair?"

He threw back his head in laughter. "Funny girl. That cheek gets me one extravagant thing. Now, let's go. The car is waiting."

CHAPTER ELEVEN

UNA

inn's idea of doing a little clothes shopping was vastly different from mine. I generally went to a few of my usual stores, headed for the clearance rack, and used my local vintage shop for the dresses I wore when I sang. And those, I rotated as well. I had been saving up everything for my future business.

Finn liked high-end. He never looked at price tags, and once he saw something he liked, he bought it. We wandered down Grafton Street and over to St. Stephen's Green, and I shopped in stores whose windows I had only ever admired. He laughed quietly when I asked where the clearance area was in the first store we went into.

"Not today, *mo chroí*. Not today."

I was grateful he wasn't pushy and he realized I wouldn't wear a lot of the extravagant outfits with my lifestyle, but he insisted on a few sweaters and a lovely dress he saw in a window. It was a beautiful shade of blue, reminding me of his eyes, and he had me try it on.

The way his eyes darkened and his hands curled into fists as if trying to stop himself from coming at me when he saw me in it made me blush.

"For when we go out to dinner," he insisted.

I refused the unreasonably expensive handbag, telling him I was too worried about carrying it on the subway.

"I'll be mugged, Finn," I pointed out.

He frowned and chose a lovely wallet instead, which I accepted, too afraid to see the price tag but knowing it was more than probably my entire closet at home.

It was in the lingerie shop he dragged me into that I lost all control of the situation. He spoke with the manager then left, saying he'd return, and I was measured and given pieces of sexy lace and silk to try on. It frightened me that none of the pieces had a price tag, and when I inquired, I was informed that the lingerie was often a gift to the man more than the woman and that this particular man wanted to spoil himself.

When I came out of the dressing room after choosing three sets, Finn was there, admiring a display. It was a diaphanous camisole, the pale pink of the fabric glimmering in the light. The embroidery was incredible, small flowers, leaves, and vines stitched in creams, golds, and red. It closed at the front with a sexy bow that matched the ones on the underwear. It looked sexy on the form, and I imagined on the right person was even more so. The barely there pieces were exquisite and delicate. I had looked at it, but with the way it was showcased, I'd avoided it as I was certain it was one of the most expensive items in the store.

Finn turned to face me, glancing at the small pile on the counter. "That's it, *mo chroí*? Really?"

"Yes," I said firmly.

He held up a silky robe, the soft fabric moving as he swung it in front of me. "I like this. It is the color of your stunning eyes."

I tried not to roll those eyes but failed as he chuckled and kissed me. "Indulge me."

I huffed a defeated sigh.

"Next door is my favorite chocolate shop. Why don't you go ahead and pick some treats for later?" he said, handing the woman his card. "I'll be along right away."

I went next door, inhaling the scent of rich chocolate and caramel. As I perused the cases, I was offered a sample, and I bit into the most decadent caramel I had ever eaten. Finn appeared, bending and claiming the last bite, flashing a mischievous smile at me.

"You found them. Two pounds of those, please," he instructed the shopgirl. He added a few other types, then instructed them to deliver a box of the caramels to Roisin. He filled out the address and smiled at me. "Her favorite, too."

I hugged his arm. "She'll love them."

We returned to the hotel after Finn bought himself some items. He loved Irish sweaters and ended up with three in various colors. He also purchased some shoes and a few other sundries, once again never glancing at a price tag, simply choosing what he liked.

Back in our room, Finn gathered me in his arms. "Thank you. Even though you didn't let me spoil you as much as I wanted."

I shook my head. "You spoiled me plenty."

He chuckled. "Now, dinner. Do you want to go out or stay in and have dinner by the fire?"

It had become overcast and drizzly. I glanced toward the window then back at him. "By the fire, I think. Just us."

He kissed my nose. "Perfect. Just us. Now, go pour a bath, and I'll arrange it. I saw how you looked at the tub earlier."

"It's incredible."

"Great for soaking." He grinned. "Or other things."

He strode away, and I felt a shiver run through me.

Other things.

I liked the sound of that.

The bath was indeed decadent. I had never soaked in a tub while drinking champagne and nibbling rich chocolate fed to me by a sexy Irishman. Or been ravished in said tub. There was no other word to describe what he did. The champagne was poured into my mouth from his. The chocolates shared, the sweetness blending between our mouths as he held his offering in his teeth and invited me closer with a wink and a crook of his finger.

Then he kissed me, the caramel and chocolate flavor still rich on his tongue. He pulled me to his lap, his cock trapped between us, his hands everywhere on my body, touching, teasing, and light. He lifted me over him, and he slid in slowly, somehow the heat of the water making me needier. He gripped my hips as I undulated, the feel of him inside me solid and perfect.

Leaning forward, he captured a nipple in his mouth, sucking, then biting it, making me gasp. He soothed the nip with his tongue, then did the same with my other breast, alternating between them. I rode him, taking him as deep as I could, moving faster as my pleasure began to build.

"You feel so good, Finn," I whispered. "So good inside me." I arched my back, letting my head fall back, my hair drifting into the steaming water. He slid his hand down my sternum, teasing my clit in the water, his other hand still gripping my hip, guiding me.

"Look at you," he growled. "My cock inside you, my fingers on your clit, your breasts red from my mouth. Who owns you, Una? Who do you belong to?" he demanded.

"You," I gasped, beginning to shake as my orgasm built. "You, Finn. Always you."

He grabbed my neck, pulling me to his mouth, and kissed me hard. It was pure possession, and I loved it. My release rolled through me, and my body locked down. He groaned into my mouth as I clenched around him, and he wrapped me in his arms, holding me close, his hips pumping fast as he climaxed.

The water splashed around us, up onto the tile, then drifting back into the tub. The steam swirled in the room, the condensation on the mirror fogging it over. I collapsed on his chest, and he held me tight. Neither of us spoke, letting the warmth of the water and the closeness of the moment settle around us. He pressed a kiss to my hair. "Una, *mo chroí*," he murmured. "What you do to me."

I lifted my head, meeting his tender gaze. In the dim light, his eyes shone a brilliant blue, and they were so filled with love, it made my breath catch. "And you to me, my love," I whispered.

He smiled. "It's been a long time since you called me that."

"It has never changed for me."

He cupped my face, his kiss gentle this time and filled with adoration. "For me either."

He pulled my head to his shoulder, pressing kisses to my crown. "And it never will."

The flames danced in the fireplace, the embers glowing. It was realistic enough to be hypnotic, and I gazed at it, enjoying the warmth. Finn handed me a coffee, sitting across from me at the small table he'd had set up. Dinner had been exceptional, the food delicious, the wine amazing, and the intimacy welcome. Just him and me alone. Music played quietly in the background, the romantic tunes matching the mood perfectly.

Finn leaned back in his chair, the firelight playing over his features. He wore a simple thermal shirt, the sleeves rolled up, exposing his forearms, and his tattoo peeking out of the unbuttoned neckline. His hair was down, brushing his shoulders. He flexed his legs, the material stretching over his thick thighs. I thought about how it felt to sit on those thighs. The strength of his body. How incredibly masculine he was.

He grinned and winked at me. "See something you like, my Una?"

"Maybe."

He chuckled and sipped his coffee, turning serious. "What happens when we get home?"

I placed my cup on the table. "We get back to life, I suppose."

"And our lives—they're entwined now, yes?"

"Yes."

"You're certain?"

I rubbed my forehead. "I'm not fighting it anymore, Finn. I realized how much I was hurting us both by denying what we felt. Do I wish you were an accountant or a teacher—something easier, safer? Yes. But you're not, and I have accepted that."

He scoffed. "I'd be a bloody awful accountant. And I have zero patience for teaching."

I laughed. "Just examples of regular jobs. But you're not, and I know now it doesn't matter. Telling myself all these years I would never fall for a syndicate man was just noise. The moment I met you, you owned me. I simply didn't know it yet."

He nodded slowly. "I did. That was why I stayed away. Gave you a chance to grow up and find a different life, but somehow I always knew you'd be mine."

He scrubbed his face. "I know you wanted something different, Una." He leaned back again, regarding me. "But frankly, *mo chroí*, a regular man would bore you to tears. You hate some aspects of my world, but you love others." He indicated the room with a wave of his hand. "An accountant couldn't give you this. Or a place to sing."

"I know, but those aren't the reasons I love you."

His smile was wide. "That's what makes it all that much sweeter." Then he winked. "I could act like an accountant for you. Wear an ill-fitting suit and have a pencil tucked behind my ear. Carry a pocket calculator. Talk taxes and budgets.”

I began to laugh, picturing Finn trying to look like an accountant.

“No, I’m good.”

He drained his coffee and stood, holding out his hand.

“Dance with me, Una.”

He wrapped me in his arms, and I nestled against him. It felt so right being in his embrace. His heartbeat was steady under my ear, his scent wrapping around me. We danced well together.

“See how well we fit?” he murmured. “We were made for each other.”

“Hmm,” I agreed.

“I wish we had more time here,” he said regretfully. “But we’ll come back for a longer stay. A happier one, I hope.”

I lifted my head. “Roisin is doing well. She’ll recover. We’ll come spend some time with her and a few nights here.”

He trailed a finger down my cheek. “I hope so.”

“I know so. She is resilient and strong. You and Niall will get her the best care, and she’ll be fine.”

"Thank you."

"For what?"

"Coming. Being with me. Caring for her. Being my light."

I smiled. "I love you, Finn."

He lowered his head, pressing a soft kiss to my mouth. "I love you."

I beamed up at him, drowning in the look on his face. His gaze was tender, his emotions open. His shoulders looked so broad in his tight shirt, and I loved seeing him so relaxed. It was a good look on him. "You are so sexy," I informed him.

He tipped his chin. "Not half as sexy as you."

I rolled my eyes. "Please. You are muscle and brawn. Hard and fit." I glanced down. "I'm..." I trailed off. "I'm not."

"Thank God for that," he grumbled. "You're perfect. I love how you feel against me. Soft and welcoming."

"I've always wanted to be tall and willowy," I confessed. "Slim and elegant. Not short and padded."

He frowned. "You're beautiful. I love you exactly the way you are. I don't want you taller or slimmer. There is so much I love. Your hair, your eyes. Your breasts. And don't even get me started on your ass." He tapped the swell of my butt, giving it a quick squeeze. "I love every single thing about you, Una. And you are sexy. So beautiful it makes my chest ache at times."

I smiled because he believed what he was saying. He thought me beautiful and captivating. "You see me with love," I said.

"I see you exactly how you are."

"Thank you."

I hummed, enjoying the moment. I snuggled closer, smiling as he pressed his lips to my crown. The music drifted into another song, and we didn't speak, simply moving together to the slow rhythm. As the song ended, he stepped back, looking determined. He lifted my hand and kissed it. "I want you to do something for me."

"Okay."

"In the bedroom, there's something on the bed. I want you to put it on for me."

"Now?"

He nodded. "Now."

Mystified, I went down the hall. On the bed was a pink bag—one I recognized from the lingerie shop. I opened it, the tissue paper crinkling as I unveiled Finn's surprise. I gasped as I saw the pale pink set I had admired earlier. Remembering how Finn had stared at it, I should have known he would purchase it. He had bought more than the items I had chosen, the bags containing many surprises.

But nothing compared to this. With trembling hands, I took off the robe I was wearing and slipped on the lingerie, crossing over to the mirror on the wall and gazing at my image. The demi cups hugged my breasts, pushing up the swells so they flowed over the top, my nipples barely hidden. The gauzy fabric ended at my waist, gathered into the bow at the front. The embroidery was delicate and feminine. The details were exquisite. The tiny scrap of silk and lace between my legs was simply an invitation waiting to be opened. The little bows that rested on my hips were a tease. I gathered up my hair in my hands, staring at myself. The pink looked pretty against my skin, the light dancing off the glimmering thread on the pieces. I looked—provocative.

Sexy.

Was that what Finn saw when he looked at me?

"Una," he growled from the doorway. "Don't move."

I froze, and he stepped behind me, our eyes meeting in the mirror. His gaze was intense and hooded. He ran his fingers down my arms, lightly grazing my sides and under my breasts, then rested his hands on my waist.

"You are so fucking beautiful. Tell me you can see that."

"I feel beautiful in this."

"You are always beautiful. In everything. In every way. But yes, right now, you are exquisite. Wearing my gift." He smiled, holding his hand out in front of me, a glinting necklace falling from his fingers. "Both of them."

I began to protest, and he shook his head. "Today is about me being selfish, remember? I want to see this on you."

He slipped the necklace around my neck and fastened it. It settled against my collarbone as if meant to be there, the metal cool on my skin. An infinity symbol set with tiny diamonds winked and glinted in the low light. It was lovely and delicate. Something I would choose, and I knew Finn had kept that in mind when picking it.

"No beginning and no end," he murmured, pressing a kiss to my neck. "Us."

"I love it."

He smiled, his eyes never leaving the mirror. "Do you see how I see you, Una?"

"I'm trying. The lingerie makes it easier."

He laughed and moved closer, wrapping his arm around my waist. "You are always beautiful. With lingerie or without. Smiling, laughing, crying. In every form."

Then his eyes darkened. "But especially when you're flushed and crying out my name, coming for me." He pressed against my back. "That is when you are the most beautiful. And I want you to see that."

"What?"

"I'm going to make you come, and you're going to watch."

FINN

Her green eyes went wide in her face at my words. A dusty pink spread over her cheeks, and her breathing picked up. She shivered, the movement feeling like a small tremor as my body reacted to her. Her nipples hardened, and goose bumps erupted on her skin.

But she didn't speak. Didn't protest.

I snaked an arm around her waist, spreading my fingers wide on her torso, and I took her gathered hair in my other hand. I pulled on it gently and tilted her head. I ghosted my mouth along her shoulder and up her neck to her ear.

"I'm going to touch you, Una. Everywhere I please. Everywhere I know pleases you. I'm going to make you come, and we're both going to watch as you do. You're going to see how beautiful you are in that moment."

Another tremor went through her, and I nipped at her neck.

"Let's clear up a few things, shall we?" I let her hair drop and drifted my hands to her hips. "What is wrong with these?"

"They're a little wide. And fleshy."

"No," I purred, keeping my voice low. "They're perfect to grab as you ride me. The exact right size to grip as I fuck you from behind." I caressed the soft skin. "Perfect."

I slid my hands to her stomach. "This?"

"It's not, um, flat," she whispered.

"It shouldn't be. I like it a little soft. I like how it feels when I lay my head on it and you stroke my hair. It's the place our children will grow, and it will protect them."

Her eyes went wide again. "Oh."

Her glance dropped, and I ran my hands on her thighs. "These are amazing. For someone so short, you have long legs. Strong ones. They wrap around my waist just right. They walk toward me quickly. Run and make me chase you." I moved my hands to the back and squeezed her plump ass. "And don't get me started on this ass. It's featured in most of my dirty thoughts. It's absolute perfection."

She blinked, and I slowly traced my fingers to her breasts, cupping them. I pushed the soft fabric down, stroking her nipples. "Your breasts are amazing too. I love how the nipples pucker under my tongue. How you moan when I suck them."

I stepped closer, pressing my body to hers. I pushed her hair aside again. "I love how smooth your skin is. How it tastes. Different here—" I licked down her neck "—than here." I dropped my hand to her pelvis, smiling as her breathing became even more rapid. The pulse at the base of her neck jumped. "And your mouth was made for me. I love kissing you. I never really enjoyed the act before, but with you, it's an addiction."

She tugged on her curls, and I shook my head. "Oh no. You don't say a word about your hair. It's wild and gorgeous. Unique. It makes you all the more special, and I love it."

That made her smile.

"And this." I dropped my hand to the small wisp between her legs. "I am totally addicted to your pussy, Una. I was the first to claim it, and it's all mine. *You're* all mine. You understand that?"

She nodded, another tremor going through her at my possessive tone.

"You know what I love the most right now?"

She gave the barest shake of her head and remained silent.

I lowered my mouth to her ear again. "I love knowing that by simply touching you, talking to you, you're wet for me. Aching. Wanting me to touch you there." I paused and tapped the material lightly. "Aren't you?"

"Y-yes," she stammered.

"Open your legs."

She did as I asked, gasping loudly as I slid my hand under the material and stroked her. She was slick, hot, and perfect, her honey helping my fingers glide over her effortlessly. Her clit was standing at attention, begging for me, and I rolled it between my thumb and forefinger, her whimper of pleasure pleasing me.

"You want more, Una?"

"Yes."

"You want to watch me fuck you with my hand? Fuck you until you come all over me?"

"Yes. Yes. Yes," she panted.

"Keep your eyes open. I want you to see yourself. You close them, and I'll stop."

"No, please," she begged.

I pressed on her stomach with one hand as I worked her with the other. I teased and pinched, sank two fingers inside her, watched as she undulated her hips, desperate to be as close to the source of pleasure as possible. And my good girl kept her eyes open, watching herself and me watching her. I pressed on her bundle of nerves with my thumb, adding a third finger inside her, letting my pinkie finger tease her sensitive pucker. Her whimpers turned into moans, then cries of pleasure, as I moved my hand faster. Pumped harder. The silk gave way under my movements, but I didn't care. I'd buy her more lingerie. She gripped my arms then reached up, grabbing at my neck and hair, her breasts spilling over, the nipples red from rubbing on the material.

And still, she watched.

Then her body locked down, her muscles gripping my fingers as she came, hot and wet, saturating my hand, screaming my name, her cheeks flushed, mouth open, and eyes wide.

Our gazes locked on each other.

Until her legs couldn't hold her up anymore.

Her body couldn't take any more pleasure.

Her eyes shut, and she slumped against me.

I bent and lifted her, sitting on the bed. I brushed her beautiful hair back and kissed her face. Hundreds of small, adoring kisses.

"Do you see now?" I asked quietly. "You are perfection to me."

She opened her eyes, meeting mine.

"I see."

"Good. Only I will ever see that beauty, Una. You're mine."

"Yours," she agreed.

I gathered her close, holding her. I wasn't surprised when she fell asleep, exhausted and sated in my embrace. I tucked her in, standing over her and gazing down. Her hair was all over the white sheets, a brilliant wave of color. Her long lashes were dark on her creamy skin and her golden freckles small flecks of sand.

She was even more beautiful now.

I bent and kissed her, a silent thank-you before I headed back to the living room to make a few calls. I would finish that and return to her, pulling her into my arms, and sleep beside her.

The way I wanted to end every day for the rest of my life.

"What sorts of problems?" I asked Roman, feeling tense.

"There was a deliberate fire set yesterday in your territory. I was there and checked it out. I know the owners from our past. They say a new gang is roaming the area. Scaring people."

"Damn."

"Then today, another." I heard a heavy sigh. "I hate to say it, Finn. But when I questioned some people, the description they gave made me think it's Murphy."

"Fecker," I snarled into the phone.

"It's typical of his sort. Petty revenge. Thinks he'll hit your bottom line. Hurt those who trust you."

"I'll deal with him when I get home tomorrow. In the meanwhile, put out the word."

"Already done." He paused. "I'll help whatever way I can. These are still people we looked after."

"I know and I appreciate it. I'll deal with him once and for all." I scrubbed my face, knowing what that meant.

Wishing more than ever I could grab Una and run with her, leaving everything else behind. I wasn't sure how she would handle this news.

"Let someone else deal with that," Roman advised. "Don't lose what you have because of him."

"Is that what you did with Effie's sister?" I asked, curious.

He cleared his throat. "Her sister was trying to kill her when I got to them. She shot me and was about to shoot my wife. Aldo took her out."

I was stunned into silence. Finally, I spoke. "I see."

"I would have taken the shot without question if I had been able to. I would like to think Effie would have forgiven me for that, but I'm glad I didn't have to find out. Let someone else handle it, Finn. That's my advice."

"Noted. I'll see you tomorrow."

I hung up, troubled. I wandered into the bedroom, gazing down at Una. How, I wondered, would she take the news? Would she beg me to give him yet another chance? Would she understand? Or would she hate me if we discovered it was indeed Brian behind the arson and the new gang?

Would she walk away—this time for good?

I hung my head. Somehow, I had a feeling I already knew the answer.

The next morning, Una was shy, not meeting my eyes, looking away when she felt my gaze on her. I found it incredibly endearing that after all the ways I had taken her, the mirror incident was making her feel exposed. I found it sexy. But then again, I found everything about her sexy.

I had woken her early this morning, kissing her awake, my cock already nudging at her entrance. She woke fully with a groan, wrapping her legs around me, bringing my cock deep inside. We rocked together, our bodies joined everywhere—chest to chest, hip to hip, mouth to mouth. It was slow and tender, and our orgasms crested close. The feel of her wrapped around my cock tightly had driven me over the edge, and I groaned my release into her neck as she shook under me.

We arrived at the airport on time and boarded quickly, the perks of owning my own plane a bonus. After takeoff, we had coffee and pastries, and I stared out the window, lost in thought.

Movement caught my eye, and I looked up, seeing Una studying me. I had been ignoring her, but her gaze was warm and open. No judgment or anger.

"Hi," she said quietly. "You've got a lot on your mind."

I sighed, knowing I had to talk to her.

I unclipped my seat belt, leaning close and taking her hands. "Una."

She tilted her head. "I don't like that tone."

"I promised you honesty. Always."

"You did. Something bad is going on in Toronto, isn't it?"

I told her what Roman had reported.

Then I said one word. "Brian."

"What does a rogue gang have to do with him?" she asked. "You think he's behind this?"

I explained about the drugs, his aggression, plus the fact that he had walked out.

As if it were a regular nine-to-five job.

Una knew better.

"And you allowed that." She paused and swallowed. "Because of me."

"I wasn't there, and Roman didn't want to overstep. He, ah, knows the complications there are about Brian."

Her eyes widened. "He was fidgety and tense the last time I saw him. Jittery." She looked angry. "I can't believe he's doing drugs. Dad always lectured both of us about that. Stay away from drugs. Too much alcohol. Use protection."

My eyebrows flew up, and she smiled. "That was directed at Brian more than me."

I smiled at her attempt at levity. I could see the pain in her eyes.

"Brian muttered something about a new venture with his roommate." She furrowed her brow. "Did he quit too? Juan?"

I shook my head. "I don't know a Juan."

"Oh. I assumed he was on the crew and that was how Brian knew him."

"No." But the name made me pause. Hadn't there been a Juan when I'd gone to see Lopez? Some young kid in the background. Was it a coincidence?

"Una," I began, but she shook her head.

"You tell me all the time that things have changed.

People leave. They decide the life isn't for them, and you let them go." Her voice held a note of desperation.

"Yes." I leaned closer, a hint of irritation seeping into my tone. "After conversations, when rules are laid out and complete respect and loyalty are shown." I shook my head. "Your brother has never shown either of those things—especially after your dad passed."

"He died because he was protecting you," she whispered.

I reared back. "And I looked after him. He showed me loyalty, and I showed him the same thing."

"But he died and you're alive."

"Your father was a good soldier, Una. He did his duty, and he knew the risks. He'd taken them for years before me." I stared at her. "You said you understood. I thought you didn't blame me."

She rubbed her forehead. "I don't. I'm just upset." She reached over and grasped my hand. "Please, Finn, can't you do something? Is this about the money he owes you? I can—"

My anger took hold, and I cut her off. "I haven't given the damn money a single thought, but since you brought it up, that pisses me off too. You will not be paying a penny of it. It's his careless debt, not yours. When will you stop protecting him and treating him like an innocent party? He needs to take responsibility, not you!" I roared.

She looked stunned at my ire.

"And what would you have me do, Una? Send him off with my congrats on a new path and let him terrorize people I protect? Burn down my businesses so he feels like a big man? He is going after me—don't you understand that?"

"You don't know that!"

"I'm going to find out, and when I do, I *will* take the necessary steps." I met her teary gaze. "I have no choice here. He is the one who has broken the rules. He is the one doing this. I cannot let it go."

"Even for me?"

I shook my head. "Even for you."

She sat back, pale and shaken.

"So, you'll kill him." Her voice trembled, and she spoke the words softly, more tears glimmering in her eyes. "My only family."

"I am your family now. We have a future. But your fucking brother keeps getting between us," I fumed. "This will only escalate, Una. He'll get bolder. He might even come after you, and I can't take that chance."

"He wouldn't hurt me."

"If he's messing with drugs, he's not the person you thought him to be. I don't think he ever was."

She wiped her cheeks. "I know him better than you."

I smiled sadly at her. "Then I need to remind you that he has hurt you. And to loosely use your own words, Una, you see him with love. He will forever be a boy to you. Your roles were always upside down. You took on the caregiver role, and you can't let it go."

"Will you give him a chance?"

I scrubbed my face. I wanted to yell at her and tell her how many chances he'd had. Remind her of the money he'd stolen. How he'd left her looking after her dad and lived his life.

"I will have my men bring him in and talk to him."

"I don't know…" She trailed off, letting the words remain unspoken. But I heard them as plain as if she had shouted them.

I don't know if I could forgive you.

I sat back, feeling defeated. "So then you'll hate me, and he wins anyway."

She didn't reply.

The rest of the flight was spent in silence. She pretended to sleep, but I knew she wasn't. I didn't know how to talk sense to her. To make her see the man who chose this path, not the boy she was trying to protect.

I passed the time working on my laptop, staring at her over the top every time she shifted, hoping she would open her eyes and we could try to reach a compromise.

Before Roman had told me what was going on, I'd planned on bringing Brian in, talking to him, putting the fear of God and me into his soul, and then sending him to another city for a fresh start. Even forgiving his debt. Maybe sending him to Ireland. I would never do that for another person, but I would do it because of Una and the deep love she had for him.

But if Roman was right and Brian had joined a gang intent on creating discord and using the knowledge of my organization to do so, he had to be stopped. He carried too many secrets I had a feeling he'd be happy to divulge to make himself a name and harm my world.

And for someone like him, there was only one way to silence him.

I rarely ever gave that order. It was always the last resort, unless my life was in danger. Or to protect those I loved. I preferred peace. Talking. Compromise. But he was tying my hands. As always with Brian Murphy, he chose the most difficult, painful path.

And this time, his decision was going to have life-altering consequences for me.

The pilot announced we were beginning our descent, and Una sat up, going to the restroom then returning. Her eyes were dull, the smile she offered me as she sat back down without any emotion behind it.

"Do you want anything before we land?" I asked.

"No, thank you."

"You haven't had a thing."

"I'm fine, Finn," she said, an edge to her voice.

I looked out the window. "I have a lot of problems waiting for me. You can head up to the suite when we get back, and I'll be up when I can."

"I'm going home."

I snapped my head in her direction. "I'm *not* playing this game with you, Una. You're angry. Fine. I am as well. We'll hash it out together once I take care of some business."

"I'm going to my apartment. I hadn't planned on going to the hotel with you before we talked. My clothes are there. My uniform. I left so quickly, I never cleaned out my fridge or took out the garbage. I need to attend to those things," she informed me.

Her words made sense, but I was still angry.

"Then I'll send a car for you when you're ready."

She lifted her chin, stubborn as hell. "I'll take the subway in the morning when I report for my shift."

I narrowed my eyes, ignoring the ache in my chest. "Una," I warned.

She glared right back. "I want to be alone for a while. You don't own me, Finn. I don't take orders from you." She turned her head. "I'm not one of your men. But if my behavior upsets you, maybe you can take care of me and my brother in one go. Save yourself some time."

Fury rolled inside me. Ignoring the fact that we were landing and I needed to stay in my seat, I tore the seat belt off and towered over her, gripping the arms of her seat. Our steward called out a warning, but I ignored her.

"Don't ever fucking say anything like that again. You know I would die rather than hurt you. You are never in danger with me. Your brother is business. You are my entire fucking world."

She stared up at me, shocked at my tone, startled at my proximity.

"Sit down," she pleaded.

"Tell me you know that. Promise me you will never think or say anything so fucking vile again."

"I know," she whispered. "I'm sorry."

I sat down, snapping on the seat belt and shutting my eyes. I took a deep breath, then another.

"I love you, *mo chroí*," I said as the plane came to a halt.

"I know," she repeated.

My heart ached at those words, because she didn't say them back.

He was already winning.

CHAPTER THIRTEEN

UNA

Finn's phone rang the instant we touched down, and he turned his back as he spoke. I passed a weary hand over my face as we exited the plane, were whisked through customs, and got into the waiting car.

Finn instructed his driver to drop me off, then head to the hotel. Silence stretched between us, the sound so loud it screamed in my ears. I clutched my purse handle so hard, my knuckles were white. It took all I had not to turn to Finn and beg for Brian. Plead with him to make an exception. I knew this world. I knew the dangers and the pain of being in it.

Which was why I had wanted out of it for so long.

But being out of it meant losing Finn, and I wasn't sure I could do that again.

The consequences of my brother's actions, however, might have ended it for me.

"Una." Finn's voice broke through my thoughts.

I glanced at him. "We're here," he stated, indicating my apartment building.

"Right." I stepped out, taking my bag from the driver. Finn watched me, not getting out of the car. Unsure what to do, I began to walk to the door, tears filling my eyes. Then I heard him call my name, and I turned, seeing him behind me. He grabbed me, bringing me flush to his body and holding me.

"We'll get through this, *mo chroí*. I swear it."

But even I heard the doubt in his voice.

He stood, ensuring I walked into the building, then I watched as his car pulled away, feeling as if my entire world had just disappeared.

I headed upstairs, entering my apartment. It smelled musty, and I got busy, emptying the garbage and the fridge, glad I hadn't been shopping before I left. There were only a few soft grapes and a mushy cucumber to toss. The sour milk, I poured down the drain. My plants were a little droopy, so I watered them and hoped they'd bounce back. I unpacked, my body on autopilot as I did. The new clothes Finn had purchased for me, I put away, the sadness bearing down on me. I paused as I ran my hand over the softness of a sweater.

Would he ever see me wear it?

I sat down, my shaky legs not able to keep me on my feet.

Would Finn kill Brian? Was my brother on drugs? Was he doing what Finn suspected?

I rubbed my aching head. In Finn's world, there was only black and white. Obedience was expected. Loyalty was demanded. You stepped out of line, you knew the consequences.

I sighed as a tear slipped down my cheek. I knew that —and so did Brian. Finn was right, and I had always coddled my brother. Took his side.

I still remembered the older brother who was sweet and funny. Who taught me how to skate. Held my hand the first day of school when I was afraid. Comforted me at night if I woke up from a bad dream. He always brought me water and sat with me.

I wasn't sure when our roles reversed. Probably when my mum died and I had to grow up fast. Help more with chores. Learn how to cook. After she passed, my dad left all that to me, and somehow I became the mother Brian had lost.

What, I wondered, would she tell me to do right now?

She always supported my dad. He used to say she was the glue that held the family together. That because of her, he was stronger. Was I strong enough to be that for Finn? To accept his decision and keep moving forward?

I wiped my face. I couldn't answer that right now. I was too tired and drained.

And I needed to talk to my brother.

I went for a run, needing to stretch my legs and clear my head. There was a trail by my building and a small park, not as nice as the one that had been in my old neighborhood, but it was fine. I noticed a man walking toward me as I headed away from my building. He looked at me, his gaze focused intently on my face as I went by. He was older, his expression cold and removed. I felt a shiver run down my spine, and I had a feeling if I looked over my shoulder, he'd be staring at me, so I kept going, grateful when I went around the corner and spotted two other women running. I kept close to them, following them around the small park and veering off once I got close to my building again. I looked around as I slowed, feeling as if I was being watched, but I didn't see anyone and I shook my head in annoyance at myself. I was tired and overwrought.

One creep with a lingering glance was all it was. He probably leered at all the women. Inside, I stepped off the elevator, running into my neighbor.

"Hey, Emily."

"Hi."

"Um, didn't you get my note?"

She frowned. "Sorry?"

"About watering my plants while I was gone?"

"I did, but I saw Brian in the hall, so I assumed he was doing it."

I was confused. "Brian moved out a few weeks ago."

"Oh." She scratched her chin. "I was sure I saw him coming out of the apartment, but maybe I was mistaken. He'd probably dropped over to say hi and he was walking away. Oh God, are the plants okay?"

"They're fine. I only buy the hardy ones," I assured her.

"Okay, great. Sorry for the mix-up."

"No problem."

I stepped into the apartment, feeling anxious. Emily thought she saw Brian leaving. I checked his keys, but they were still on the hook, the dull bronze matching the one I had. I knew the super wouldn't let him in. Emily must have been mistaken, as she said. I hadn't told him I was away, so he must have dropped over to say hi. Unless he'd had a second key I didn't know about. Why would he come inside, though?

I went to his old room, pushing open the door. I sniffed, the air a bit stale with a slightly odd scent mixed in. Everything was in its place. I crossed to the closet, opening the door. The backpack he'd put in it was still tucked into the corner of the shelf. With a shake of my head, I shut the door then headed for a shower, leaving the bedroom door open to air it out a bit.

A while later, I came down the hall, stopping in confusion. The bedroom door was almost shut, but I had left it open, hadn't I?

I pushed it open, looking inside. Everything was normal. No one was there. I headed to the front door, checking that it was closed. It was locked, the dead bolt firmly in place. The bedroom door probably drifted shut on its own and I was making too much of it.

I sat down, staring at the floor. I rubbed my eyes. I was tired and overreacting. I was sure I was, but I decided I would ask the super about changing the locks the next time I saw him.

I was tired the next morning, having hardly slept that night. I tossed and turned, thinking of Finn. Worried. Upset he hadn't called.

Then I realized not once in my worrying had I wondered about Brian.

And I wondered if my subconscious was telling me something.

I went to work, feeling the weight of the world on my shoulders. As I stepped off the subway, I got the feeling again of being watched. I looked around, but the station was busy—packed with morning commuters. I thought I glimpsed the same man from the day before, but he was gone too quickly for me to be sure.

Then I shook my head and ran for the bus, not wanting to be late. I was nervous as I walked in, wondering how the staff would treat me. If Finn would be waiting. But I was greeted in the same warm fashion, and Finn was nowhere to be seen. The morning was busy with checkouts and getting reservations organized for a large group arriving on the weekend, and it flew by. I had my lunch by the fireplace, feeling strangely bereft. I glanced at the cameras, somehow aware that Finn wasn't watching me back.

I recalled his words. *"I'm not playing this game with you, Una."*

I had to swallow the lump in my throat. Had he given up this time, knowing the bumps ahead were too large to smooth over between us?

On the way home, I sensed eyes on me, but when I looked around the crowded subway car, I saw no one I recognized. No mysterious man leering at me.

I was overtired and upset and seeing things that weren't there. Jumping at shadows.

I stepped out of the elevator, rounding the corner, shock stopping my feet when I saw Brian outside my door.

"Brian?"

He blinked, looking surprised. Or was that guilt?

"Hey, Una. I was just leaving. I knocked, but you weren't home."

"I was at work. You know that. And you didn't answer my call or text last night."

"Yeah. I don't have the old phone anymore. I, ah, had to give it back."

"When you quit."

"Guess I'm not surprised you know about that." He scratched his head. "Can we talk?"

I went past him, glancing down. He had some keys in his hand. "What are those?"

He looked down. "My keys."

"Do you have a key to my place?"

He looked annoyed. "No. I gave it back, Una." He held up the ring. "These are to my new place and my car. Jesus," he muttered, pushing them my way. "You want to check?"

"No." I huffed a sigh. "Come in."

He went past me, and I wrinkled my nose. "Have you started smoking again?"

He rolled his eyes. "You're not my mother. I bummed one earlier. I was tense."

I looked at him. He was thinner, his dark eyes almost black. He seemed on edge. Unhappy.

"Are you on drugs, Brian?" I asked.

"Fuck's sake, Una," he snapped. "Not you too. You and the mighty Finn. So fucking moral." He snorted.

"You saw Finn?" I gripped the back of the sofa, relief pouring through me. He'd seen Finn, and he was alive.

"He sent his men after me, so yeah, I went and saw him." He winced as he sat down. "We had words." He leaned back. "Really, Una. It's been a day. Can I have a whiskey?"

I poured us each a finger in a glass and handed him one. He tossed it back and held out his glass for more. I poured him another and he frowned, so I added a splash more then sat across from him.

"What happened?" I asked quietly.

"Oh, your boy was full of questions and accusations. I had to prove to him I wasn't some sort of low-life arsonist. I've been busy with Juan, building our business. I don't give a flying shit about Finn or his world anymore. That fucker Roman Costas filled his head with lies." He sat back with a smirk, an ugly one. "I set the record straight." He took another sip of whiskey. "And I paid him the money I owed him, so I am free and clear of him." He reached into his pocket and withdrew an envelope. "And there's yours."

I gaped at him, not touching it. "Brian, what are you doing to get that sort of money?"

"We got an investor in our company. I told him everything. And you know what? He didn't care. He fronted us the money, and Juan let me take this to pay off my debts. I'll draw a lesser salary to pay it off.

Without fucking interest. I owe nothing to you or your fucking precious Finn."

I shook my head. "What sort of investor does that? What have you gotten yourself involved with?"

"Why am I not surprised that my sister has zero faith in me? First, I had to listen to Finn all afternoon. Get tossed around. Swear my fucking fidelity to someone I hate." He took a drink of whiskey. "And now, you're all sanctimonious, as if you're so fucking pure."

He narrowed his eyes, and I shivered at the look of them. Empty. Cold. Angry. And far too black. He leaned close, the scent of cigarettes and something else washing over me. It was all I could do not to gag or lean back.

"You think you're all high-and-mighty, my little sister? Fucking big bad Finn? Throwing me to the wolf and walking away? You think he can always protect you?" he laughed, the sound unpleasant. "Yet I'm here with you. Alone. I could slap you around, hurt you, and he could do nothing."

My stomach rolled at his words and his implied threat. Then he sat back. "But I never would."

His words should have calmed me, but the fact that he'd uttered them frightened me.

"I asked Finn to let you go," I whispered.

"And he did. But you didn't ask him to forgive the loan. Or to make sure it was known I wasn't to be touched. That only applies to you, doesn't it, sister dear? I guess you need to suck his cock for protection." He stood. "At least I haven't lowered myself to that. Sleeping with the man who killed our dad."

His words and the hatred with which he spewed them shocked me.

"Dad was doing his job. He took that bullet out of loyalty."

"And got nothing for it but pissing and shitting himself until he died," he snarled. "Finn did nothing."

I stood, angry now too. "He paid all the medical bills. The mortgage. For nursing care. He made sure Dad never went without. He looked after him."

"And what about me?" he roared, his whiskey-soaked breath hitting my face. "I should have been promoted. Given special treatment to make up for it."

I gaped at him. "Oh my God, that's what you think? Dad got hurt, so you should have it easy? What makes you think you should be entitled that way?"

He grasped my arms, shaking me. "Finn O'Reilly owes me."

"No," I gasped. "He doesn't. You owe him."

His grip tightened to the point of pain. Then with a snarl, he pushed me away. I fell to the floor, hitting my hip, staring up at him with new eyes.

"He is going to pay. He thinks this is over, but it's not. One day, he will bow to me." He grinned, an evil, twisted grin I had never seen on him before. "And I'll show him the same mercy he showed me." He picked up his whiskey and drained it, throwing the glass against the wall. Then he picked up the envelope. "You know what? Ask Finn for your money. You're his whore now. I'm going to take this and enjoy myself. See you around, sister."

He left, slamming the door behind him. It took me a moment before I got off the floor and raced to the door, throwing the dead bolt.

Whoever that person was who had left in such anger wasn't my brother. I didn't recognize that man.

I covered my face as I sobbed.

Finn had been right all along.

But it might be too late for me to tell him.

CHAPTER FOURTEEN

FINN

I scrubbed my hand over my face, cursing inwardly. I studied the picture Roman put in front of me and shook my head.

"That isn't Brian Murphy."

Roman frowned. "Are you sure?"

"You've seen him. His hair is red, and he has so many freckles his face almost looks the same color at times." I tapped the grainy picture. "This guy's hair is too dark, and his skin is clear. Not Brian."

I sat down, feeling relief. I still had to deal with him, but I didn't have to kill him—yet.

"The guy on the crew swore it was him. Said it sounded just like him."

"I have lots of men with a trace of an accent. Brian picked it up from his dad and hanging with the crew. The guy heard someone who sounded like Murphy during a panicked arson attack. He could have been mistaken." I looked at the grainy picture. "This guy is clean-shaven. Murphy isn't. He's always sporting a beard. Or what might pass as one."

Roman grunted.

"Are there any other pictures?"

"No, the camera was knocked out of place. In both cases, which makes me think it's someone who knows your business."

"Murphy wasn't up on all the details. Especially lately since I had him doing grunt work."

"You've got men looking for him?"

"Yeah."

I looked out the window, feeling weary. I hadn't stopped since I'd stepped back into the hotel. The arson and the gang attacks were my priority. Without Niall, I was burning the candle at both ends, and I hadn't been to my suite except for a quick shower that morning.

And I hadn't talked to or seen Una. By the time I could call her last night, it was too late, and I assumed she'd be sleeping. I didn't want to text her, thinking I would see her in the hotel and we'd be able to talk for a moment, but that hadn't happened. Another business was raided and a lot of damage done, and I'd been there with my men since three a.m. trying to figure out what was happening and why.

As soon as I was done with Roman, I planned on calling her. Except my phone rang, and the last words I expected to hear were uttered.

"Brian Murphy is at the warehouse, and he's asking for you."

"I'm on my way."

I stood, pulling down my sleeves. "This should be interesting."

"You want backup?"

I shook my head, holding out my hand. "I've got my men. You've been more than generous with your time, Roman. Go home to your family with my gratitude. I owe you."

He stood, accepting my handshake. "I've always prided myself on sizing up a person quickly, Finn. Whatever he has to say, watch Brian Murphy. He's a wolf in sheep's clothing. His sister is amazing, but he is trouble. If you need me, call me. If you need backup, it's yours. Someone is messing with you, which messes with our old territory, and it still means something to me. And Luca. We'll have your back."

"I appreciate it."

He nodded and left. I grabbed my jacket, looking longingly at the monitor. I knew Una would be at the front desk. I wanted to see her, but I was afraid if I did, I wouldn't be able to resist going to her. I missed her so much it was a physical ache.

But the bottom line was her brother was still standing between us, and I needed to handle that before I could deal with the problems he brought to our relationship.

I picked up my phone and walked away.

Brian looked like shit. He was paler than usual, his freckles a bright map of color all over his face. His spartan beard was even more so today, patches of white and red on his chin and jowls.

I studied him, thinking how upset his father would be. Jim prided himself on honor and loyalty. Working hard. He passed that on to his youngest. It apparently had skipped right over Brian. Even on the thin ice he was skating, he was sitting down, picking at his nails as if he hadn't a care in the world.

Without a word, I grabbed him by the scruff of the neck, pinning him to the wall.

"What the fuck game are you playing, Murphy? You're lucky I haven't simply ended you."

"You won't," he smirked. "Because you like fucking my sister."

I didn't hold back as I punched him. He doubled over, gasping for air. I gripped his neck, pushing his head into the hard wall. "One more word like that about your sister and I'll end you, regardless of the consequences."

He stared at me, his mouth opening and closing as he struggled for breath. I squeezed, enjoying the way his eyes bulged and he clawed at my hands. Then I pulled back, letting him drop to the floor. I sat behind the old desk.

"You have five minutes to convince me not to kill you."

He struggled to his feet and sat on the scarred wooden chair. "I'm sorry."

I lifted an eyebrow. "That's the best you've got?"

He glared but took a deep breath. "I was angry the other day when Roman was at the warehouse. Out of line. I said a lot of shit. I apologize."

"You were high."

"I was in pain, and I took too many pills."

I didn't believe it for a second, but I let it go. I didn't care if he drugged himself to death. It would make my life easier.

"And? You need to start talking, Brian, before I start shooting."

He held out his hands. "Come on, Finn. Let's be honest. You hate me. I dislike you. You're happy to see the end of me."

"You know it's not that easy."

He huffed. "I swore an oath, and I'll keep it."

"What do you know of the new gang that has suddenly appeared?"

"Nothing. I'm busy with my new venture."

"Which is?"

He lifted his shoulders, rolling his neck. "I don't have to tell you what I have planned except it has nothing to do with you or your world."

I counted to ten. If Niall were here, Brian would already be dead from the tone he was speaking to me in. Once again, it was Una and her love for this useless boy in front of me that protected him.

"You owe me a huge amount of money."

Brian nodded and reached for a bag, placing it on the desk. "Here it is in full."

I stood, opening the bag carefully, and stared at the contents. "Who have you borrowed this from?"

He shook his head. "I've paid my debt. I gave you my word."

"Which means nothing to me," I snapped.

He stared at me without blinking. "I swear on my father's grave."

A beat passed.

"You know what he meant to me," he added.

That was probably the most truthful thing Brian Murphy had ever said.

I looked at the money. Then at him.

The debt was paid. I could release him and watch him for a while. Add extra security to my territory and be vigilant. Make sure he wasn't part of it.

Maybe he would find his own path. Maybe he would fail. Maybe he'd get mixed up with something else and meet his end. I had no expectations that he would actually work hard and stick to whatever plans he was hatching now.

But it wouldn't be at my hands.

I could tell Una honestly I'd let him go. That I did as she asked, but tell her it was the last time.

Surely she could see how hard I was trying for her. This might be the only chance for us.

So, I grabbed it.

"You break your word, I'm coming for you. No holds barred. It won't matter who you're related to."

"You won't have to."

"Who is Juan?" I asked out of the blue.

He looked surprised and cleared his throat. "My roommate."

"Where did you meet him?"

"At the bar through some friends."

"Is he part of Lopez's crew?"

He frowned. "Lopez? No. I'm staying away from his place."

"You better. Keep your nose clean, Brian. Try working hard. Applying yourself."

He rolled his eyes as he stood. Resentment poured off him, all pretense of being contrite gone. "Thanks for the pep talk. One day, you might find you need my help, Finn. I'll be only too pleased to tell you to go fuck yourself."

"Watch your tone," I snarled, standing. "I'm still—"

He waved his hand. "You're nothing to me now but my past."

I gripped the desk, the edge of the wood splintering under my hands. I wanted to kill him. "Get out."

He sauntered toward the door.

"I'll be watching, Brian."

"Yeah. Say hi to my sister while you're doing that."

He walked out.

I stared at the money, then at the door.

He was lying. I knew it as sure as I knew my own name. Whatever he'd done to get this money was bad news. He was too brave suddenly. As if he had a secret.

I shook my head, knowing I had just made a mistake, and I had no one to blame but myself.

And that made me angry.

I headed back to the hotel and went to my suite. I stood in the shower, feeling the heat on my skin. I scrubbed myself, as if washing away the grit of the day. Wishing I could wash away the past couple of days and not have argued with Una. Refused to let her walk away. I stepped from the shower, towel-drying my hair, feeling the exhaustion catching up with me. I glanced at my watch, deciding I would order some food, then go see her. Talk to her and clear the air. Lay it all on the table without any other ears listening.

I ordered a sandwich and poured myself a whiskey, calling Niall to check in.

"They're releasing her tomorrow," he informed me. "I've set up all the care, and I plan to stay a couple of days to make sure she's settled."

Knowing the line was secure, I told him everything that had happened, including a shortened version of the fight with Una.

He sighed. "If I'd been there, I'd have put a bullet in him. Una could have hated me instead."

I chuckled, draining my whiskey and pouring another generous finger or two into my glass. "I've never been so torn."

"You aren't with anything else. It's just this fucked-up situation." He paused. "I hope you don't regret this, Finn. More than if you had taken him out. Or put out the word to do so."

"I think I will," I replied honestly. "Something is up."

"Then we need to figure it out. Fast. And take Roman up on his offer. Get some extra men on security."

"I'll call him in the morning."

"I'll be there as soon as I can."

He rang off and I sighed, going to the door when I heard the discreet knock. I took my sandwich and ate it, barely tasting it, running my finger over my phone constantly. I wanted to call Una, but the need to see her was stronger. I finished my sandwich and stood, my phone ringing as I did.

"O'Reilly."

"Boss, we got another one."

I shut my eyes. "On my way."

The next morning, I was almost delirious with exhaustion. I hadn't slept in days. Last night, two businesses had been torched in my territory. Neither was mine, but they were local owners who watched their lives go up in smoke. By the time I dealt with the fire department, the families, and relocating them since they lived over their stores, it was dawn. Neither of them had good enough surveillance, so I spent a significant chunk of time with my team and a company arranging more cameras in various areas. I needed to catch whoever this was. I added extra men and called Roman, asking for additional help.

"I still have lots of men who would work," he assured me. "I'll get some to your place, and you dispatch them where needed." He paused. "You need me to send Aldo? He can help run the crew."

I paused. "No. Niall is back soon. But if I change my mind, I'll let you know."

"I'll be in touch."

I smelled of smoke and ash. I was covered in soot and dirt. I headed to my suite and once again stood under the showerhead, but the spray didn't ease the tension. Until I figured this out, I couldn't relax.

Brian Murphy wasn't smart enough to plan and execute something like this. But someone hated me enough and was raging a vendetta against me.

I needed to figure out who before more people were hurt.

I stepped from the shower.

But first, I needed to see Una. The rest of the world could wait.

CHAPTER FIFTEEN

UNA

I blinked at the guest standing in front of me, tapping his fingers on the wooden surface impatiently. He was older, with heavy jowls, and red-faced, almost sputtering in his indignation. His voice had been increasing in volume over the past moments.

"Did you hear me? I want some satisfaction. I demand my money back, and I want to speak to a manager."

"Sir," I replied in my most soothing voice. "I have called the manager, who is dealing with another issue. He will be here momentarily. If you'd like to sit, I can have some coffee brought to you and your, ah, wife."

I was certain the young buxom blond wasn't his wife.

"I don't want any fucking coffee, you redheaded snippet! I want to be treated with the respect I deserve!" He slammed his hand this time, making the desk shake with the force of it.

I forced a smile on my face. But before I could speak, another voice from behind him spoke up, icy and firm.

"I own this hotel. How can I be of service?"

The man spun, craning his head back to look Finn in the face. Finn scowled down at him, his gaze penetrating and cold. "I do suggest, however, that you speak to me with the same level of respect you are demanding."

Mr. Flynn drew himself up, squaring his shoulders. "I have been insulted, and I want restitution. This girl isn't helping."

Finn angled his head to the side, staring at him, his stance and expression intimidating. "How odd. Ms. Murphy is one of my best employees. Perhaps it is the disrespect you are showing her that is rendering her unable to help you with your problem." He switched his gaze to me, lifting an eyebrow, his expression less hostile. "Which would be, Ms. Murphy?"

"Oh, ah, Mr. Flynn says the waiter eyed his wife inappropriately and splashed him with coffee while doing so. He is very upset. Philip—Mr. Watson—is upstairs inquiring with the manager to figure this out."

"I see." Finn stared down at Mr. Flynn. "Una," he said quietly. "Comp Mr. Flynn's room and any subsequent charges. Arrange a car to the airport."

"I have my own car."

"Then we'll have it out front right away." Finn tilted his head. "If I might have a moment with you in private."

Mr. Flynn turned my way. "That is how you treat an important guest."

I peeked over the monitor as Finn took Mr. Flynn to the side. His back was to me, but I saw the way Mr. Flynn's face drained of color as Finn spoke. He laid a hand on his shoulder in a friendly gesture I assumed was anything but friendly. Finn only spoke briefly, but Mr. Flynn was nodding so quickly, he reminded me of a bobblehead doll. I cleared his account, and a few moments later, they returned to the desk.

"All taken care of, sir," I said with a forced smile. "Your car is ready."

Mr. Flynn cleared his throat. "Thank you. I'm sorry if I was rude. I was upset. Maddy gets offended easily."

I wanted to tell him maybe Maddy should wear something that covered her breasts instead of showing them off. Her nipples were barely concealed. Her ass cheeks were in danger of exploding out of her tight skirt as well. But I kept my thoughts to myself, handing him the folded bill.

"Have a safe trip home," I murmured. "Thank you for staying at O'Reilly's. We look forward to seeing you again."

He shook his head, side-eyeing Finn. "Probably not."

Then he scurried away, grabbing Maddy. "Let's go."

She tottered behind him on high heels, towering over him. "Can't we gamble now, Howie? I like the machines that make noise!"

"No!" he roared, looking back, seeing Finn again. "We have to go, Maddy. *Now.*"

Philip stepped off the elevator, meeting Finn across the lobby. They spoke for a few moments, and Finn nodded, shook his hand, and headed for the elevator. I fought back the tears as the doors shut, hanging my head. He was still angry with me.

I hadn't slept all night. I'd tried to call Finn, but it went straight to voice mail. I'd dozed in my chair, too afraid to go to bed in case Brian came back.

I had taken a cab to work this morning, too exhausted to care about the cost and not prepared to deal with the subway. Or worry about anyone staring at me.

I had hoped to see Finn and talk to him.

Philip came behind the desk. "Well, that was interesting."

"Hmm," I hummed, not trusting my voice. My throat felt thick.

"Mr. O'Reilly wants to see you in his office, Una. Now."

"Oh."

He took the pen from my hand. "Don't keep him waiting."

I knocked on the door, fear gripping me. This was it. Finn was fed up with my brother and with me. He was going to let me go. End us once and for all.

Would he let me tell him what Brian had said?

Would he care?

"In," Finn called.

I took a deep breath and straightened my shoulders. Whatever happened, I had my pride. I would figure it out.

Except when I walked in and saw Finn leaning against his desk facing the door, my bravado left me. He appeared to be furious, his arms crossed over his chest. He had dark circles under his eyes and looked as exhausted as I felt.

We stared at each other in silence.

Finally, I blurted it out. "I was trying to soothe him, Finn. He was impossible to deal with. I mean, I'm sure Logan did ogle her, but I think I did too. It's rather hard not to."

He blinked then shook his head.

"I don't give a fuck about that asshole. He'll never be welcome here again. In fact, he's going to find it hard to book a room in any decent hotel by the time I'm finished with him."

"What?"

He stood straight. "Are you all right, *mo chroí?*"

I started to tremble. Tears gathered in my eyes.

He frowned, taking a step toward me. "Una," he murmured, his voice tender and low. He opened his arms, and I ran straight into them, feeling myself shudder with relief as he held me in his grasp. For the first time since he'd let me walk away, I felt completely safe. My tears came, hot and heavy, and all I could do was clutch Finn and let him hold me.

I realized right then that Finn O'Reilly was my home. His embrace was my soft landing.

And I never wanted to leave it.

FINN

I held her tight, myriad emotions coursing through me. Relief she was in my arms. Comfort from the feel of her nestled against me. Worry over her emotional state. Fury in the knowledge that something aside from the asshole at the front desk had caused the tears currently soaking into my shirt.

And pain knowing a lot of her tears were no doubt on account of me.

I bent slightly, picking her up and heading to the sofa. I sat down, still holding her, running a hand up and down her back, making low noises in my throat, trying to figure out how to comfort her the best. I needed her to calm down enough to tell me what was happening.

She was shaking, her body a mass of tremors. Her skin felt too cool under my touch, and I stroked her arms, feeling her tense even more. I ran my hands along her head, rocking slightly.

I hated her tears. I hated them even more because they were almost silent. Her shoulders shook, and the softest of pained sounds escaped her mouth, but there were no harsh, loud sobs the way some women cried.

Somehow, I thought I would have preferred that. Her low cries cut me to the quick, my chest aching with her pain, as if I were feeling it with her.

I found my phone, calling the front desk.

"Yes, Mr. O'Reilly," Philip answered, ever the professional.

"Ms. Murphy will not be returning this week," I informed him. "I need you to replace her."

"Of course." He paused. "Friday night?" he asked, letting the words hang between us.

"I think she'll perform."

"Very good." He cleared his throat. "Maybe some tea to be delivered to the office?"

"Good idea. Thank you."

"Of course, sir. Right away."

I hung up, grateful he was in charge. Tea would be good for Una.

I pressed a kiss to her head, crooning her name. "It's all right, Una. I have you."

She kept crying, and I kissed her again. "Please, *mo chroí*, I need you to tell me what's wrong. I can't fix it if I don't know what's happened."

She shuddered, dragging in a deep breath. "That's it," I encouraged. "Another one, Una. Take another breath."

She did, the sound almost painful, and she let her head fall back. She was beyond pale, her freckles standing out on her skin. Dark circles were under her eyes, and when they fluttered open, they were red-rimmed and distressed. I traced a finger down her damp cheek.

"Hush now," I murmured. "I'm here, and everything is going to be okay."

A discreet knock on the door startled her, and I shook my head. "Tea. Go wash your face, and I'll get it."

She slipped from my lap, and I waited until she had gone into the washroom to open my office door. I took the tray, not surprised to see a plate of small sandwiches and treats on it. I offered a silent thanks to Philip, mentally reminding myself to send him and his wife on a weekend away. I'd arrange something with Roman, who had commented more than once on Philip's capabilities.

I poured tea, adding some honey the way Una liked, and she returned. Calmer, but still obviously distressed. I patted the cushion beside me, and when she sat down, I handed her the cup, pressing a kiss to her cheek. "I'm here," I repeated.

She nodded, sipping her tea, a slight tremble to her hand.

I spoke, telling her what had happened since I had left her at her apartment. "I wasn't ignoring you, Una, or still angry. I was desperately trying to figure out what was happening. To help the people who needed me. Do you understand that?" I asked gently, somehow worried about pushing her over an edge I couldn't comprehend.

"Yes," she replied.

I took her cup, filling it again. She accepted it, and I was pleased to see the tremble had lessened. I inhaled. "I saw Brian at the warehouse."

"I know."

I frowned. "How?"

"He came to see me."

"And, of course, gave you his version of the story."

"He said you roughed him up and talked down to him."

"He's lucky I let him go."

"You did that for me," she whispered.

"Yes," I stated honestly.

"I won't ask that of you again."

Something in her voice, the way she tensed, gave me pause.

"What happened, Una? What else did he say?"

She began to tremble again.

"Una?" I asked, trying to stay calm. "Tell me."

"It was awful," she replied. "He seemed okay, and then suddenly, he was a different person. Angry and bitter. Nasty. He said terrible things. Threatened me. I was so scared."

"Tell me exactly what he said," I demanded through tight lips. "Every word."

She replayed the visit, and my fury burned hotter the more she spoke. He had fucking been lying the entire time, and I had allowed him to leave. When she repeated his threats, it was all I could do not to throw something. I wanted to pick up the phone and order him found and killed.

"Did he touch you?"

She hesitated.

"Una, did he hurt you?"

She slipped off her jacket, showing me her upper arms. Each one bore the same black-and-blue marks of a handprint. I knew the kind of pressure it would take to leave imprints that dark.

I had to count to ten. Twice. Curl my fists hard enough that my knuckles cracked. Brian Murphy had just signed his death warrant.

"You were right, Finn. All along. I refused to listen, but I know now you were right. My brother is gone, and I don't know the man who replaced him."

"That doesn't give me any satisfaction."

She nodded, still not meeting my eyes. I stood and tugged her jacket back into place. I lifted her chin. "Your brother is the one responsible here. He has made his choices. He was tense yesterday, no doubt needing a hit of whatever he's on. He held his temper in check to buy himself some time. Then he got high and came to see you, letting his real agenda out. You can't be around him anymore."

"No," she whispered, her lips quivering.

I bent and kissed her soft mouth. "I need to make sure you're safe."

"I think someone is watching me," she blurted.

I tightened my hand on her chin. "What?"

"I went for a run, and there was a man. He stared at me. Not just a casual look, but intense. Angry. It gave me goose bumps, and I joined a couple other women because I was afraid to run alone."

"What did he look like?"

She frowned. "Dark hair, average height. But it was his eyes, Finn. They were dead. And he looked cold. Emotionless. The hair on the back of my neck stood on end with one glance. I looked away really fast, so I didn't get a good look at the rest of his features. I thought I saw him again the next day, but I wasn't sure if it was my imagination or not." She laughed, the sound nervous. "Maybe the whole staring thing was my imagination. I was upset and everything."

I shook my head. "You aren't prone to fits of imagination, Una. If your gut said he was dangerous, I'm glad you listened to it." I frowned. "Why didn't you call? Or, even better, why didn't you come here? You'd be safe."

"I wasn't sure what you would do if I showed up here. I called but it went to voice mail, and I didn't want to leave a message when I was so upset."

I pulled her into my arms. "I would never be angry enough to not be concerned for your safety. Ever. And I don't care where I am, what I'm doing—you are my priority. If I had heard that voice mail, I would have come and gotten you or sent my men to watch over you until I could." I tightened my grip. "I promise you that, Una. Always."

She sighed, nestling close, her ear over my heart. It was racing, simply the thought of her in danger making me crazy. "You're staying here," I announced. "Until we figure this out, you're staying here. With me."

She didn't argue.

"You have the rest of the week off. You can perform on the weekend if you want, but no more front desk this week. We're going to the suite now, and you're going to sleep."

"You need to sleep too."

"I'll see what happens. There've been too many incidents for me to sleep."

We headed upstairs. I was intent on tucking her in. I would watch over her and work from my desk up there. She looked as if she was ready to crash any second.

"When is Niall back?" she asked in the elevator.

"Soon."

"You said Roman is sending you some men?"

"Yes. That will help. I can add men to patrol and watch." I swiped my pass.

"Do you think there's a reason they're hitting only in the one area?"

I paused, turning to look at her. "I never gave that any thought." I put my hand on the small of her back, urging her forward. I thought about what she had asked. "You're right," I muttered.

"It's where I lived when I came here. I cut my teeth in that area. I know it the best. They know me."

She frowned. "Whoever it is, they're making it personal."

"Not many would know all that. Unless they knew my history." I ran a hand through my hair. "Someone in my own crew."

She looked troubled, then spoke. "Or was in your crew and knew your history because their father spoke of it often. With pride. How you rose in the ranks. The way people, especially in that neighborhood, looked up to you. Regarded you as a hero, not a criminal, because you made sure they were safe."

I nodded slowly. "And by attacking it, they make me look incompetent and careless."

"Someone like Brian."

I huffed out a laugh. "Sorry, my girl, but I don't think your brother is smart enough to plan and execute such an in-depth plan."

"Unless he had help. He has the knowledge. Someone else has the men and the money." She gripped my arm. "Someone with enough money to pay you back, so Brian isn't beholden to you—but rather, to them. He's become their soldier."

I stared at her. "You are brilliant."

CHAPTER SIXTEEN

FINN

"But who?" Roman asked, rubbing his chin. I had tucked Una into bed and set up a private video call. Niall joined us.

"Someone who wants to take over. These rogue gangs aren't that rogue. And it wasn't Brian in the photo, but I think you were right. He's part of this."

"You've put out the word?" Niall asked.

I knew what he was asking. Brian Murphy now had a price on his head. "Yes."

"No more leniency?"

"None."

"I'll get some inquiries out there," Roman offered. "Discreetly, of course. Luca will reach out too."

"I need him alive to find out who is behind this and why. I've spent years building bridges, peace." I scrubbed my face in anger. "Why?"

"Some people don't want peace. They thrive on conflict. They believe in taking what they want and will do whatever they need to in order to get that. Can you think of anyone you've been at odds with?"

"Lopez?" Niall questioned.

I snorted. "Hardly at odds. I paid him his money, so he didn't continue to make his ridiculous interest. Hardly a reason to go after me."

Roman looked thoughtful. "He's an unknown. Worth checking into. You said yourself he was a cold bastard. Maybe he takes things to the extreme." He rubbed his chin. "Let me handle that part. I have an incredible hacker. The dark web is his specialty."

"Fine."

With a nod, he signed off.

"I'll be there tomorrow," Niall informed me. "Mum is home, and all is good. I think she wants me gone. She says I'm hovering too much."

"Sounds like her."

"This is serious, Finn. You need me. You look like hell."

"My territory being torched is keeping me busy."

"Well, now you know to concentrate everything in the one neighborhood. Maybe we'll catch them and can work our way up the chain."

"I hope so."

I signed off, called one of my captains, and rearranged the schedule. "Keep it on the down-low, but we're sticking to the Waverly area."

"Got it."

"They see anything, they move. Anything. Better safe than sorry. And be on the lookout for Murphy."

I hung up and went to check on Una. She was curled into the bed, huddled under the covers, asleep but not peaceful. I felt exhaustion bearing down on me, and I decided to lie down. My phone would wake me when I was needed.

And I had no doubt I would be needed soon.

I woke to the feel of Una on my chest, her hair tickling my nose. I glanced at my watch, shocked that five hours had passed. I grabbed my phone, scrolling. I had messages, but no calls. No emergencies.

The sleep had rejuvenated me. I brushed the hair from Una's face, pleased to see she seemed to be deeply asleep. I wondered if the fact that we were together and close helped us both find the rest we needed.

I slipped from the bed, heading to my desk. I ordered coffee and food, suddenly starving. I made some calls, checked in with my men, pleased all seemed quiet, but I worried about what would happen when night fell on the city.

A short while later, I heard Una get up, and she appeared by my desk, her hair a mess of curls, looking incredibly sexy in a T-shirt of mine that hung down her thighs and off her shoulders. I smiled at her sleepy expression. "Hello, *mo chroí.*"

She ran a hand through her hair, smiling ruefully. "Hi. Did you sleep?"

I reached for her, wrapping my arm around her thighs and pulling her close. "Very well. You?"

She nodded, covering a yawn. "Yes."

"I sleep better beside you," I acknowledged.

"The same for me," she said with a shy smile.

"I ordered some sandwiches and coffee. Do you want me to get you some tea?"

"No, I'm good right now."

"Let me know if you change your mind."

"I will."

We gazed at each other, the air around us beginning to warm. I traced the soft skin of her thighs, smiling as she shivered. "I'm glad you're here," I murmured.

She bent, pressing a kiss to my mouth. "I love you."

I smiled against her lips. "The same for me." I pressed back to her lips, groaning as she opened for me, and our tongues slid together. I pushed my chair back, pulling her to my lap so she straddled me. I held her tight, kissing her harder. Deeper. Letting her feel how much I loved her. How glad I was that she was there with me. She whimpered, tugging on my hair, gripping my neck, slowly undulating as my cock grew stiff between us.

"Finn," she whispered, a plea in her voice.

"Una," I groaned. "You need to eat."

"I need you more."

One moment, I was sitting in the chair, her astride me. The next, she had shimmied from my lap and was between my legs, tugging on my pants. I lifted my hips even as I shook my head.

"You don't—"

"Hush," she replied. "You said I needed to eat."

Then she wrapped her lips around my cock and drew me in.

I let my head fall back. The heat and wetness of her mouth surrounded me. She sucked and teased. Licked up and down my shaft, cupping my balls as she hummed. Teased the crown then took all of me in, swallowing as I hit the back of her throat.

Then she started again. I was lost in a vortex of sensations. The warmth of her mouth, the cool of the air when she would pull back. The glide of her tongue on the underside of me. How she suckled the crown in the sweetest way possible. The way she lapped at me, sucked me in. The vibrations as she hummed, singing a love song deep in her throat as she took me to heaven. The gentle tugging of her fingers on my balls, the grip of them when she cupped me.

I wound my hands into her hair, loving the feeling of the silk as it fell through my fingers. I gripped a fistful of her tresses, praising her, cursing, begging. Wanting more, needing more of everything she was doing to me. Begging her for relief, yet never wanting the experience to end.

Until it became too much. "Una," I gasped, tightening my hands. "You need—"

She swallowed around me, taking me so deep I climaxed, my back arching, her name falling like a symphony from my lips as I thrust into her mouth, riding a wave I never wanted to reach shore.

Then I collapsed. Gasping, out of breath, shocked by her actions, but delighted at the same time.

I stared down at her, then bent, pulling her back to my lap. I kissed her, tasting the sharpness of my release in her mouth. Her stiff nipples rubbed on my chest, and I dropped my hand between us, feeling her slick folds.

"You liked that, Una?" I groaned. "Sucking me off at the table? Are you aching, needing your own release?"

"Yes," she panted. "Touch me, Finn. I'm already close."

I plunged two fingers inside her, her gasp loud. I pressed on her clit with my thumb, and she began to ride my hand, our mouths fused together, her whimpers and moans swallowed by me. I went faster, strumming her clit as she cried out, her body primed and ready. When I added a third finger, she let her head fall back and cried out, her muscles locking down. I kissed the arch of her neck, licking my way to her collarbone and sucking her breasts through the material of the shirt. She rode my fingers to completion, whimpering when the sensation became too much. I pulled her into my arms, her head tucked under my chin, her ear pressed to my pounding heart.

I could feel her pulse racing under my touch, and I stroked her hair.

For a moment, we basked in the stillness, our bodies sated, minds at peace, and souls entwined.

Then she lifted her head, smiling.

"Tea now."

I kissed her.

"Okay."

The night was quiet. Not a fire, a robbery, or a sighting of the gang that had suddenly appeared. I slept fitfully, checking my phone, certain I was missing alerts. I spoke to my men, and, like me, they were surprised by the quiet. I was sure it was a temporary lull and advised them to be vigilant.

In the morning, I showered, planning on leaving a sleeping Una in my bed. She woke as I dressed, sitting up and looking startled.

"I need to get ready!"

I shook my head, meeting her gaze. "You aren't working today," I stated firmly. "Your shift has been covered."

"What am I supposed to do, then?"

"Read. Sleep. Relax. I'll be in the office or here at my desk once I've done some rounds."

"Can I come with you?"

I frowned. "I'm not sure that's a good idea."

"You'll keep me safe."

I pulled on my suit jacket as I thought it over. "You promise not to leave my side and do exactly what I say?"

"Yes."

"Fine. You can come. I'll go do some work until you're ready."

"Oh." She looked down. "My clothes are in my locker."

"I'll get them sent up."

She toyed with the blanket. "Everyone will know I was sleeping up here."

I bent and kissed her. "I don't care. You're mine. I don't give a shit who knows and what they have to say about it. Unless they're disrespectful, then they'll feel my foot in their fucking arse."

"Well, okay, Mr. O'Reilly. No need to get all sweary about it."

I began to laugh. "Go shower. You have an hour."

"I only need thirty minutes."

UNA

It took me forty, but Finn didn't seem to mind. He had toast and tea waiting for me, and I ate as he spoke to his men and updated Roman.

"He is being very helpful," I commented.

He sipped his coffee. "This was his brother's city. His as well. They still care. They want the neighborhood back and thriving." He stood. "Ready?"

"Yes."

He held out his hand. "Beside me, Una. I tell you to duck, you duck. I tell you to stay in the car, that's where you stay. You won't be alone a moment—if I have to leave your side, a man will be with you. And you listen to him since he is there to keep you safe. You got me?"

I squeezed his fingers. "Got it."

His gaze softened. "Okay, then. Let's go."

We arrived, Rory pulling over and cutting the engine. "You want me to wait here, Mr. O'Reilly?"

Finn glanced around. "Yes."

He looked my way, intense and focused. "Remember what I said."

I nodded, taken aback by his sudden demeanor change. He tapped on the window, and the guard with us opened the door. Finn stepped out, his shoulders back, head held high. He scanned the area before offering me his hand. I stepped out, and he gripped my fingers with his. "Walk close. Tom will be behind you. John is in front. They will protect you."

"Who will protect you?" I asked.

He flashed me a quick smile. "I can protect myself, but they can handle both of us."

I was fascinated watching Finn as we went around to the shops and spoke with people. I knew him as my Finn. The loving, passionate man under the fierce exterior. I saw him daily as the owner of the hotel—charming and handsome, confident. I had seen glimpses of the syndicate boss, but he was front and center today. Calm, in control, intimidating. He spoke intelligently, choosing to listen intently, rushing no one who approached him. He nodded as people told him of their worries. Assured them quietly of taking their concerns seriously. Stressing the added security and the desire to end this sudden situation and restore calm to the area.

The older couples, especially the women, made me smile. They offered him sweets, drinks. Fussed over him. He accepted their flutterings with a patient expression, never refusing anything they offered. It would, I realized, hurt their feelings, and he had no desire to do that. I hung back as he spoke with his men, had a long, low discussion with a fire marshal who was on-site checking into one of the buildings that had been on fire. Finn looked furious, shaking his head, his fists tight. He was determined to end this, and he was frustrated it was even happening.

What I saw opened my eyes a little. I recalled my dad talking about rounds with Finn. The people. Brian only ever talked about the darker side, almost reveling in it. Dad liked what Finn and his generation brought to the table. Coexisting with other families, looking out for their people, and not fighting over territory. Not everyone saw it that way, but so many did, and today, I was observing it firsthand.

And most of all, I saw the mutual respect. He treated people as if they mattered—from the old man still rolling dough in a bakery he'd owned for years, to the younger woman running a small convenience store, trying to raise her kids. There was no one ethnic group in this area. Portuguese, Chinese, Vietnamese, Italian, and other shops all existed here, their worlds mixing and creating a beautiful harmony. One that Finn wanted to restore.

As Finn spoke with the fire marshal again, I sat on a bench across from the bakery, eating a sweet bun a woman had insisted I take earlier. It was buttery and soft, the filling a rich cream. A group of four young men strolled past me, a pair of bright-red sneakers catching my eye as they headed across the street and into the bakery, loud and boisterous. A moment later, another group walked in behind them, this one with three. In a short time, they filed out, and for some reason, I counted them. Six. The one with the bright-red sneakers wasn't with them. They went past me again, talking, eating buns, and a few moments later, I noticed someone walk out from the alley down the street. He was empty-handed and headed in the opposite direction. It could have been a different person, but the red on his feet caught my eye again. I wasn't sure why I noticed it, but I did.

I turned and watched the young men enter the convenience store. A few moments later, they came out, a couple of them carrying bags. I counted again, noting a missing body. I waited, but he never appeared. I realized he could work there or maybe he was taking longer than the others, yet somehow it struck me odd again. I took another bite of my bun, wondering why I had noticed anything.

Tom noticed my gaze. "Everything okay, Ms. Murphy?" He looked around. "Something bothering you?"

I sighed. "No. Just watching the locals."

Finn shook the fire marshal's hand and came over, sitting beside me. He leaned over, touching the side of my mouth and drawing his hand back. A little cream sat on the end of his finger, and with a wink, he licked it off. "Delicious."

I rolled my eyes, offering him the bag. "Have your own."

"Won't taste as good," he teased.

"I don't think I've ever been to this part of the city," I mused.

He sat back with a sigh. "When I lived here, it was pretty bad. Mostly immigrants like me, lots of violence and no structure. Fighting over the neighborhood. The Italians wanted it to be theirs. The Koreans wanted to claim it. Same with the other groups. My cousin was one of the first to suggest they work together and make it everyone's. There was already a Little Italy, a Portuguese part of town. Chinatown. Why not have a melting pot? Make it safer. Let the businesses flourish."

He huffed a laugh. "There was a lot of pushback, but others agreed. And so, it started. The neighborhood got cleaned up. Crime went down. The streets were safer. Businesses did well." He waved toward downtown. "You can see where our territory ends. Housing prices go down. More transients. Less employment and stores. More graffiti."

"I love the murals here."

"We hire local kids to paint them. Most street artists won't destroy others' works. We keep them busy changing things, and it keeps the locals happy." He sighed. "Usually."

I turned to him, meeting his eyes. "Finn," I murmured. "I know you think people are losing confidence, but they're not. I saw how they reacted to you. The way you treat them. You're still their hero. They know this is upsetting you as well. They know you're working on it." I leaned closer. "And you're my hero. Forever."

He smiled and touched my cheek. "Thank you, *mo chroí*. I needed to hear that. You always know what to say."

He stood and held out his hand. "Time to go."

I let him pull me from the bench, and we headed to the car. A flash of red caught my eye, and I saw a man hurrying away, his back turned. It made me think of the groups I'd seen earlier. I was about to say something to Finn when his phone sent him an alert.

"Niall just landed. I need to get back to the hotel. Roman is going to meet us there."

"Okay."

CHAPTER SEVENTEEN

UNA

I sat at the table, listening to the men talk. Roman's guy had pulled security images for every traffic camera and the ones the businesses had, and they were studying them, clearly frustrated.

"My man in the fire department says they are all deliberately set. But no one is seen going into or coming out of these buildings before the fires start. No alarms. No unusual sightings."

"Can they be setting off some sort of bomb remotely?"

"Yes, but how are they getting them in without being seen?" Niall asked, scrubbing his face. He looked tired, but he refused to budge, insisting this was more important than sleep.

I sipped my tea, looking toward the bag on the table and thinking I might have another bun. That sparked the memory of the young men in the street. It suddenly struck me as odd that after they'd rounded the corner, I hadn't seen another grouping.

My hand froze as I recalled a long-forgotten memory involving Brian.

"Oh my God," I gasped.

They all glanced my way. "Una?" Finn asked. "What is it?"

"As a kid, Brian used to love to steal things. Chocolate bars, bags of chips. Then he moved on to bigger things."

Finn lifted an eyebrow. "This doesn't shock me."

I stood. "No, he didn't just pocket them. His friends would go in, and they would distract the owner. Ask for something on the shelf or whatever. While they were busy, he would take what he wanted and leave before the owner even knew he'd been there. He'd wait outside until the owner wasn't paying attention, so it was as if he had never even been there."

They stared at me.

"What if that's how they're doing this? With distraction? I mean, it's simple and effective." I explained about the groups I'd seen today. "One has the device and plants it where it won't be seen. Or knows where the basement is and hides until it's time.

The cameras are all on the front of the store and the road. They could start the fire, slip out a window or door at the back and run along the alley, coming out blocks from the fire. I saw a guy today—his bright-red sneakers caught my eye. He was with the first group but then appeared farther down the street alone, as if he'd stayed back."

Finn exchanged a glance with Roman and Niall. He stood, his phone in his hand. Niall and Roman were already on theirs, and they were all talking, issuing orders. "Una, which stores were they in?" Finn asked, his eyes wild.

"The bakery and the convenience store."

He snapped instructions into the phone. "I'm on my way."

He grabbed his coat, stopping in front of me. "You are a fucking genius, Una." He bent and kissed me hard. "Wait here. Don't leave this room."

They left, a flurry of movement. Roman squeezed my arm as he went past me. "Brilliant observation," he breathed.

Niall winked at me. "Clever girl."

I sat and waited.

I dozed, waking when gentle fingers trailed along my cheek. I sat up, Finn sitting beside me.

"Well?"

"We found two different devices," he said, looking exhausted but relieved. "The bomb squad dismantled them." He smiled, shaking his head. "You saved the bakery and the convenience store. The bakery would have burned, but the convenience store would have blown up and killed everyone in it."

"Oh God."

"Roman's guy and mine searched the cameras during the daytime. They found what you saw and went back. Similar MOs happened on those days."

"The same men?"

"Some. Every business was checked, and from now on, no groups are allowed in. We're searching for the men."

"How old were they?"

"Older than they looked. It was a simple plan. Make them look like kids. Locals. Go in and buy something. Order food to make them busy or take their time picking cupcakes—whatever. One hid the device. Or slipped away and hid it later." He rubbed his face. "And you noticed it."

"Because I was looking and I noticed his sneakers. And the neighborhood was new to me, so I was paying attention."

"I've sent word to everyone about what is happening and to watch in their territories. I'm not sure if this is personal or if they're trying to take over other areas."

"What now?"

He showed me his phone. "This guy. He looked familiar, and I think I saw him at Lopez's track."

I studied the picture, my breath catching. "He looks like the man I saw watching me, but younger. But they have the same eyes."

He looked upset and swiped his phone. "We found this too."

I squinted at the screen. The same man was with another person, deep in discussion. I couldn't see the face, but I recognized the hair. "Brian," I breathed out.

"I think we found Juan, and despite Brian's denials, I'm certain he's part of Lopez's circle and he's giving them information. Your brother is in something deep, Una. Dangerous." He waited, then said the word I knew was coming. "Unforgivable."

My heart lurched, but for the first time, I said nothing. No pleading, no begging for another chance. Even I knew Brian had come to the end of the line.

"I don't want to know, Finn. Don't tell me," I whispered. "Please."

He was silent then nodded. "All right."

I searched for a change of subject. I couldn't handle what was going through my head.

"I need to go to my apartment tomorrow."

"Why?"

"My dresses are there for performing. The super has installed a new lock, so I need to pick up the key. I want to get a few things."

"Can you buy a dress here? Tomorrow is going to be —" he paused "—hectic, with everything I need to handle."

"Couldn't Tom come with me? I won't be long. Get my dresses and the new key. Gather a few things. I won't be alone."

He sighed, the sound heavy. "I'll see what I can arrange."

"Thank you."

He held out his hand. "Come to bed, *mo chroí*. I need to rest, and I need you with me to do so."

I went willingly.

I didn't sleep much, and neither did Finn. My mind was on Brian and what was going to happen. I felt as if I were already mourning him.

I knew Finn had even more on his mind, and I didn't ask. I didn't want to know. I admitted to myself I wasn't sure I could stop myself from warning Brian, and I felt ashamed.

We were both quiet as we had breakfast. I nibbled on my toast, even my tea not holding any appeal.

"Una," Finn said, breaking into my thoughts.

I met his eyes, feeling torn.

"I understand," he said quietly. "He's your brother. You still want to protect him."

"You can't trust me," I whispered. "I can't trust myself."

He smiled, tracing a finger down my cheek. "I do trust you. But again, I understand. The way you love is an incredible gift, Una. Some people, however, don't deserve it."

"He did once."

"You can't separate the boy from the man he's become. And I know you're hurting."

I had to look away, blinking.

"This isn't an easy life at times," he admitted. "I would rather hurt myself a hundred times than see you in pain. But my hands are tied here. He has physically hurt you. He's on some sort of road of destruction and is coming after me. But I promise you this." He took my hand. "I will find whoever put him on that road, and they will be punished."

"And if you find out in some way it isn't him?" I asked, even though I knew better.

"Then I will act accordingly."

It was all I could ask from him.

FINN

I went to my office after agreeing to allow Una to go to her apartment and get her things. Tom would accompany her to keep her safe. I escorted her down to the car, disliking that she'd be out of my sight but knowing she needed to stay busy. I knew she was struggling. I hated the fact that I was responsible for that struggle, even though I had no choice.

And I hated that her tender heart still hoped.

Niall and Roman were in my office, and I was surprised to see Aldo as well. I shook his hand and sat down. "Something tells me I need to sit for this."

"Pedro Lopez isn't his real name. And he's a black hole," Roman informed me, not bothering with a greeting. "One of horror."

"Fuck."

"Wanted in several countries. He's into some dark stuff. He'd disappeared off the map for a while. There were rumors of his death." He paused. "Until now."

Aldo shook his head. "Busy setting up shop here."

"Tell me."

"Hard-core drugs. Sex trafficking. Kidnapping. Weapons. Auctions—and not antiques."

"How did you find him?"

"That picture you had of Juan. You said Una mentioned the resemblance between them was strong. I had my guy age it and start scanning on the dark web. He got a hit on the face. And Juan is his nephew. He is very much like his uncle. Sick, greedy, and twisted. They like to get their informants hooked and dependent."

"Where is he getting the drugs? I haven't heard any rumblings."

Niall ran a hand through his hair. "I had our guy do some recon." At Roman's look, he shrugged. "You have your guy for the web. We have ours for drones. Exceptionally undetectable ones."

"What did you find?" I asked.

"A barn set way out back on the property by the racetrack in a grove of trees. Almost impossible to see on the ground. Looked run-down, almost deserted. There was a small window open, hanging off as if the building was empty."

"But it's not," I guessed.

"No. He directed the drone in and scoped it out. It looks new. Not used as a stable, though. Too far away from the track."

"Any ideas?"

Niall looked grim. "I had him do another check. There were heat sources. A lot of them. Yet no one in the barn."

"Underground," Roman mused.

"A hidden lab," I said with a curse.

He nodded.

"You think he's manufacturing his own drugs?"

"Yes. His MO is to kidnap people and force them to make his drugs. They rarely are ever seen again. One guy escaped and told his story, and Pedro's place was raided and destroyed. Pedro disappeared, just resurfacing now under a new last name and country."

"We need to take him out."

Roman nodded. "We need to plan this carefully. There are a lot of people's lives at stake if we're right."

"I'm getting more drones over it today. And tonight. With cameras."

We discussed ideas, plans. Luca joined in via video, offering his counsel, as horrified as we were to discover who Lopez was.

"We need him taken down," he growled. "Fast."

My phone rang, and I saw I was Una. I walked to the corner, answering.

"*Mo chroí*. Is everything all right?"

Her gasping breaths let me know it wasn't.

I held up my hand, effectively silencing the men behind me and switching to speaker.

"Una," I said, keeping my voice calm. "What is it?"

Niall was on his feet, his phone to his ear. He stepped in the hallway, and I knew he was calling Tom.

All I heard was her panicked breathing. I could feel her terror.

"Una," I repeated.

Niall walked in, shaking his head furiously. My heart dropped. I pointed to the door, and he nodded, knowing what I needed.

Backup at Una's.

Now.

Then I heard it. A low, ugly laugh. Then a voice I recognized even with his over-the-top accent as he mocked me.

"Top o' the morning to ya, Finn."

I shut my eyes, reining in my fear and my anger. "Brian."

"Isn't this cozy?" he said, his words fast and hard. "Me, my little sister, and your dead guard."

I heard Una whimper.

"Don't hurt her, Brian. Jesus, man, you know how much she loves you."

His laugh was bitter. "To a point, sure. But did she use you for what I needed? No. She got her cushy job. Her fucking place to sing. A nice place to live."

"She worked for all that," I said, not wanting to argue with him and make him angrier, but needing him to stay on the line. I needed time to get to her.

"I fucking worked too. Did I get the recognition? The bump up the ladder? No, it was always 'fuck Brian.' You think I don't know that?"

"I'm sorry," I lied. "I'll come there, and we'll talk it through."

"Yes." Una spoke, her voice shaky. "Finn will help you. I told you that. He'll figure out what to do with the drugs you have hidden here, help get you clean, and we can forget all this!"

Drugs he had hidden?

I ground my teeth as I heard the sound of a slap and a pained gasp from Una.

"Brian," I warned.

"Brian," he mimicked. "I'm done listening to either of you. I want to just shoot her."

My blood ran cold. "You can't kill her. Your dad would be horrified. That's not what he taught you. And I would hunt you down, Brian. I swear to God—"

He interrupted me. "Ah, don't worry, Finn. I ain't gonna kill her. She's worth far too much alive for me to do that."

"What?"

"She's my ticket to the good life." He sniggered. "Finally good for something."

Niall walked in, pantomiming with his hands. Men were on the way. I nodded. Roman looked up with a jerk of his chin. He had some on the way as well.

"But you aren't getting her back. I sold her."

I grabbed the back of the chair in front of me.

"What the fuck did you just say?"

"You heard me." He paused. "Remember the other day, Finn? I said one day you'd ask for my help and I'd say fuck you."

Una was sobbing somewhere behind him, the sound sending rage through me. I struggled to remain in control. I wasn't above begging. Not for her. Anything for her.

"You sold her. Your sister."

"Well, traded, really. My life for hers. Plus, a bunch of cash."

"Don't do this." I swallowed. "I'll give you anything you want. More money. Anything."

There was a beat of silence.

"Fuck you."

And he hung up.

I lost it. I picked up a mug close at hand, hurling it at the wall, cursing.

He had her. He had sold her.

Sold her. Like an inanimate object with no feelings.

And I knew who he had sold her to.

I turned, staring at the three men in my office.

"Fuck the casualties. This is war."

CHAPTER EIGHTEEN

UNA

We pulled up to my apartment, and I looked at Tom in the front seat. "I don't suppose I can convince you to stay here or go for coffee while I run upstairs? There's a great little café around the corner."

He chuckled and shook his head. Tom got out of the car and opened my door, looking around before he did.

We entered the building, the superintendent meeting us. "I put the new lock on as soon as you called, Una. Mr. O'Reilly had someone sweep the apartment to make sure it was safe. Here's the key."

"Thanks."

"Sad to think you won't be living here anymore."

I kept my expression carefully neutral. "Why would you say that?"

"Mr. O'Reilly told me you were moving out soon."

I lifted my eyebrows but kept my mouth shut. In the elevator, I glanced at Tom, who was trying to hide his grin. He met my gaze with a shrug. "The boss," was all he said.

The new key slid in easily, and I opened the door, Tom following me in. "I'll be right here," he said, sitting in the chair by the door.

I went to my bedroom, finding the dry cleaning bags with the dresses I liked to wear for my singing gigs. I carried them to the living room, draping them over the back of the sofa. "It's more comfortable," I informed Tom, patting the back. "You can sit here. That's the most uncomfortable chair in this place. I only use it to put on my shoes."

He smiled and stood. "It is awful."

"I know, but it looks nice. Aesthetics, you know."

He sat on the sofa, unbuttoning his suit jacket. "Much better."

I returned to my room, taking the only suitcase I had and filling it quickly with clothes and toiletries. My uniforms were in my locker, so I was covered there. I added some shoes and all the clothing Finn had bought me, including the lingerie. I looked around, deciding I had enough and I would return.

After I'd had a long talk with Mr. O'Reilly.

I reached for a photo on my bedside table. It was of my mum and me when I was little. I tucked it in the bag and carried that to the living room.

Tom glanced up from his phone. "Almost done?"

"Yes. I want to dump the trash. It smells a bit odd in here."

He stood. "I'll take it."

"It's just down the hall."

He held out his hand for the key. "Really?" I asked.

"Yes. I'm not to leave you unprotected, and I'm not leaving the door unlocked. Even for a couple of minutes."

I handed him the key and he left, the door clicking locked behind him.

An idea hit me, and I went into Brian's old room, stopping for a moment at the scent. The odd smell lingered in here the strongest, and I wondered if I had missed something when cleaning.

I reached into the closet for the backpack, intent on taking the picture Brian had shown me. I would copy it, take it somewhere, have it digitally enhanced, and put it back in a couple of days.

I heard the door as I pulled the backpack off the shelf, the unexpected weight causing it to slip from my hand. It landed on the floor with a thump. "I'm fine," I called out. "I'll be right there."

I bent to pick up the bag, not surprised to see the zipper had broken. The bag was stuffed. More than I recalled it being when Brian had shown it to me. Curious, I pushed the plaid material of what I assumed was one of my dad's shirts to the side and blinked at what I was seeing.

Clear bags. Hundreds of them. Some looked like flour. Others like shards of glass. The odor I had been smelling was stronger now that the backpack was open.

Drugs.

The bag was full of drugs.

I heard a noise behind me.

"Tom, we need to call Finn. Right now," I said.

"Tom has a bit of a headache right now."

I spun on my heel, meeting my brother's black-eyed gaze. He was pale, his mouth turned up in a twisted sort of grin. My heartbeat sped up as I took in the gun in his hands, the silencer on the end of it adding an even scarier threat than his casual stance.

Or the blood on his shirt.

"But by all means," he continued. "Let's call Finn. I have so much to tell him."

He grinned.

"And neither of you are going to like it."

I stared, and he tilted his head. "Cat got your tongue, little sister?"

"Brian—what—how—"

He laughed, the sound frightening. "Never thought I'd see the day you were speechless."

I gathered my courage. "Where is Tom?"

He smiled. "Dead. I pushed his body into the garbage can where he belonged." He held up a shiny key. "Not before retrieving this, of course." He tutted. "You've made my life difficult the past couple of days, Una. My new boss thinks I lifted a few of his drugs, which I had planned on doing until he figured it out. I had to convince him I was simply storing them for easier deliveries. Lots of users not far from here." He winked as if we were sharing a joke. "Imagine my dismay when I couldn't get in any longer."

"I-I'm sorry."

He shook his head, and I noticed a twitch in his eye I hadn't seen before. "I don't think you really are."

"So, you had a key all along?"

He rolled his eyes. "Everyone thinks you're so smart. You're dumb. Far too trusting. Did you really think I only had one copy of the key? I've been coming and going—even while you were asleep. Stashing the drugs and the money. A few times, I was here, seeing you get ready for work, thinking how easy it would be to hurt you. And I really wanted to sometimes."

A shiver went through me. He hated me. Or at least this drug-induced version did.

"Why—why would you kill Tom?"

He shrugged as if it was no big deal. "He was always an ass to me. Thought too much of himself. And of Finn." He studied me. "But of course I shouldn't say anything bad about the perfect Finn O'Reilly, should I?" He ran the end of the gun over his chin in a jerky motion. "Is he a good fuck for you, Una?"

Somehow that question shocked me more than anything. "Brian Murphy! That is *none* of your business. Stop this nonsense now. Where is Tom?"

Suddenly, he was moving. Stalking toward me, anger

radiating from him. I backed up, hitting the wall. He pushed the gun against my temple.

"He is fucking dead, just like you're going to be."

I whimpered, now really scared. "Why?" I whispered.

"Because you deserve it." Then he stepped back. "But I can't." He looked truly upset by those words. "I have to take you to him."

"To whom?" I asked. "Finn?"

"Finn?" he laughed. "So he can kill me? No. I have to take the drugs and you to him. Juan and my new boss. Prove myself."

I swallowed. "No, Brian. Let me call Finn. He can help you."

"How?"

"He can help you with the drugs. Dispose of them. We can get you into rehab, and I'll convince Finn to send you somewhere new. You can start over again," I babbled.

He laughed as if my words were the biggest joke. "Right, Una. I'm high, not stupid. He'd blow my head off before I could say a word."

"No, no, he won't."

"Of course not. He'd have someone else do the dirty work so he could tell you his hands were clean. Take you upstairs and fuck you so you'd forget."

"Stop saying that."

"Where's your phone?"

"In my pocket."

He waved the gun at me. "Call him. Now. I've got a message for him."

I hesitated, and he pointed the gun at me, his hand suddenly steady. "Now."

I pressed Finn's name and began to pray.

I woke up groggy and disoriented. The feel of fingers running down my cheek made me sigh as I sifted through my foggy brain.

"I must have had a nightmare," I mumbled, wondering why my voice sounded so scratchy.

"Oh no," a voice said, sounding amused. "Your nightmare is just beginning, sister."

I sat up, every nerve in my body screaming terror as I jerked away from the fingers on my skin. In front of me was the man I had seen before. The one who'd frightened me with just a look. Up close, he was even more terrifying. His eyes were dead. Emotionless. Emanating from him was malice. Pure evil. He was older, his hair slicked back, and unattractive. Everything about him oozed danger.

I scrambled back, hitting a wall and looking around, confused and dazed. Scared.

Brian was leaning against the opposite wall, looking smug. Beside him was a man his age who looked like the person crouching in front of me.

"Brian?" I whispered, searching my mind. The events of this morning hit me. The apartment. Tom. Brian and the gun. Calling Finn and the words Brian had used before hanging up and tossing my cell phone to the bed. *"You won't be needing that anymore."* Then he'd shoved the gun into my back and told me I was going with him.

I had tried to struggle, and he shook his head. "The easy way or the hard way, Una. You come with me, no one else gets hurt. You struggle, and I will shoot every person who looks our way."

I thought of Mrs. Meyers down the hall whom I often saw. My neighbor Emily. The super and his kind wife.

"I'll behave."

"See that you do."

We took the stairs, waving at Mrs. Meyers across the lobby as he pushed me out the back door, his gun jammed into my back. I struggled with him at getting into the trunk, and before I knew what was happening, I felt pain on the back of my head, and the world went black.

Now, I was in a dark room. With three men who all threatened me in different ways.

My brother looked unconcerned. "I can't help you, Una. It's you or me, and this time, I'm choosing me." He pushed off the wall. "You'll figure it all out. You always do."

He sauntered away and disappeared around the corner.

"Who—who are you?" I asked the man still crouched in front of me. He eyed me like a piece of meat, his gaze cold.

"Your future."

Fear twisted around my spine, and I felt nauseous. My head ached and I was cold. I pulled my arms around my waist, horrified to realize my ankle was chained to something.

"Please. I know someone who will pay you. Whatever you want," I begged, knowing my words were true. Finn would do anything to get me back safely.

He stood, staring down at me. "The great Finn?" He began to laugh. "He is of no use to you anymore."

I swallowed. He began to pace back and forth in front of me, mumbling, talking to the younger man still leaning against the wall, eyeing me with disdain.

"Is she what you really want, Uncle?"

"Yes, Juan. Almost perfect."

I blinked. *Juan.* This was Brian's roommate?

"I'm sure she'll be perfect once the Russians are done with her."

"Uncle" laughed. "Oh, she will be."

"Wh-what?"

"You're not ready for me yet. You will be in a few months."

"No," I gasped, shaking my head. "No."

"See that right there? Your denials and pleas will be removed. Your thoughts and desires will be gone. You'll live to serve me. Only me."

My breathing became panicked. I looked around, desperate to find a way out.

"You don't like me now, but once your training is done and you're returned to me, I'll be your world." He tilted his head, studying me. "My perfect slave. I will own every inch of you. Your body. Your voice. You will serve me. Sing for me." He flashed his teeth. "Forever."

He began to walk away, glancing over his shoulder. "And there is nothing your precious Finn can do to stop it."

He went around the same corner Brian had, and I heard the clang of a metal door.

I was left alone with Juan, who stared at me.

"I don't see his obsession," he said. "But then, I like blondes. Uncle got me one of those."

"*Got* you one?" I said, finding my anger. "Women aren't things you pick up at the store. We're not for sale."

He laughed, the sound echoing in the damp, dark space. "Oh, for those of us who can afford it, you are." He crossed his arms. "My uncle saw you weeks ago. Someone had videoed you singing at the hotel. He became obsessed. Your voice. Your red hair. He's always had a thing for red hair. Then he found out you were connected to O'Reilly, and his obsession reached a new level. He hates him," he stated calmly, bending to brush some dirt off his sneaker. They were red with a tiger face stitched into the front, the eyes glittering even in the low light. They were hideous, and I recognized them. He was the one I had seen the day I was out with Finn that I'd told him about.

"Why?"

He shrugged. "I don't know what drives my uncle, aside from money and power. Some slight, some offense, and he takes it personally. Some deal he was involved in that O'Reilly somehow killed. It cost him a lot of money. He's been waiting. Not how I'd run things, but my time will come." He lifted his arms in a bored yawn. "So, he decided to take you, and here you are."

I stared at him. He was so casual. As if it was no big deal and he did it all the time. A frightening realization hit me. He did.

"I have to admit, it's been fun. Befriending your brother. Making sure to stoke the flames of anger he felt toward O'Reilly." He smirked. "The money, the drugs, stringing him along, and getting him hooked. He has quite the ego on him, doesn't he? As if Uncle would give him his own territory to run. All part of the plan to get to you. Plus, rattling the Irishman's cage was an added bonus. Disrupting his world and costing him money."

He stroked his chin. "Once he knew Finn was as obsessed with you as he is, there was no stopping Uncle."

"Is he Lopez?" I whispered, trying to process

everything he was saying. He certainly liked to talk. Brag.

He shrugged again. "To the world, yes. To me, Uncle. To you—" he smiled wide and evil "—*master*."

I began to thrash, pull on the chain holding me. "I will never!" I shouted. "I will fight you every step of the way. I'll—"

He cut me off, stepping forward and jabbing a needle into my arm. "You're all the same. So tiresome. I prefer it when you return without a personality or the will to even speak."

The room began to spin, and my tongue felt thick. He walked away, stopping and turning around. "There is no escape and no rescue. Finn can't find you, and law enforcement can't help. You won't even be in this country soon. And everyone—even your precious Irishman—will forget about you. You'll forget who you were. All you will know will be pain and servitude." He looked around with a smirk. "Enjoy the accommodations while you can. You're not going to like where you're going."

And darkness descended again.

CHAPTER NINETEEN

UNA

I woke, this time suddenly and alert. I was on the damp ground, but I wasn't alone. I blinked up at the woman sitting beside me in the dim light. She had my head on her lap, and she offered me a wobbly smile.

"Hi."

I sat up, everything spinning. "Careful," she warned. "The drugs they pump into us linger."

I pushed my hair off my face. "Who are you?"

"Annabelle Lewis."

"What are you doing here?"

Her bottom lip quivered. "Same as you. They took me."

"From where?"

"I had just arrived at the bus station. I was heading to the hotel, and they grabbed me and dragged me into an alley. I woke up here." She paused. "Two weeks ago. Or maybe more. I can't keep track." She wrapped her arms around herself. "It's always dark here."

I shivered.

"You're Una."

I narrowed my eyes, shifting away. "How did you know that?"

"I was here. In the corner where I like to sit. I don't think they can see me there, but even if they can, it's as far as my chain stretches."

"Oh."

She met my eyes, hers glazed with tears. "I heard what he said. That younger, dark-haired one. I thought I was scared before, but now that I know what's happening, I'm more terrified than I've ever been in my life."

I studied her in the dimness. I could see she was about my age. Long blond hair that I was sure at one point was lovely and wavy. Now, it was a dirty, ratty mess. Her skin was grubby, her cheeks raw from wiping them when she cried, no doubt. She was thin and looked exhausted.

"*The same way you'll look soon*," a little voice in my head whispered.

My chest ached with repressed tears, but I refused to let them out.

"Are there others?" I asked, wondering if we could work together and somehow surprise whatever guards they had checking on us.

"Yes. But they're down that way. And if we try to talk, they come in and hurt us." She turned her face, and I saw how swollen her cheek was. I could make out the bruises, even in the dull light. "I think there are six of us being held."

"How many men are there?"

"I'm not sure." She shuddered. "The one who wears the red sneakers is the worst."

"Do you know where we are?"

She shook her head. "No."

I tugged on the iron bar around my ankle, feeling along the chain to the end. It was screwed into the cement of the wall, and the only way I could loosen it was with a tool.

"There is nothing," she whispered. "I looked. I tried."

"Finn will find me," I stated firmly. "He'll rescue me and you. The other girls too."

"I hope he gets here soon. I heard them say we're gone next week."

"How long was I out?" I asked, wondering how much time had elapsed.

"He gave you a heavy dose. I'd say a day."

A week. Finn could find me in a week. Right?

"It was supposed to be sooner," she confided. "But I heard them say the Russians were delaying things."

I frowned and she shrugged. "I pretend to be asleep a lot if I hear someone coming. He, the younger one with the ugly shoes, is always staring at me, and I hate it."

"Juan," I told her.

"Well, Juan talks a lot. He and the other redhead just stand there and try to outdo each other. They forget I'm there at times."

"The other redhead is my brother."

She gaped at me. "And he's part of this?" She grabbed my hand. "Oh, Una. I'm sorry."

"Me too."

"He—Juan—keeps telling me I'll be his. I hate him."

I squeezed her hand. "We have to try to help each other."

"Do you really think your Finn will find you?"

"Yes."

"I hope you're right," she replied as she sighed out a shaky breath, pulling her knees to her chest and laying her head on her hands.

I looked around the dark, damp space, sending up a prayer.

"Please, Finn. Please."

FINN

I was going crazy. I couldn't sleep. Couldn't eat. I paced, spent hours with Niall and Aldo chasing down leads. More hours on the phone and in front of the computer.

I tugged my hands through my hair. It had been forty-eight hours since Una disappeared. I had no idea where she was. If she was okay.

My imagination ran rampant when I thought about it too much.

Was she scared? Hurt? Crying for me? What horrors was she enduring?

Would I ever see her again?

I was ready to storm the racetrack, infiltrate the building we were certain was a hidden lab, and force Lopez to talk, but it was Roman who stopped me.

"If we go in there and blow up his lab and not find Una, Finn," he said, his voice steady, "you will have signed her death warrant."

His words made me stop.

"You need to stay calm. She needs Finn O'Reilly right now. Syndicate man. Not her lover."

Two hours later, Luca Costas walked in, adding more power to our search. But it seemed fruitless. Lopez hadn't moved off the property. Brian hadn't shown up that we'd been able to see. Una's purse and phone had been left behind in her apartment. We'd discovered Tom in the garbage room, dumped into a wide, lidded garbage bin. He'd been shot but was miraculously not dead. Brian was as inept with a gun as he was with his brain. The bullet had grazed Tom's head but buried itself into the wall of the garbage room. He was furious and upset when he came to in the hospital, but he was unable to give us much detail.

The car Brian had been driving was found in a deserted parking lot. There were no cameras around, so we had no idea what sort of vehicle he'd transferred Una to or where they went. Niall currently had a man tracing every car we could pick up in that area, trying to track which one might have Brian behind the wheel.

And then Roman and Luca disappeared. I hadn't seen them since last night, and neither of them answered their phones. I was angry, frustrated, and pissed off. All I knew was they said they had to follow up on a lead. Since then, it was as if they had vanished.

Niall came in, looking as exhausted as I felt. He sat down, pouring a coffee and tossing it back like a shot of whiskey.

"Anything?" I asked.

"Rumors. Nothing we can substantiate."

"I've reached out to everyone. Offered rewards. Favors. Called in favors." My shoulders fell forward in defeat. "Nothing."

He nodded.

"Where the fuck are Roman and Luca?" I asked. "I don't understand."

Niall began to speak just as the door opened, and they walked in. They wore the same clothing as they had been wearing when I'd seen them yesterday. They were both somber and looked tired.

Before I could speak, Roman held up his hand. "I know you're full of questions. I had a lead I had to follow fast, and I didn't have time to explain. I didn't want to give you hope in case it didn't pan out."

"Did it?" I asked, my voice tight.

Roman and Luca shared a glance. "We need to sit down, Finn. This is gonna be hard to hear."

I swallowed the sudden lump in my throat. "Tell me."

Roman drew in a deep breath. "We went to find Greg Santini."

"Who is that?" I asked.

He rolled his shoulders. "The man who had my wife kidnapped and planned to sell her."

I gaped at him. "Why would you do that?"

"He had a lot of contacts with people I would never deal with. If anyone could help you, it would be him. He owed me."

At my questioning look, he explained.

"His brother broke the truce, and he died. Greg ran, leaving this world behind. We knew where he was, but we left him alone. But I thought he could help in this case. And he did."

I leaned forward. "How?"

Roman rubbed his lip, glancing at Luca. "He had deep connections. Still has a few. He called in some favors after I persuaded him it was in his best interest." He flexed his hand, and I saw the torn knuckles, understanding how the persuasion had gone down.

"Lopez calls himself a Dominant. One of the worst kinds. I just call him a sick fuck. But he doesn't like to train his subs. He, ah, doesn't have the patience. He likes them...broken."

I couldn't speak, indicating for Roman to keep going. I gripped the arm of the chair, knowing I needed to stay strong.

"There is a group of men in Russia that specializes in training. That's all they do. Buy them. Men, women, boys, girls. Train them until they are a shell of their former selves." He met my eyes, his filled with sympathy. "They're particularly brutal."

I could feel my chest contract rapidly. It felt as if I couldn't get enough oxygen into my lungs.

"Lopez finds people. Sells them to this group. Part of his reward is they train subs for him and gift them back. It happens frequently since they never last long. If they make it out of Russia." His tone was low. "He has a reputation for cruelty. And he has a thing for redheads."

I was out of my chair in a flash and out of the room. I bent over the toilet, and the meager contents of my stomach were ejected, bitter and searing. Tears filled my eyes, and I struggled for breath.

Una.

My Una.

Mo chroí.

I stood, wiping my mouth. I looked in the mirror, my reflection almost unrecognizable. I was pale, sweating. I looked older. Defeated.

Then Una's face drifted across my mind. I heard her voice in my head.

"Hero," she whispered. "My hero. I love you, Finn."

I straightened. Splashed my face with water. Stiffened my shoulders.

"How do we find him?" I snapped as I walked back into the room, my emotions locked down and my focus on one thing. Finding her. Saving her.

Or die trying.

Roman looked me over and nodded, the pity gone from his eyes.

"Greg found out they're headed here. The group. There's an auction happening in a few days. Six women. One of whom I am certain is Una."

"Do we know where?"

"Not yet, but Greg is finding out. They only disclose it the day before."

Niall spoke up. "What if the lab and the place they're holding Una are the same?"

I frowned at the thought. "The lab is a bomb waiting to explode. Would he risk that? Having—" I had to swallow "—the merchandise so close to a possible disaster?"

"It's Lopez. Think about it the way he would. Everything in one place. Fewer men, less attention. More profit."

Luca spoke. "I think he's done it before. From what I've read, he takes a lot of shortcuts, so it would make sense." He looked at Roman before finishing his thoughts. "Frankly, as much as he is obsessed with Una, if something happened, he would just move on. There would be no mourning for his loss."

I had to turn away for a moment. It all made sense and, in some ways, made things easier for us. Planning. But the thought of Una being trapped underground, close to a dangerous lab, made me feel ill again. And until we had the place confirmed, we didn't know if we were right. If we stormed it now and she wasn't there, she was as good as dead.

I had to pray nothing happened until we had confirmation.

"How do you know this Greg is telling the truth?"

"He owes me," Roman said firmly. "I'm collecting. He is going to find out the location and let us know."

"He won't double-cross you?"

"No," he said firmly.

"Then, gentlemen, we're about to crash the party once we have a location." My hands tightened into fists. "And everything goes. The lab, wherever he's hiding her. We hit it all at once. He is left with nothing. I want him to know I took it all before he dies."

Everyone nodded.

"Let's make a plan."

UNA

I had no idea how much time had passed since I'd been chained up in the dark. We were left there, the occasional bottle of water tossed to us, barely enough food to even begin to satisfy the hunger pangs that were constant. We had a bucket for a toilet. No place to wash.

Once, we were dragged to another room and hosed down, the water barely tepid. The scrap of cloth tossed our way was not enough to get dry. I hid my necklace from Finn in my pocket, praying they wouldn't find it. It was all I had of him, and I held it in my hands in the dark, rubbing the metal between my fingers, knowing he had touched it.

My hope was fading. The longer I sat there, scared and alone, the fainter my spirit became. The only thing keeping me from total despair was Annabelle. Or Anna, as she had asked me to call her in a hushed voice. We always spoke quietly, our heads bowing close together, unsure if we were being overheard. She told me about growing up in the north. Spending summers on the lake, helping her parents run their small camping ground.

"Wouldn't they be looking for you?" I asked.

"No. Dad died a few years ago and Mom this past winter. I sold the campground and planned on using the money to start in the big city." Her shoulders slumped. "Big mistake, I guess."

"Your friends?"

She shook her head. "We lived out of town. I didn't have a lot of them. Those I did wouldn't think I was missing not hearing from me yet. They'd think I was busy getting settled."

Her eyes glistened with fresh tears. "No one will remember me soon."

"We'll get out of here. Finn will come," I assured her.

But I was beginning to think maybe Finn couldn't find me.

I told her about my dad, growing up as an only daughter with Brian. I shared good memories, trying to stop the dislike I was feeling toward him. It felt as if I were talking about someone else. A different person from the man filled with hate and greed that he had become. I talked about my mum and how I missed her after she was gone.

And I told her about Finn and how much I loved him. How I regretted wasting the time I had on a stupid promise I had made to myself as I grew up.

"I'll never leave him again if we get out of here," I whispered. "I'll show him every day how much I love him."

Lopez and Juan showed up at various times. Lopez was always leering and hurtful. He liked to pinch and slap; although he did it and then stepped back, the coward that he was, so I couldn't retaliate. He had a lot to say, all of it meant to frighten me—and it did—but I refused to show him. He loved to use the words broken, doll, and possession. He talked about how he looked forward to me pleasing him. Serving him. He grinned, staring down at me, kneeling in the dirt.

"On your knees—you will always be on your knees now. My own little whore."

It was all I could do not to tell him I looked forward to Finn killing him. Preferably slowly.

Juan was even more impatient, often tugging on Anna's hair as he hurt her and said things to her I couldn't hear but made her cry. He liked that. He also liked to kick. I wanted to grab a red-covered foot and knock him off-balance, but I knew he'd take it out on Anna. Both men enjoyed building our terror. Emphasizing their position with physical pain.

Sick fucks. Both of them.

Brian never came. I wondered if he was still alive. If they were still using him.

And I wondered how much longer I would live. If what Lopez and Juan kept telling us was true, I wouldn't survive.

It was only the thought of never seeing Finn again, never feeling his arms around me, that could make me cry. And I hid my tears so no one could see.

At least those were still mine.

The sound of footsteps and voices made me sit up straighter, and I gripped Anna's hand. Juan appeared, looking unusually animated. "Stand up."

We did, and he aimed a gun at us. Instinctually, I stepped in front of Anna, and he sniggered. "You can't protect her."

"Someone has to," I replied.

He only sneered.

Another man appeared and unlocked our ankles. We were pushed down the hall and into the room with the showers. But it was different. Now, there were towels. Robes. Shampoo.

"Clean yourselves up. You have fifteen minutes."

We did as we were told, neither of us wanting to risk being hit or shot. My hair was knotted and hard to wash, but I did my best. After drying off, I pulled on the robe, hating the fact that it was short, white, and left nothing to the imagination. There was a small tear inside the lapel, and I slipped Finn's necklace into it, feeling it fall to the hem. Even though they were wet, I put my underwear back on.

Anna did the same. Then we waited, knowing our lives were about to change.

And not for the better.

CHAPTER TWENTY

FINN

"We're certain?" I asked.

"Greg assures me the information is accurate."

"It makes no sense. They're having an auction at the racetrack? In front of people?"

I paced the room. "No, there is something we're missing."

Roman and Aldo began to speak in Italian. Fast—their hands gesturing, words tumbling. Luca listened then clapped his hands. "Yes. Hiding in plain sight!"

"What?" I asked.

"You get to the racetrack, and you'll be escorted elsewhere on the property. It's a busy night, and no one will notice people coming in or disappearing. The normal crowd is only concerned about the horse racing. The noise and mob cover everything. They've added a late-night race for that very purpose. All smoke and mirrors."

"But where?"

"The barn." Niall looked at the screen, studying it. "See how this piece of the back of the racetrack is like an extended wing? I think this structure beside it has a dual purpose. Those golf carts parked there? Enough to get staff around, but I would bet my last dollar there is more. And I think underground tunnels from a couple of the empty buildings lead under the stable. In and out, no one sees a thing." He sat back, running a weary hand over his face. "There was more activity around that barn set back on the property last night. Lights. But no people outside. No one coming and going. That's how they get in and out." He traced a path on the screen. "People slip away in small groups, heading to the wing and out to the golf carts. It's dark, and no one is looking. The path we saw in the grass? It is going to have a fork not many use that leads to the trees and to the barn. Others will go through the tunnels. No one will notice the movement."

I studied the screen. "You're right. That stupid fecker. Doesn't he know how dangerous—" I stopped my rant, knowing it would do no good. "We can do it all at once, then. Rescue the women and blow his lab."

"So, how are we doing this?" Aldo asked. "Will we follow them?"

"No. We need to surround the building earlier. Be in the trees behind it in camouflage. Surprise them. We need men. Guns." I looked up from the screen. "Night goggles. And tech. We surround the building, verify Una is there, cut the lights, and move in." I drew in a long breath. "Kill everyone involved. Blow the barn and the lab once we get the innocents out." I looked at Luca. "Between us, we have the right people to make sure it's called an accident, right?"

"Consider it handled."

"Men?"

"I'm on it," Aldo said, walking away with his phone to his ear.

"I'll get on the equipment," Niall muttered. "We're going to need a lot of explosives."

Roman held up his hand. "I've got a guy."

For the first time in days, I smiled. "Of course you do."

"We need supplies. Vans to move the victims. Blankets. A place to take them for medical attention."

Roman smirked at me. "Good thing your hotel was built with a private parking lot underneath and an elevator, isn't it? We can set up a makeshift hospital."

"Yes. I'll get the floors cleared and the public elevator locked off."

Luca glanced up. "Others will help. We have enough men to make sure this goes off without a hitch. We're not the only ones sickened by human trafficking. Kidnapping and forced labor."

He sighed. "We'll find the victims all a safe place or get them back home, if that's what they want." He scrubbed his eyes. "From the heat sources, we figure about twenty people, plus the women. We can handle that. More, if needed."

"Good. Whatever we need to do."

The room was busy for a while, one of us always stepping into the hall or in a corner to talk.

Finally, we looked at one another. "Everything is set. Men, plan, backup, vehicles, medical, weapons," I stated.

"Auction is at ten p.m."

"I have our guy planting small drones on the beams inside the barn. Should be done in the next couple of hours as long as that window is still open. No one will notice them, but we can have a visual. He'll connect to the power outside and cut it on our signal. We go in, secure the women, and start taking out the bad guys."

Aldo rolled his shoulders. "It's been a while. It's gonna feel good."

He was right.

I faced them. "Lopez doesn't come out alive. None of them do."

Everyone nodded in accord.

Turning, I shut my eyes, inhaling deeply. I would have her back tomorrow, and I was never letting her out of my sight again.

I'm coming, Una. Hold on.

It was dark, the clouds cooperating and covering the moon. We watched in silence as people would appear and slip into the barn. Beside me, Niall would identify them as he got the intel in his earpiece.

"Boris and Olga," he murmured. "The very worst of the worst. Husband and wife team known for their brutality." He was quiet for a moment. "Jesus, these people are sick."

There were eight of them in total. Plus guards. Lopez and Juan, in addition to a few others.

Aldo crackled in my ear. "First wave takes out the guards. Only four outside the barn. We've got others covering the tunnel exits we know of. All shoot to kill. The only ones safe are those of us with the green stripes our night goggles can pick up on. We're the second wave. The third will move in and get people out, then the bombs get planted, and we're done."

I grunted in reply, shifting a little, making sure my bulletproof armor was in place.

"Everyone, protect the women—that is our highest priority," Roman rumbled across the group.

Bright lights suddenly exploded in the darkness, spilling out from the higher-up windows and under the doors. The auction was about to start. My nerves tightened in anticipation, a rush of calmness tearing through me. The end goal was Una. I needed to concentrate on that. Nothing else.

"We have a visual on Una," Roman breathed out. "She and five others on the left side of the barn, held behind bars."

My chest constricted. I would have her back soon. In my arms. Lopez would pay for this with his life.

"We go in five," Luca breathed out. "On my count. The power will be cut in three. Then we have control."

I pulled my night goggles down and checked to make sure my silencer was tight. We didn't want to attract any attention.

I was ready.

We crept forward, surrounding the structure. There were plenty of us here—good guys—more scattered on the property, waiting if needed. I watched as the guards were swiftly dealt with, and our men took their places, ready to open the doors for us.

Luca drew in a deep breath. "Five..."

And two seconds later, the power went out.

UNA

I had never known terror the way I was feeling it. Waves of cold rushed over my body as I looked at the people staring at us. We had been dragged up some stairs into a stable, pushed into stalls, metal bars rolling from the ceiling, keeping us locked in. Anna and I clung to each other's hands, both of us trembling in fear. But I refused to cry. To let them break me already.

People had strolled around as if attending a party. No one spoke, but they circled in slow strides, their dead eyes never leaving the cages that had effectively been constructed. Icy stares, smirking lips, and unbridled evil were in front of us. We were merchandise. Not even human to them. Once they were all there, the doors shut, and I felt all my hope drain away. This was it. My life ended now. I knew I wouldn't survive whatever came after this evening.

Lopez droned on, his words insulting and degrading. Brian leaned against the back wall with Juan, and the one time I met his gaze, he looked away as if suddenly uncomfortable. I hoped he was. He looked terrible, although I was certain I looked worse. Juan looked smug, his ankles crossed, his stupid red sneakers out of place.

Lopez clapped his hands. "Let's begin, shall we?"

I wanted to scream. To fight and to run. But I had no chance. Locked behind bars, barely clothed, and with no weapon, I would fail. I had to stay in place and pray that somehow, some way, I could get out.

Pray that Finn would find me.

And then the lights went out. There was a startled murmur, and suddenly, it was chaos. I heard the sound of thundering feet and bodies dropping. Muted shooting. Screaming. Cursing. A line of men appeared before us, one shouting, "Get down!"

I grabbed Anna and pulled her to the floor. I crawled with her to the back of the stall. "Keep your head down," I ordered.

"What's happening?" she gasped.

I could feel it. *Feel him.*

Finn had found me.

"My hero," I responded.

FINN

Lopez was too comfortable with his hidden auctions. He'd been doing them in secret, and his ego was big enough to think he had everything in hand. He'd become lax.

He didn't expect us.

Our plan was executed without a hitch. We had accounted for every contingency. Our element of surprise and the darkness worked as we needed them to. Immediately, ten men lined up in front of the women, their guns pointed to the crowd. Another group guarded the doors, guns ready. We followed the first group, shooting as we went, eliminating the world of scum with each bullet. We took out the inside guards first, then aimed at the buyers and Lopez's group. They didn't stand a chance against our firepower.

I had one fast glimpse of Una in the darkness. She looked terrified, but she was alive, and that was all I needed.

It was over quickly, and we tore off our night goggles as the lights were turned back on. Bodies littered the floor, the scent of bullets and blood filling the air. I felt nothing but contempt as I looked at the dead around me.

Lopez was against the wall, shock on his face at the blood saturating his ill-fitting suit jacket. Juan was not far away, facedown, his red sneakers identifying him. All the guards were dead.

I sprinted to the side where our men still guarded the makeshift cages. "Get these open," I shouted, dropping to my knees in front of where Una lay, huddled in the corner, her arms wrapped around a small blond woman.

"Una! *Mo chroí*—it's over. You're safe."

She didn't move, and I felt the panic that flooded my body. "Una," I begged. "Please, look at me."

Finally, she raised her head, and I held out my hand, tamping down my horror at her appearance. She was bruised and battered, her face, arms, and legs showing marks. She was whiter than paper, her eyes sunken. Her hair was tangled, and the robe she was wearing barely covered her torso. She was shivering and terrified, her eyes unable to focus.

Ignoring the commotion behind me, I reached out again. "Come here, my love," I urged. "Come to me."

She startled as the bars were raised. Then she met my eyes. I pleaded silently for her to realize it was me— she was safe and I was here.

"Finn," she breathed out.

I couldn't wait. I stood and went to her, scooping her into my arms. She made a sound of distress, gripping the other woman's hand, and I called for Niall, who appeared beside me. "Help," I instructed, somehow feeling her need. "They have to stay close right now."

Niall bent, saying something to the woman before lifting her into his arms. She didn't fight him, burrowing into him instead, her head on his shoulder.

He had an odd expression on his face as he pulled her close. "She's freezing." He turned, yelling for blankets, and we wrapped the women we were holding as best we could.

Una was a shivering mass of fear in my arms. I had a feeling Niall was experiencing the same reaction.

I lifted Una higher, my lips close to her ear. "I have you, *mo chroí*. You are safe. No one will touch you now but me."

The adrenaline began to fade, and I realized how badly I was shaking. I fell back to my knees, holding Una, whispering comforting words, soothing my hand up and down her back.

Around me, our team was busy. Luca led one group down to where we suspected the lab was. Others were checking bodies, removing IDs, prepping for the next step. It was carnage and horrible, but I didn't care. The world was better without the scum we had eliminated.

Una lifted her head and made a sound of distress. She pushed against my chest.

"Don't look, sweet girl."

"B-Brian," she stammered.

Looking over, I saw her brother. He was sitting against the wall, his head lolling to one side. Blood was seeping rapidly from his stomach. He was staring at her, his expression pleading, his trembling hand stretching in her direction.

Standing, I took her to him, knowing she needed to say goodbye. It was hard to let her go from my arms, and I made sure the blanket was wrapped around her. She dropped to her knees, tears streaming down her cheeks. She tenderly pushed the hair off his face. "Help is coming," she cried, her voice rough. She turned to me, desperate. "Right, Finn?"

There was no hope for him, but I nodded. "Yes."

He tried to smile, blood trickling from his mouth. He shook his head, his eyes suddenly going wide with fear. "No," he groaned, lifting his arm, the effort costing him the last of his strength.

I spun to see what he was looking at. Lopez was staggering toward us, a gun held in his unsteady hand and aiming for Una. Before I could draw my weapon, Brian shot, the bullet hitting Lopez. The impact spun him around, and he fell face first beside Juan. The sound of the gun going off echoed in the room, startling everyone.

Brian gasped for air, and Una's sobs became harder as she reached for him, pulling him close and cradling his head in her lap. He looked up at her, an expression of deep sorrow on his face.

"Sing," he gurgled.

Lowering her head, she sang for him, her voice thick but still beautiful. I watched as the life faded from his eyes, his mouth forming a word before he died.

"*Sorry.*"

Then he was gone. Una bent, still singing, stroking his hair like a child. I looked around, everyone pausing in their duties to watch the poignant moment.

I was helpless in the face of her pain, wondering how much more she could endure before breaking. I touched her shoulder. "Una, we have to go."

She looked up. "What?"

"We need to clear everything out. The building is going to blow soon."

She shook her head wildly, clutching Brian. "No! You can't—he's not—"

"*Mo chroí,*" I murmured. "He's gone."

Her voice was drenched in horror and so loud she was almost screaming. "*You are not burying my brother with these people.*"

Behind me, Roman spoke, his voice firm and calm. "No. We'll take him, Una. You can bury him properly with your dad. We'll make sure he gets the respect he deserves, right, Finn?"

"Yes," I said, meeting her pain-filled gaze. "He saved your life. Tonight, he became a hero. He died protecting you."

"Promise?" she asked, her voice sounding like a child's.

"Yes. But you have to let Roman take care of it."

She finally loosened her hold. Roman leaned down. "Take her, Finn. Leave this all to us. You need to get her out of here. The others have been dispatched and are already on their way to the hotel. Niall has someone he is refusing to let go of. Take them and Una and go. We'll follow shortly once we finish here." He met my eyes. "It won't be long."

Time was of the essence. We needed to get everyone out and cleared before the explosions began. Before someone heard or saw something. We didn't want any civilian deaths on our hands.

I didn't argue. I stood and picked up Una, pushing her head into my neck. The squelch of pooling blood under my feet made me shudder. I covered her ear with my palm, pushing her head into my neck. I didn't want her to hear it. To look around and see the carnage, the dead bodies and the blood. She had enough to recover from. I walked to Niall. "We need to go."

He nodded, still holding the small blond woman Una had called Anna. I didn't ask why.

Clutching my girl, I carried her out of that barn, praying one day her mind would release her from it as well.

I would do everything in my power to make sure it happened.

CHAPTER TWENTY-ONE

FINN

No one spoke in the van that met us at the designated spot. I held Una, her quiet sobs painful to hear. At the hotel, the self-contained parking area was busy, and we took my private elevator to my floor. Niall had a room there as well, and I stopped by his door, indicating the woman he held. "Let her get cleaned up, and you can arrange to take her downstairs."

He only grunted slightly, entering his room. I carried Una to mine, heading right to the bathroom. I turned on the shower, letting it heat, then set her on the vanity as I stripped. I left my boxers on, unsure about how unsafe she was feeling—even with me. I tugged off the blanket, pausing at the sash of the robe. "Una?" I asked quietly.

She nodded, and I pulled it from her, discarding it on the floor. In the shower, I sat her on the bench, letting the hot water pour over her. I washed myself as she remained still, huddled on the seat, her head lowered and shoulders bent.

I kneeled in front of her. "Let me help," I murmured.

Again, all I got was a nod. I washed her hair twice, adding conditioner the way she liked, then I spent long minutes pulling a comb through the wet strands, finally working out the knots. I rinsed it and picked up the body wash.

"No," she whimpered as I reached for the loofah.

I froze. "Okay," I assured her. "You want to do it?"

"Yes."

"Do you want me to go?" I asked, fighting down my hurt. How I was feeling didn't matter. How she felt was paramount.

She didn't look at me. "Not far."

"I'll be right outside the shower. I'll get us some fresh clothes and be right back."

"Okay."

I slipped out, wrapping a towel around my waist. I waited until she was on her feet and soaping herself, then I hurried to my closet, pulling on sweats and a casual shirt before heading back. She was standing under the spray, moving slowly.

I picked up the clothes from the floor. "I'll burn these."

"No!" she gasped, turning. "My necklace."

I tried not to let my rage show. She was covered in bruises. Cuts and welts were on her ankles, and I realized she'd been chained up. She had marks everywhere. I swallowed my anger.

"Where?" I asked.

"In the lapel. There is a little slit, and it fell to the hem."

I found it, holding it up. "I have it, *mo chroí.*"

"It was all I had of you," she whispered. "I had to keep it to remind myself you were out there."

I held out my hand. "Una."

She stepped from the shower, her marked skin wet. I wrapped a towel around her and pulled her close. She melted into me, shaky but still standing.

"I will always be there for you." I pressed a kiss to her head. "Always."

"I know."

Her hands shook as she held a cup of tea. She was dressed and bundled in a blanket. Dr. Barnes had been to my room and checked her out, with me standing beside her the entire time. He'd been my private physician for years and I trusted him completely, but she needed me close. And he didn't ask me to leave, understanding her frame of mind. He'd made and overseen all the arrangements downstairs for the victims we'd brought in for care as well.

"Dehydrated. Bruised and battered. She needs liquids, food, and care. Tylenol for the aches. This cream for the cuts on her ankles." At the door, he met my gaze. "You did a good thing, Finn. All those people. We'll look after them."

I glanced back at Una. "I'm worried about her mental state. All of this, and her brother was one of the casualties."

He handed me a small bottle. "To help her sleep if needed. Nonaddictive," he assured me. "I can arrange some counseling if she desires it."

"Thank you."

"Now, next door. I understand Niall has another one."

I frowned. "I thought he was taking her downstairs with the others."

He shrugged. "Change of plan, I suppose."

He left, and I returned to Una.

I pushed a bowl her way. "Please eat something."

She looked at the soup, shaking her head. I sat beside her, lifting the bowl and pressing a spoon to her mouth. "Please."

She let me feed her, some of the creamy soup slowly disappearing. She hadn't spoken much, but she made sure she touched me. Every time I got up or moved, she became agitated, reaching out for me. I had a feeling it would be that way for a while. I was fine with it—I felt better touching her as well.

I set aside the bowl, offering her some toast. She took the lukewarm bread but made no move to eat it.

"Anna," she suddenly said.

"Is safe," I soothed. "With Niall," I added.

She blinked. "Niall?"

"Apparently."

"I want to see her."

I wouldn't deny her anything she wanted. I helped her to her feet, hating her grimace of pain. She wore a pair of soft leggings, a warm sweater, and socks, plus the blanket wrapped around her, which helped ward off the constant chill she was experiencing.

We went down the hall, knocking on Niall's door. He opened it, looking unusually ruffled.

"Una wants to see Anna," I stated.

He opened the door wider, indicating for us to come in.

Anna sat on the sofa, bundled much like Una in a blanket. Her hair was washed, hanging down her back almost to her waist, and it glinted a soft golden blond in the light. She had creamy skin, and her doe-like eyes were a deep brown. She was small and looked vulnerable. She carried the same marks of abuse as Una did, but hers were even more plentiful.

She cried out Una's name, and the two women clung to each other, whispering and comforting the other.

I looked at Niall, and he shook his head. "I can't get more than five feet from her and she becomes upset," he said quietly. "I couldn't take her downstairs. I stood inside the fucking bathroom facing the wall while she showered to keep her calm."

"Una is reacting the same."

"But Anna doesn't know me."

"Una probably talked about you. You carried her out of hell, Niall. It makes sense she feels safe with you."

He didn't say anything, his gaze locked on the small woman. There was something in his expression I had never seen from him before.

A look I recognized. I wore it every time I looked at Una.

I turned away, trying not to smile.

This could be interesting.

The women sat beside each other. I could see Anna was wearing a T-shirt of Niall's and a pair of his sweatpants. Thick socks covered her feet. Every item was too big on her.

"Get her some clothing from the boutique tomorrow," I murmured.

"Yeah, already thought of that. I gave her what I could."

"Has she eaten?"

"Tea. Toast."

I chuckled. "These two are alike. Although I did get some soup into Una."

"Damn it," he swore. "I never thought of soup."

I clapped him on the shoulder. "You'll figure it out."

"Doc Barnes says she's severely undernourished. Dehydrated. She needs care and rest."

I nodded. "She'll get whatever she needs. Una is very fond of her. Protective."

He muttered something that sounded like, "*I fucking get that.*" But I couldn't be sure.

"Have you heard from them?" he asked, meaning Roman, Luca, and Aldo.

"A text saying it was done. They should be here soon." I had arranged suites for them. In fact, I had blocked off two entire floors for the next while, unsure what to expect. I'd had the hotel staff move people, comp rooms, offer casino cash, free accommodations on another date, and dinners. We'd invented a false electrical problem on the two floors as a cover story. The victims and those who helped us tonight had a place to rest and recover for as long as they needed.

"We need to meet."

"In my suite. I can't leave Una."

His gaze drifted to the sofa.

"Bring Anna with you. She can stay with Una." I looked at them, holding hands, quietly talking. "I think they need each other right now."

"Okay."

I looked around the dining table I rarely sat at. Roman, Luca, and Aldo joined me, drinking coffee and whiskey. Platters of food and carafes of coffee filled the table. Niall was to my right, where he could see the living room.

Una and Anna were on the sofa. Across from them were Effie, Vi, and Justine. They had arrived at my invitation. I knew the men were missing their wives and would find comfort in having them close. The unexpected bonus was the friendship and comfort they were giving to Una and Anna. They had experienced traumas and were able to offer insights I never could.

I sat back, sipping coffee. "Fill me in."

"Almost everything went according to plan," Roman stated. His gaze flickered to Luca. "Almost."

"What didn't?" I hissed, leaning forward.

"Juan escaped."

"I thought he was dead!" Niall protested, his anger evident.

"No, the coward was pretending. He was shot and played dead. In the aftermath, he somehow got away.

We don't know how badly he was hurt, but we have eyes out looking for him."

"Fuck," Niall muttered. "Anna told me he was obsessed with her. She was there for over three weeks."

"We'll keep her safe and hope he's crawled away to die somewhere," I assured him.

Aldo looked grim. "I hope he dies painfully."

"And the building?"

"A pile of rubble. The fire was so intense, the bodies will be unidentifiable. The rumor has already started that there was a fire in the lab, and the entire place went up with them all in it so quickly that no one could escape. All Lopez's fault for having an auction in the same place as a dangerous lab," Roman informed us.

"The racetrack was shut down, citing being too close to a chemical fire. Lopez didn't have a big crew since he kept his shit hidden. Most of them perished tonight. The few who got away are running so fast they won't stop for a long time and were low-level. The real employees he kept to cover his illegal shit are accounted for. The horses were all transported safely."

"You accomplished a lot."

"The syndicate did. We all worked together. Once again proving we're stronger as a group than on our own. We ended Lopez's evil culture."

"And since we're in no way connected with the track or Lopez, no one will look our way," Luca added. "We're safe."

I glanced toward the women. "Even Santini?"

"He won't utter a word," Roman said, looking fierce.

"We need to find Juan. Or his corpse."

"We will."

"Brian?" I asked quietly.

"At the morgue. Awaiting instructions."

"I'll handle it."

I heard some laughter and looked over with a smile. "Your women seem to be the best medicine right now."

"They understand," Roman replied, a look of adoration in his eyes as he looked at his wife.

"I am obligated to all of you," I said. "I owe each of you a debt I can never repay, and I will be there if you need me."

Luca grimaced. "Getting rid of him was in all our best interests. But we're happy to have helped. I think this has made the syndicate tighter with a common goal. The message will be heard, however it is delivered." He stood. "But I need my wife and some sleep. We'll talk more before we leave tomorrow."

I stood and shook his hand. "Thank you."

Una curled up on her side, a soft sigh escaping her lips. She looked drowsy, the sleeping pills she'd agreed to take relaxing her. I was beside her, unsure what to do. I wanted to pull her into my arms, sleep with her on my chest the way we usually did, but I didn't know if she wanted to be touched that way. Tenderly, I brushed the hair back from her face, trying not to scowl at the bruises on her skin. I wished I could have Lopez in front of me. That I could cover him in marks and bruises. Let him feel real fear before he died.

The sensation of Una's fingers on my face brought me out of my musings.

"Hi," I murmured.

"Are you going to leave?" she asked, sounding fearful.

"No."

"Why aren't you under the covers with me?"

"I didn't know if you wanted that," I admitted honestly.

"Your touch doesn't frighten me, Finn. It soothes me."

I slid under the blankets, my entire body relaxing as she shifted, laying her head on my chest, her torso pressed to mine. We were quiet for a moment.

"While I was there in the dark, I couldn't sleep. But I would drift, and I dreamed you were holding me. It was awful waking up cold and alone."

I pressed a kiss to her head. "Never again. I will always be here. No one and nothing will harm you again, Una. I swear it."

She snuggled closer, and I snaked my arm around her waist, holding her tight. "I love you, *mo chroí.*"

"Same for me," she whispered, making me smile.

"Sleep. I have you."

"I know."

The next day, Niall walked in with Anna. Neither looked rested. Considering how often Una had cried out and woke screaming, I felt the same way.

It was going to take a while until either woman felt safe.

We left them together, heading to the table. That was as far away as I was comfortable at the moment.

"Rough night?"

"Jesus," he replied, his voice low. "I have no idea what I'm doing. Her terror is fucking killing me. I can't take the screams...or the tears."

"Time," I replied. "They have to heal."

"How do you stand it? I know how much you love her. I don't have the connection to Anna you have, and her pain is ripping me apart."

"Are you so certain about that, Niall? No connection?"

He scoffed, taking a sip of coffee. "I feel badly for her. I want to help her. She obviously means a lot to Una."

I let it go. This wasn't the time for personal exchanges.

"You saw the news this morning?"

"Yes. The reporting is perfect. An explosion led to the discovery of a hidden drug lab. Assumed set off by an accident in the highly flammable facility. All casualties were thought to be employees but are unidentifiable." He sat back. "Those who knew where the Russians were will assume they were caught in the inferno."

I nodded. "The racetrack is closed permanently. I think the feeling is the syndicate will purchase it and reopen so they can keep tabs on it. Any news on Juan?"

"No sightings. We'll keep searching."

"Good."

"Any decision on Brian?"

"Yes. Una said he is to be cremated, and she'll bury him with her mum and dad. She wants a private funeral. Our crew has been informed he died a hero helping us. I am doing that for her. And I already informed the morgue. It will happen quickly before questions are asked."

"All right."

"My focus is back on the territory and the hotel. My priority, though, is Una and helping her through this."

"Of course."

"She told me Anna grew up in a family that ran summer rentals. She has experience in the industry—at least loosely. I am going to offer to put her in our apprentice program here and give her a room to live in until she's ready to face the outside world." I looked over at the way the women were sitting facing each other, quietly talking like old friends. "She helped Una. I owe her." Then I smiled at Niall. "I like her too."

He looked at them, a softening of his eyes telling me what I needed to know. But he kept his voice neutral. "Whatever you think is best, Finn."

"Where did she sleep last night?" I asked out of the blue.

He frowned. "In the bedroom. I thought she'd be more comfortable than on the sofa."

"Ah." I leaned over the table. "Where did you sleep?"

He narrowed his eyes, standing and pushing his chair back. "Feck off. She was screaming. I had to stay with her."

Then he stalked away.

Leaving me hiding my grin.

Interesting, indeed.

CHAPTER TWENTY-TWO

FINN

I had always thought of Una as brave. Fearless. She handled her problems and the world she'd been forced to live in with a determination and acceptance that belied her young age.

Watching her the day we buried her brother only proved she was all that, as well as pure grace under pressure.

I had let it be known that her brother's past, especially the last weeks of his life, was buried with him. His death was the result of fighting *with* us. He saved his sister's life, and that was how he was being remembered. I would allow nothing else to be said about him. With that single act, he had cleared away his past deeds, and I would always owe him for that.

I had a feeling that even without Brian, Lopez would have gotten to Una, his obsession for her that deep. The information Roman's man had found on the deceased criminal made the hair on my neck stand on end. I was grateful he was dead.

I watched as she thanked people for coming to the service. Made sure they had a drink and food. Much like the day I had seen her at her dad's funeral. Looking out for everyone but herself. Only this time, I was beside her, a silent sentinel, my presence signaling to everyone who she belonged to. And I looked after her, making her sit, ensuring she ate. Handling any detail that happened so she could mourn quietly and listen to the good things people had to say about Brian. His humor. Stories of him and his dad. I was grateful when those made her smile. To allow her to recall there had been some good in him. I had to believe there was, given how she loved him.

It wasn't a large crowd, but many from the syndicate were there, paying their respects and shaking my hand, our united front clear.

Una requested a private graveside gathering, so it was only us as she placed the small urn beside her parents' graves. I stepped back, giving her the privacy she needed. Her lips moved in a low whisper as she crouched by the small plot, and I knew she was telling her brother words she wanted to share with him and no one else.

I looked around the mostly empty graveyard. It was overcast and gray. Drizzly. The somber weather matching the occasion.

Una stepped back, taking my proffered hand. She was pale, quiet, and still so beautiful in her grief. I knew she was struggling to find her feet, and I also knew there was a conversation we had to have.

One I dreaded.

Back at the hotel, she changed into warm leggings and one of my sweaters. She felt constantly cold these days and needed as much warmth as she could find. I changed as well, ordering tea for her and coffee for me. She wrapped her hands around the mug, inhaling the bergamot fragrance.

"You could save a lot of money and make the tea in the room yourself," she murmured.

I smiled at her gentle scolding. "It's all my money, Una. It doesn't really matter."

She glanced around. "Your condo had more life in it. Pictures, that sort of thing."

"I told you before this was just a place to sleep. I haven't really considered it home. Nothing felt like home after you left."

She frowned, studying her mug but not saying anything. I took a long sip from my coffee, needing the bracing caffeine.

"Una, we need to talk."

Her gaze flew to mine, panic flaring in them. "Finn?"

"No, everything is all right. But the future, Una. We need to talk about the future."

"The future?" she whispered.

I nodded, gathering the words I needed to say. Knowing her reply might once again leave me alone and without her. A reality I was prepared for. Expecting, in fact, after what had occurred.

"How you foresee us going forward."

She frowned, looking around. She rose from the sofa and walked around the room, staring and seemingly lost in thought.

"Honestly?" she asked.

I nodded, bracing myself. "Honest. We are always honest with each other."

"For starters, I'd want to bring some color in here. Personality. I don't want to live in a hotel room. Well, one that looks like a hotel room—even an expensive one."

Something in my chest tripped. A small ripple went through me. "You want to stay here with me?"

"Well, first off, I can't bear the thought of going to my apartment, and frankly, I can't see you living there. It's too small. We could look for another place, but I know you like being on-site here. But if we could make it more personal…"

At the look on my face, she trailed off, and an expression of anxious disbelief crossed hers.

"Oh. *Oh God*, you don't want me here."

I was on my feet instantly, crossing the room. I cupped her face, shaking my head. "I want nothing more. I didn't know if you wanted to stay with *me*."

"You mean stay *here* with you?"

I frowned. "I thought you were going to leave me again, Una."

Her eyes went wide. "Leave you?"

"You have always hated that part of my life. You left me once because of it. This time was worse because it was you. I wouldn't blame you."

She covered my hands with hers, pulling our clasped fingers down to her chest. "Finn," she whispered. "I told you I would stay. I trust you to keep me safe. I know what happened was because of a sick individual, not because of who you are."

"You hate this world."

"But I love you more."

I bent my head, kissing her fingers. Then I pulled her into my arms and kissed her sweet mouth.

"I thought I'd lost you. That you'd tell me you had to go," I confessed.

"And you'd let me?"

"I would give you anything to make you happy. I planned to buy you a hotel in a small place and let you go to follow your dreams." I paused. "With trusted men close and my eyes on you from a distance."

"You would have let me live my life without you?"

"I'd never be far. And the instant you asked for me, I would come."

"What if I didn't?"

"I would be content knowing you were all right and happy."

"I'm never happy unless you're with me."

"*Mo chroí*," I whispered.

"I love you," she said again. "Do you still love me?"

"How can you ask me that? Of course I do."

She opened her mouth, then closed it.

"Say it, Una. Ask me whatever you need. Tell me whatever you have to tell me."

I didn't expect her next words.

"Lopez never touched me, Finn. Not sexually."

I frowned. "I know."

"You haven't touched me since I came back."

"I hold you every night. I'm touching you now," I argued.

"Before I was taken, you couldn't be in the same room with me for ten minutes without trying to ravish me." She blinked up at me. "You don't want me anymore?"

I shut my eyes, pulling her close and pressing my lips to her forehead. "I want you every second of every day. But you've been through so much. Hurt. I didn't know if you were ready—if you wanted to be touched that way, Una."

"I want it from you, Finn. I want your touch to erase all the bad ones they inflicted. So all I remember is how good it feels to be touched."

I swept her into my arms, carrying her to the bedroom.

"Then let me remind you."

I laid her on the bed, hovering over her.

"This is going to be slow, Una. And I want your words. If you're scared or feeling anything but pleasure, you're going to tell me."

"And you'll stop?"

I shook my head. "We'll start again. I won't stop until you're mine again. Completely."

I peeled off her clothes, kissing every inch of flesh I uncovered. Every bruise or laceration that still marred her skin. I touched her with reverence, grateful that she was still mine. That she survived. That she was ready to be with me again. I kept my mouth gentle and my touch light as I caressed her. I praised her, wanting her to hear my voice.

"You are so beautiful."

"I love your freckles—all the little grains of sand all over your skin. Sexy little dots only I can see. It makes you even more mine."

"You have such elegant feet. Delicate, yet so strong. Just like the rest of you."

"Are you still ticklish, mo chroí? *Here?" I let my fingers*

drift over the backs of her knees, delighting in her low giggle.

More than once, I felt her tense, and I refused to move on until she relaxed again. I didn't grip her wrists or hold her down, certain those would trigger her panic. I kissed her slowly, deeply, letting her feel my love. She began getting lost in the moment, falling into her passion. She grabbed the hem of my shirt, tugging it off me. The feel of her fingers on my back, stroking and gripping me, was indescribable. I licked at her neck, nuzzling my face into the fragrant spot at the base of her throat, groaning her name.

"You taste so sweet, *mo chroí*. I've missed you."

"Finn," she whispered. "Please."

"Tell me what you want."

"I want you. On me. I need to feel you."

I carefully laid my torso to hers, allowing some of my weight to press down on her. She wrapped her legs around me, drawing me close. We kissed, drawing breath from each other, our bond tightening as our mouths moved, our bodies melded, and our passion began to blaze. I buried my hands in her hair, feeling the silk of it. She clutched at my back, fisting my hair, tugging on it as I kissed and licked my way across her collarbone to her breasts, sucking the tight buds into my mouth until she was begging, tugging my hair harder, pleading in a breathy voice for me.

I notched my cock to her entrance, feeling the slick heat welcome me. Slowly, I slid myself in, kissing her the whole time. Feeling the hitch of her breathing as I reached down, lifting her hips and burying myself as far as I could go. She shivered in anticipation as I withdrew and pushed back in. I shut my eyes at the overwhelming rightness of being with her. I rocked into her, keeping her close. Whispering my love. Showering her with kisses. Touching her. Groaning at the pleasure of her wrapped around me. Hot. Wet. Perfect.

She began to shake, crying out my name. She grasped my neck hard as she succumbed, her eyes wide, her muscles gripping my cock, milking my own release from somewhere so deep inside me I was certain I would burst from the intense pleasure.

Until I collapsed into her arms, spent and exhausted.

Wrapped around the woman I loved, knowing she was mine forever. She would stay with me.

I pressed a kiss to her head.

"Marry me, Una."

UNA

Finn fell asleep before I could totally comprehend what he had said—or breathed out before he'd tucked me close and slumbered.

I shifted a little, staring at him. I wondered if he knew how beautiful he was. He'd scoff and brush away my word, but he was. His features were bold, masculine, and defined. His height and breadth made him even more so. With his long, wild dark-red hair and imposing stance, he was an incredibly sexy, ruggedly beautiful man.

I knew what he was. Who he was. I saw firsthand what he was capable of. A cold-blooded killer when needed, a fearless leader, a loving nephew, and a tender, giving lover.

And he was mine.

I wasn't sure when I had made peace with the light and dark that lived inside him. But somehow I knew, despite all the thoughts to the contrary, no one else would ever complete me the way he did.

Thinking of his words, of how he planned to let me go in order for me to be happy, touched me. Except I knew before he uttered them I could never be happy without him. I'd tried, and it didn't work.

Finn O'Reilly was it for me.

And he would keep me safe.

I stroked the arm holding me tight to his warm body, looking around. I had never thought of living in a hotel. But I supposed it wasn't much different from a condo. Finn had a terrace where I could grow some plants. He owned the place, so I knew he'd let me bring in different furniture. Add color and pictures and make it our home.

The added bonus was room service when I didn't feel like cooking.

And housekeeping.

A small laugh escaped my mouth, and I covered it with my hand, feeling silly.

"Don't," he rumbled, tightening his arm. "Whatever is making you laugh, let it out. I love hearing you laugh."

He lifted his head, still half asleep. "You haven't laughed in a long time."

"I was thinking living here would have some benefits."

One eyebrow rose in query.

"Housekeeping. Room service."

A grin split his face. "By room service, you mean me and sex anytime you want it."

"And housekeeping."

"I'll clean up after."

I laughed again, this time louder. "Whatever, Finn."

He smiled, then kissed me. "Marry me, and you can have it all, Una."

"You meant that?" I asked against his mouth.

"Not overly romantic, but yes, I meant it. I love you. I want you to be my wife."

"It would make you happy?"

"*Mo chroí*, it would make me the happiest man on earth. The universe, even."

I cupped his cheek. "Then yes."

He rolled, pulling me with him and holding me tight. He kissed me until I was breathless, his erection growing between us.

"Let's celebrate," he murmured.

"What did you have in mind?" I asked, teasing him as I cupped his balls.

"Room service. Now."

I was good with that.

CHAPTER TWENTY-THREE

FINN

The next morning, I sat at my desk, immediately turning on the security feed. I zoomed in on the waterfall, smiling at the monitor.

As I was getting ready, Una squared her shoulders and told me she wanted to leave the suite. It was the first time she had said that since I'd brought her back from the racetrack.

"I really need to work. You can come to the office?" I asked, pausing in pulling on my pants.

"No. I want to go downstairs." She drew in a deep breath. "By the waterfall and the fire. I can read there. Maybe Niall can bring Anna down. You two can work, and we can read and just enjoy it."

"Are you ready for that?"

She hesitated but nodded. "You can see me, right?"

"Yes. And I have extra men around. You would be perfectly safe."

"Then I want to try."

I had left her there with a tray of tea and toast. Her Kindle and her phone. A blanket across her lap. Instructions with my men she was to be watched.

The staff were pleased to see her. For the first few moments, I watched as they came to say hello, one by one, talking to her, hugging her. They were told she'd been in a car accident, explaining her bruises and absence. She smiled up at the camera and texted me a smiling emoji and a thumbs-up.

Niall and Anna appeared, Anna sinking into the chair next to Una's. Niall looked unsure, and then he bent and said something to her. She nodded and patted the hand he had resting on her shoulder. He paused, then walked away. Unable to resist, I tracked him across the lobby. He stopped twice, looking back, then again by the elevator, peering around the corner, his gaze locked on her. He tried to be casual about it, but he was anything but.

I switched back to the women, pleased to see them holding their mugs and munching on toast. Anna looked better. Still pale and thin, but she'd been a hostage longer, and she would need more time to recover. I was going to talk to her today about my idea. But first, I needed to discuss it with Niall. I had a feeling he would be involved in the majority of her decisions from now on.

He walked in a few moments later. I tried to look busy, my laptop open, the security monitor back on Anna and Una. I watched as he got a coffee then ambled over, trying to appear casual as he looked over all the monitors, his gaze resting on one the longest.

He sat down, taking a sip of his coffee and setting it on the desk.

"I have news."

I sat back. "Let me hear it."

"Our contact at the cop shop told me they found a body about a mile from the racetrack."

"Juan?"

He nodded. "They think so. General description fits." He picked up his cup. "Died from blood loss. There was a bullet hole."

"Can they do DNA? Fingerprints?"

"They tried. No hits, but he was an unknown. He called Lopez his uncle, but that wasn't his real name.

Could have been a son or a cousin or just some kid he recruited." He took a sip. "Fingerprints aren't, ah, possible."

"Why?"

"His right arm is mostly missing—and part of his left. And his leg was being chewed on."

I grimaced. "Part of me hopes he was still alive when they started chewing."

"I have to agree." He paused. "And our guy said he was wearing red sneakers. The same ones we saw Juan wearing with the tiger embroidery."

"Well, that rather seals the deal." I sat back, regarding him. "Have you told Anna?"

"Not yet. I will later. It might help her relax, knowing he's not out there."

"I'm going to talk to her later about my idea. Tell her she can stay in a room here until she's on her feet and feels safe to live elsewhere."

"Yeah, about that. She doesn't need the room."

I lifted one eyebrow. "Oh, why is that?"

"She can have Mum's room."

I tried to hide my smile behind my mug. "You mean the adjoining room to yours?"

"She'd feel safer being close. It's private—she can keep the door locked. But I'd be close if she needed me."

"Will it be locked on your side?" I asked.

He narrowed his eyes. "I'm doing this because she is Una's friend. To help."

I nodded. "Right. Of course. *Una's friend*. To help."

He leaned forward. "I haven't shot anyone for a few days now, Finn. My finger is suddenly feeling itchy. You want to risk it?"

I chuckled and pointed to the monitor.

"She's lovely, Niall. Intelligent. Sweet. Roisin would love her."

"I don't do relationships, Finn. I'm simply doing my part."

"So, you're not attracted to her?"

He opened his mouth then snapped it shut when I waved my finger at him. "Truth."

"You can't help but be attracted to her," he huffed. "She's incredible. But not for me. I'm not interested in something serious. And she's the serious sort of girl."

I picked up my phone and scrolled through it.

"What are you doing?"

"Marking today on my calendar."

"What the hell for?"

"I'll be reminding you of this stupid conversation, and I want you to know the date you denied how you feel."

"I can't deny something that's not there."

"You have no feelings for her?" I asked. "None?"

"Aside from concern, no," he insisted. But I saw the way his gaze strayed to the monitor. And I swore I saw a flash of pain.

"Well then, working with her, sleeping that close, shouldn't be a problem, should it?"

He stood. "I'm out of here. I have things to do."

A few moments later, I began to laugh when I saw him back on the main floor, staring at Anna. The longing on his face was transparent. He glanced at the camera, knowing I was watching, and flipped me the bird, making me laugh again. Then he headed toward where she was sitting, and she looked up, her smile warm and wide when she saw it was him. I wondered if he knew how his expression changed. It morphed into a tender look and a smile that echoed hers.

"Goner," I said to no one. "I wonder how long until he admits it?"

I had Una bring Anna upstairs for lunch. We met in the pub, the warm ambiance relaxing her. I wasn't surprised when Niall strode in and joined us. He sat beside her, leaning over and asking her something quietly. She nodded.

"I'm fine," she murmured.

"Good."

We ordered, and I sat back, tapping Una's leg under the table, indicating the couple on the other side with a slight tilt of my chin. She tapped me back, a small grin on her face.

After we ate our bowls of delicious Irish stew and fresh brown bread, I told Anna my offer. She stirred her coffee, frowning.

"It's only an offer, Anna," I explained, wondering why she looked so upset. "Maybe you had plans to return up north or another idea?"

"Oh no," she said. "I had been dreading trying to find a job, and I would love to stay here. I'd get to work with Una?"

"Yes, and the other staff. You'd be in guest services.

Trained and paid while doing so." I looked at Niall, lifting my eyebrows to indicate for him to talk.

"And you'd get to live in the hotel," Niall added, turning to her.

"I would?"

I cleared my throat. "I'm indebted to you, Anna. You and Una developed a friendship while you were, ah, trapped. She told me if it weren't for you, she would have gone mad."

"She was equally good to me," Anna said. "She tried to protect me from, um, *him.*"

Her hand shook as she reached for her coffee, and she paled simply at the mention of Juan. Niall shifted closer, draping his arm over the back of the chair she sat in.

"He can't hurt you anymore," he assured her.

"But what if he comes looking for me?" she asked, her eyes wide. "And hurts Una? I can't stay here and risk that."

Niall met my gaze, and I nodded. Leaning forward, he spoke quietly, telling her and Una that Juan was dead.

"You're sure?" Anna asked, her voice thick.

"They can't ID him since there was no way to fingerprint him and no DNA in any system. But the fact that he was so close to the track and had a gunshot wound, the coincidence is too great," I replied with confidence. "Plus, he was wearing those hideous sneakers."

"Why no fingerprints?" Una asked.

I cleared my throat. "Mother Nature has a way of removing them."

Una looked confused, and then her eyes went wide. "Oh. *Oh.*"

Anna looked at her, and Una mimed biting her nails. Theatrically. Anna looked startled, then turned her face, coughing to cover a little laugh.

"He deserved it," Una stated.

Anna nodded, shifting in her chair to face Niall. I couldn't help but see his fingers tangled in her hair that fell over the back of the chair. He saw my glance, pulling his arm back, but I'd caught him.

"Maybe we should discuss it?" she asked.

"It's your decision. I think you'd like it here. Great staff. And you'd be safe."

She turned back to me. "I accept."

"Great. I'll get the paperwork in order with HR. You can take a little more time to recover and start next week."

"Okay."

Niall stood. "You look pale and should probably lie down."

She stood as well, hesitating, then leaned down and hugged me. "Thank you, Finn. I see why you're Una's hero."

Niall glared at me, and I patted her back. "Thank you."

They left, Niall's hand on the small of her back, the gesture oddly intimate since he rarely touched anyone.

Una turned to me, lifting her eyebrows. "Are they…?"

I shrugged. "Niall says no. He is only helping."

"Bullshit. He's as protective of her as you are of me."

"I agree." I leaned closer. "And he insists she use his mum's room. Which adjoins his."

She clapped her hands in delight. "Oh my God, they are such a cute couple. He's all big and strong. Dark and broody. She's little and golden. Like night and day."

I chuckled. "Good description."

"We need to help them," she decided.

"We need to wait and see what happens."

She frowned but didn't argue. I wondered how long until she asked Anna what was going on.

I hoped she'd tell me.

She picked up her coffee and sipped. Then she turned to me, looking serious. "Finn."

"*Mo chroí?*"

"I want to go back to work this week. Well, at least Friday and Saturday night."

I smiled widely. "You want to sing?"

"Yes. I need to move forward. Do something that gives me joy."

"Your voice gives me great joy as well," I murmured, stroking a line up her throat.

"You'll be there, right?" she asked.

"Always."

"My, ah, dresses," she paused and swallowed, the memories of the last time she was in her apartment no doubt racing through her head.

"You're buying new ones," I informed her. "I'll take you down to the boutique later. You pick what you want."

"I have to go back—"

"No. I'll have it cleaned out and your personal stuff brought to the suite. You never have to go back there again." I didn't want her to face those memories.

She paused. "You told me Tom wasn't dead, but I haven't seen him."

"He'll be back tomorrow."

"And you're sure he's okay?"

"Yes," I assured her. "He's fine. I made him take a few days off, that's all."

I practically had to have his wife tie him down, but I kept that to myself.

"Oh, good. I look forward to seeing him."

"He is looking forward to seeing you too."

UNA

Friday night, I sat at the dressing table, finishing my makeup. The soft fragrance of Finn's flowers drifted over, and I inhaled, stopping what I was doing and stroking the soft petals. The arrangement was huge, and this time, there was a card.

Mo chroí,
Sing for me.
Always, Finn

I stood, crossing to the screen by the door and sliding the new dress Finn had picked out for me over my head. I looked in the mirror. It was a soft green, flowing and elegant. The long sleeves hid the fading bruises, and the delicate shimmer of the crystals drew your attention to the bias cut of the skirt and the swirl of the material that swept the floor. It was modest and pretty, and I felt like a million dollars in it. Careful makeup covered the marks on my collarbones and face. They no longer hurt and would soon be gone.

I only hoped the painful memories would fade as well. The therapist I had started seeing was helping. She was insightful and down-to-earth, and we got along well. She was the wife of one of Finn's men, so nothing I told her came as much of a shock. And it was nice to say things without filtering them. I didn't have to worry about upsetting Finn if I was having a bad moment and said what was on my mind.

There was a tap on the door, and Tom stuck his head in. "They're ready for you."

Finn insisted on a guard for me at all times. I asked for Tom and had been happy to see him return to my side.

We got along well, and I trusted him. I still felt awful about what Brian had attempted to do, but he'd waved me off and we hadn't spoken of it again.

I hesitated before going onstage, a small flutter of nerves hitting me. I had to remind myself the danger was gone. No one was watching who wanted to hurt me. No one was stalking me.

I took a deep breath and walked out.

I was greeted with a warm round of applause, my eyes widening at the large table set up at the front. Roman, Aldo, Luca, and their wives were all there. Niall and Anna. Finn sat closest, his pride evident, beaming at me, nodding in encouragement. His intense gaze met mine, flooding me with warmth. I felt his love, his strength, surround me.

He was here.

I was safe.

I shut my eyes, and I began to sing.

FINN

As always, Una's voice transported me to another

time. Her song choices tonight were those of love. Hope. Happiness.

And she sang them all to me.

I fingered the small box in my pocket. Tonight after she stepped offstage, I would ask her to marry me properly, then take her upstairs and surprise her with a dinner with our guests. We'd celebrate the moment with the people who'd made it possible for it to happen. Who'd stepped in and helped me get her back.

She was only doing the one show tonight and tomorrow. She would resume her schedule next week. And working in her new role in the office.

She would be safe in the hotel. Guarded when she left the property.

Never far from my sight.

And she would be loved.

Endlessly.

She finished her set, and the entire room stood, clapping and calling for an encore.

They couldn't get enough.

I smiled proudly, knowing I had to share her for a little longer.

Then I'd ask my question, and she'd say yes.

I was sure of it.

Later in the elevator, I pressed a kiss to Una's head. "You were incredible," I murmured. "So amazing."

"It felt good to sing," she replied.

In the suite, I indicated the terrace. "A little fresh air?"

"I'd like that."

Outside on the table, I had more flowers for her. A bottle of champagne chilling. When she looked at me, I smiled. "To celebrate your return to the O'Reilly's stage."

"Ah," she breathed, walking to the railing. She rested her arms on the metal, looking out over the lights of the city. "Always so busy," she murmured. "So big."

I joined her, wrapping my arms around her. "It is. Easy to get lost in."

"Or found," she murmured.

I pressed a kiss to her neck, drawing in a deep breath, but before I could speak, she turned in my arms, looking up at me.

"Will you marry me soon, Finn?"

I was stunned. "Soon, *mo chroí*? May I ask why?"

"Life is too short. I wasted too much time with doubt. I love you. You love me. I want to belong to you. I want everyone to know you're mine."

I grinned at her possessive words. "Funny," I mused, pulling the box from my pocket, flipping the lid open. "You took the words out of my mouth."

She looked at the ring nestled in velvet. The large center emerald twinkled in the light. It was flawless, perfect. The diamonds surrounding it were brilliant and protected the middle stone, the way I planned to do to her the rest of her life.

She gasped at the ring.

"The emerald reminds me of your eyes," I murmured.

"It's so beautiful." She glanced up at me. "I love you."

"I'll start the preparations," I said, slipping the ring on her finger and wrapping her back in my arms. "I want the world to know you're mine too."

"Finn?" she whispered against my lips.

"Hmm?"

"Use your contacts. I want it to be soon."

I grinned as I captured her mouth. "Done."

Then I kissed my fiancée with utter abandon.

Because she was finally mine.

My Una.

Mo chroí.

WAIT A MINUTE, you say? No Epilogue from me? Yes, there is an epilogue, but you are going to have to read it in NIALL.

Thank you so much for reading FINN. If you are so inclined, reviews are always welcome by me at your retailer.

If you'd like to read more about Aldo and Roman, their stories are in the Men of the Falls duet available in ebook, paperback and audiobook.

Enjoy meeting other readers? Lots of fun, with upcoming book talk and giveaways! Check out Melanie Moreland's Minions on Facebook.

Join my newsletter for up-to-date news, sales, book announcements and excerpts (no spam). Click here to sign up Melanie Moreland's newsletter or use the QR code below:

Scan To Sign Up Now

Visit my website www.melaniemoreland.com
Enjoy reading! Melanie

ACKNOWLEDGMENTS

Many thanks to many people.

My team and admins work together to ensure my group, page and SM runs while I am busy creating. Their tasks are endless, their jobs thankless. But without them I would be lost.

Emily, Atlee, Karen, and George thank you.

My Hype team is filled with wonderful people who shout about my books, squeal over arcs and keep me uplifted when I'm uncertain. I am so grateful for you ladies—much love to you.

Beth, Deb, Sisters D & D—thank you for your eyes, your support, and your suggestions. They make my books better.

Lisa—you rock. That is all I have to say. That and the diet coke is always on ice for you.

Karen—there are no words—even for me. My right hand, my left, my sister from another mister. You make my book world easier and my real world brighter. Love you.

The bloggers, the readers, the posters and the reviewers. Thank you for being part of this journey.

And to my Matthew—Love. Always Love. Thank you for the thousand and one things you do to make sure I get to spend time with my characters, even if it means less time with you. I am lucky to call you mine.

ALSO AVAILABLE FROM MORELAND BOOKS

Titles published under Melanie Moreland

The Contract Series

Marriage of Convenience- Same Couple

The Contract (Contract #1)

The Baby Clause (Contract Novella)

The Amendment (Contract #3)

The Addendum (Contract #4)

Vested Interest Series

Billionaire - Different Couples

BAM - The Beginning (Prequel)

Bentley (Vested Interest #1)

Aiden (Vested Interest #2)

Maddox (Vested Interest #3)

Reid (Vested Interest #4)

Van (Vested Interest #5)

Halton (Vested Interest #6)

Sandy (Vested Interest #7)

Vested Interest/ABC Crossover

A Merry Vested Wedding

ABC Corp Series

Second Generation - Different Couples

My Saving Grace (Vested Interest: ABC Corp #1)

Finding Ronan's Heart (Vested Interest: ABC Corp #2)

Loved By Liam (Vested Interest: ABC Corp #3)

Age of Ava (Vested Interest: ABC Corp #4)

Sunshine & Sammy (Vested Interest: ABC Corp #5)

Unscripted With Mila (Vested Interest: ABC Corp #6)

Men of Hidden Justice

Vigilante Justice - Different Couples

The Boss

Second-In-Command

The Commander

The Watcher

The Specialist

Men of the Falls

Canadian mafia duet - Different Couples

Aldo

Roman

The Irishmen

Happily Ever After Collection

Heart Strings

A Simple Life

Titles published under M. Moreland

Insta-Spark Collection

Low Angst and all standalone

It Started with a Kiss

Christmas Sugar

An Instant Connection

An Unexpected Gift

Harvest of Love

An Unexpected Chance

Following Maggie

The Wish List

Wrapped In Love

ABOUT THE AUTHOR

NYT/WSJ/USAT international bestselling author Melanie Moreland, lives a happy and content life in a quiet area of Ontario with her beloved husband of thirty-plus years and their rescue cat, Amber. Nothing means more to her than her friends and family, and she cherishes every moment spent with them.

While seriously addicted to coffee, and highly challenged with all things computer-related and technical, she relishes baking, cooking, and trying new recipes for people to sample. She loves to throw dinner parties, and enjoys traveling, here and abroad, but finds coming home is always the best part of any trip.

Melanie loves stories, especially paired with a good wine, and enjoys skydiving (free falling over a fleck of dust) extreme snowboarding (falling down stairs) and piloting her own helicopter (tripping over her own feet.) She's learned happily ever afters, even bumpy ones, are all in how you tell the story.

Melanie is represented by Flavia Viotti at Bookcase Literary Agency. For any questions regarding subsidiary or translation rights please contact her at flavia@bookcaseagency.com

facebook.com/authormoreland

instagram.com/morelandmelanie

bookbub.com/authors/melanie-moreland

amazon.com/Melanie-Moreland/author/B00GV6LB00

goodreads.com/Melanie_Moreland

tiktok.com/@melaniemoreland

threads.net/@morelandmelanie

www.ingramcontent.com/pod-product-compliance
Lightning Source LLC
Chambersburg PA
CBHW070310310726
48976CB00005B/1646